Bolan came out braced to attack

But the enemy gunner was down, bloody tracks stitched across his chest. Bolan glanced at Kasm, watched slow-leaking crimson discolor one sleeve of his robe.

"How bad are you hit?"

"Just a scratch."

"Okay. Let's go." Bolan picked up the Uzi and wrestled the cartridge belt free of the lifeless body. He took a minute to buckle it on, double-checking the stuttergun's load, then followed Kasm to the stairs.

When they were halfway to ground level, two figures appeared at the head of the stairs, guns in hand, blotting out the dim light from above. Bolan sidestepped and flattened himself to the wall, taking one-handed aim with the Uzi, his finger already depressing the trigger.

By Bolan's calculations it was almost midnight. More delays would spell certain death. Any second, Grimaldi and his Phantoms would rain hellfire on the strike zone. Any second, the roof would cave in on their heads, and they would die in the tunnels....

MACK BOLAN®

The Executioner

DON PENDLETON's EXECUTIONER
MACK BOLAN®

Cold Judgment

A GOLD EAGLE BOOK FROM
WORLDWIDE®

TORONTO • NEW YORK • LONDON • PARIS
AMSTERDAM • STOCKHOLM • HAMBURG
ATHENS • MILAN • TOKYO • SYDNEY

First edition June 1988

ISBN 0-373-61114-5

Special thanks and acknowledgment to
Mike Newton for his contribution to this work.

Fanatics have their dreams, wherewith they weave
A paradise for a sect.

> —John Keats, 1819

There is no place in a fanatic's head where reason
may enter.

> —Napoléon I

If it is impossible to reason with fanatics, then I'll
have to speak the only language they understand—
brute force.

> —Mack Bolan

To all American servicemen on peacekeeping duty in the war-torn Middle East. God keep.

PROLOGUE

Jabez al-Malik settled on a wooden bench and scanned the baggage-pickup area of Orly International. The cavernous chamber was nearly deserted, and he felt terribly conspicuous in his bulky military-surplus jacket, sitting by himself with no apparent business in the terminal. If he was outward bound, he should have been killing time in Departures; if meeting someone, then Arrivals was the place to be. He worried that security police might take an interest in him, pause to ask him questions he could never hope to answer. If they asked about the jacket, tried to check beneath it, he was finished.

As he waited for the others, Jabez al-Malik experienced his first real doubts about their mission. It was planned for everyone to get away in the confusion, but he knew that plans were insubstantial things, perpetually altered by the whims of fate and circumstance. It was entirely possible that some of them—or *all* of them—would die this afternoon. In theory, he was ready for it. In practice, though...

His eyes picked out the figure of Nizam Mihdi, leader of their band, emerging from the mens' room on the far side of the baggage chamber. Their eyes met, neither man displaying any sign of recognition.

Within five minutes the other members of the team arrived. Without a sign to either of his comrades, Hakim Buzurg moved past the baggage carousels, homing in on a newspaper vending machine. He could not read or speak a word of French, but Buzurg bought a paper anyway, opening the pages up at random, scanning with a rapt expression on his face as he leaned back against the wall.

Omar Melekshah entered the area holding a steaming cup of coffee in one hand, the other tucked inside a roomy pocket of his topcoat. A wispy mustache, slick hair and mirrored aviator glasses gave him the appearance of a Mexican *bandito* or a trafficker in drugs. Jabez al-Malik cringed as Omar made his way across the baggage chamber, fairly strutting past the porters, nodding once and flashing his teeth at a security policeman on rounds. The idiot would get himself arrested—get them *all* arrested—if he kept on playing games.

Four-thirty.

Flights were due from Italy and the United States, arriving almost simultaneously. In a few more minutes, close to seven hundred passengers would be descending on the baggage carousels to jostle for their luggage, juggling satchels as they tried to fight their way back through the crowd. Today, some of them would not make it to their destinations.

Rumbling footsteps, babbling voices, from above him and behind, the sounds of human cattle moving in a herd toward stairs and escalators. Slipping one hand underneath his jacket, he double-checked the Skorpion machine pistol by touch. Magazine in place. Safety switch released and fire selector set for automatic mode. A live round in the firing chamber. Two spare magazines inside the lining of his jacket, on the left, where he could reach them easily at need. The Makarov 9 mm automatic, tucked inside his waistband, in the middle of his back, was currently beyond his reach. Its bulk, the stony jab against his spine, was reassuring all the same. He had rehearsed the draw a hundred times, and he had checked the backup gun no more than forty minutes earlier. It would perform upon command.

The tourists from America and Italy were crowding past him, their voices joining in a babble that al-Malik could not understand. Before the mission each of them had been compelled to learn some basic French—enough to answer simple questions, ask directions, hail a taxi—but he was assaulted now by jabberings in languages he could not identify. The Hindu family, with its shrouded women, red dots painted on their foreheads, was identifiable on sight, but who could tell the Turks from Greeks or Spaniards, the Americans from Englishmen or Scandinavians?

It did not matter, finally, if he could tell the sheep and goats apart. Collectively, without regard to race or nationality or creed, they were his enemies, potential targets in the holy war that was his life, his reason for existence. It was not for him to understand why Allah had selected Orly International, this day and these targets to reveal himself and offer an example to the infidels. It was enough that he had spoken, through his earthly representative, decreeing that it must be so. Jabez al-Malik recognized divine instructions, and he would obey.

He felt some apprehension all the same, and with the knowledge of his weakness came an overriding sense of shame. He was embarrassed by the doubts that lingered in his mind, afraid that he would prove himself unworthy when the time arrived.

He could no longer see the baggage carousels—too many sweating bodies in the way—but he could hear the hum of the conveyor belts as they began their endless circuit, luggage surfacing as if by magic from its subterranean collection point. The jostling began, some of the tourists laughing at themselves or their companions, others cursing underneath their breath, the vast majority content to wait or struggle in heroic silence. Now the lucky few were bulling through the mob toward numbered exits, bags clutched in their hands or trailing after them on wheels.

He glanced at Nizam Mihdi, received the silent signal they had all been waiting for. He was digging underneath his jacket for the Skorpion when hell erupted in the baggage chamber, automatic weapons blazing in a wicked cross fire. They were armed with a motley collection of hardware—his Skorpion, two mini-Uzis, a Beretta Model 12—but all of them were lethal at short range. Jabez al-Malik was not forced to choose a target. He simply pointed in the general direction of the panicked crowd and squeezed off short bursts, the thrill of combat singing in his blood.

He saw a woman fall. Another, huge with child, was thrashing on the floor. Beside her, kneeling in a pool of blood, was a Catholic priest, his collar flecked with crimson. The Skorpion stuttered its lethal lead, bullets slamming into random targets, dropping them without regard to age or sex. With thunder ringing in his ears, al-Malik offered up a prayer, calling on the God of all creation to accept his sacrifice.

A grenade exploded in the crowd, its shrapnel knifing through the crush of bodies, the stench of smoke competing with the smell of cooking meat. Omar Melekshah lobbed a second fragmentation bomb across the vaulted chamber, grinning as he fired his machine pistol one-handed, raking the crowd.

They were surging back in *his* direction now, the mob behaving like a huge, amorphous single-celled organism, flanked by pain on every side. A vast amoeba attempting to escape, aware within itself that no escape was possible.

A teenage girl lurched toward him, blouse and sweater torn to reveal her breasts. It was her face, however, that commanded his attention. It was stripped of flesh along one side, the naked bone and muscle visible beneath. The terrorist raised the Skorpion to finish her, and panicked as the hammer fell upon an empty chamber.

She was on him now, her bloody fingers groping for support, the blind eyes unaware that she was clutching at her mortal enemy. He slammed the muzzle of his weapon across her skull and drove her to her knees, retreating as he ripped the lining from his jacket. He lost one magazine but saved the other, wrestling it into place. He must destroy her, wipe the accusation from her ruined face with fire and steel.

Before he had a chance to aim and fire, the sharp reports of automatic rifles echoed through the baggage chamber, challenging the sputter of machine guns. Security police were responding to the attack, converging on all sides, their uniforms like punctuation marks throughout the crowd.

And they were firing for effect. He saw Hakim Buzurg go down, the tall man's life terminated by a round that drilled his forehead, peeling back the cranium as if it came equipped with hinges. Nizam Mihdi was concentrating on the uniforms, his Uzi spitting short precision bursts, but there were other officers behind him, closing, and he would not make the exit.

Al-Malik was up and running, dodging through the crowd, intent on finding cover. Ahead, the women's rest room beckoned, and he shouldered through the door, cheeks flaming with embarrassment, humiliation, as two frightened women stood before him, screaming. He was screaming, too, before he shot them, and a sudden ringing silence fell inside the rest room. From the slaughterhouse outside, a final burst of rifle fire informed him that the officers had dealt with Omar Melekshah.

He alone remained, and they were coming for him. He could not hear them yet, would not be able to communicate with them in any case, but he could still extract a price before they killed him. Shamed by cowardice, the fact that only he had broken, only he had run, Jabez al-Malik braced himself to make a final stand and kill as many of the infidels as possible before they cut him down.

Behind him, from the nearest stall, he heard the snuffling sound of bitter weeping. Startled, recognizing opportunity as he recovered from initial fright, he threw his weight against the door, defeated by its latch. The woman moaned in terror as he backed off, aimed his weapon at the locking mechanism and squeezed off a burst that slammed the door wide open.

She was terrified to move, but he removed the element of choice, the fingers of his free hand tangled in her hair as he dragged her, unceremoniously, away from the commode. She faced the door on her knees, with Jabez al-Malik standing at her back, the muzzle of his Skorpion pressed hot against one ear.

The first man through the door was braced to kill him, could have done so with a single burst, but there was still the woman to consider. Jabbering in French, he held his rifle leveled at al-Malik, calling to his backup, standing rigid as the others crowded in behind him. Three. Then four. Now five.

Enough.

If he could salvage anything from this humiliation, it would be through dying, offering his life for the glory of Allah. There was nothing on the other side to fear and everything to wish for. In another moment he would join Nizam Mihdi and his other comrades in the garden. If he earned the right, redeemed himself in time.

His free hand snaked around to find the Makarov, released it from its holster in the middle of his back. He flicked the safety off, thumbed back the hammer in a single fluid motion and raised both it and the submachine gun. Thunder exploded in his ears and in his blood. A marching cadence. He could see the garden in his mind; he recognized it instantly. And he was smiling as he died.

1

"Five minutes to the drop zone."

"Right."

"You sure this trip is necessary, man?"

"I'm sure."

"I was afraid of that."

Mack Bolan could appreciate the pilot's obvious concern. Jack Grimaldi had been with him from the early days of Bolan's private war against the Mafia, and they had seen some hairy times together. Jack would grouse and bitch about a job from time to time, but he would always see it through.

"Suppose your contact doesn't make it?"

Bolan frowned. It was a possibility, of course, and he had made allowances. "I go in by myself," he answered. "We don't have the target fixed, but I can still approximate. With any luck, I'll stumble over something."

"Just so something doesn't stumble over *you*."

"I'll do my best."

"Four minutes."

Time to check his gear. He wore a single parachute, which he had packed himself. A backup would have been superfluous, considering the altitude at which he planned to jump, and he would have his hands full burying the gear he had in the rocky ground.

Aside from the essential parachute and goggles, Bolan wore a pack with three days' rations, a first-aid kit, canteens, collapsible entrenching tool and a wicked Tanto fighting knife. His side arm was the sleek Beretta 93-R, fitted with its special silencer, complete with half a dozen extra magazines. Across his chest the soldier carried a Kalashnikov assault rifle, the same AK-47 distributed by agents of the KGB to terrorists and "armies of liberation" the world over. A bit heavy for Bolan's taste, the rifle had proved its reliability in unforgiving desert terrain... and it preserved deniability—as did the Soviet grenades he carried, scavenged by the CIA from would-be terrorists in Yucatán. If he was killed or captured in the course of what he was about to do, his weapons and equipment would not give his nationality or personal identity away.

"That's three."

He double-checked the harness of his parachute and the catches specially designed for quick release on touchdown, and found the rip cord with his eyes closed. Just in case. A half moon rode above the mountains, northward, bathing sand and stone in cold, relentless light. The rocky foothills lay ahead, an alien environment, hostile to intruders, etched in shades of black and gray.

They had approached the barren land from the sea, after taking off from Israel on the heels of midnight. Grimaldi had set his course for Cyprus, playing to the radar tracking stations in Beirut and Port Said, giving them fifteen minutes before he dropped off-screen and swung back to the east. They crossed the Syrian coastline south of Baniyas unobserved, Grimaldi homing on the rugged Elburz Mountains, north of Hamah. Somewhere up ahead, among the rugged peaks and valleys, Bolan's target waited for him, marking time.

"You've got the homer?"

"Yes."

"You still need forty-eight?"

"No change."

Two days. It might not be enough, but on the other hand, two days could be a lifetime.

"Two."

Bolan shed the earphones, stood in the open door. Without the jumper's goggles, wind rush would have blinded him immediately; as it was, his cheeks were filled with rushing air, the jumpsuit molded to his body like a second skin. He gripped the doorframe to prevent himself from being prematurely blown away.

"One minute!"

Jack Grimaldi's voice was nearly lost, a whisper in the gale, but Bolan caught the message and crouched slightly in the doorway as he braced himself. Their plane was still below the altitude for radar, and he caught sight of boulders, brush and stunted trees thrown into clear relief by moonlight. If he veered off course by so much as a fraction—

"Go!"

Bolan pushed off, let the slipstream carry him below the fuselage and clear of impact with the plane. Arms tight against his sides, he hurtled toward the rocky ground below, a sentient projectile on a hard collision course with Mother Earth.

Five hundred feet. He spread his arms and legs to heighten wind resistance, subtly changing course. He had seen a light, winking in the darkness below him. A beacon, beckoning him back to Earth, prepared to guide him home.

Except that home was not below him. *Home,* if it existed after so much time, was half a world away. His target was the killing ground, and he had come to teach an object lesson in the politics of death.

The beacon had been right on time, but there was still the possibility of ambush. Given Syria's connections with the terrorist fraternity, betrayal and exposure of his mission were potential facts of life—or death. Committed to the job in any case, he would expect the best, prepare to face the worst and forge ahead without regard to what might happen on the ground.

Three hundred feet. He found the rip cord and deployed the special parachute, his rate of fall decelerating as the nylon canopy took wind. He played the risers, hauling first to starboard, then to port, negotiating currents as he targeted the beacon, homing on the light that was the only sign of welcome in a hostile landscape.

Impact. Bolan tucked himself into a textbook shoulder roll and came out of it on his knees, the AK-47 in his hands, his chute spilled out behind him like a giant's soiled, discarded handkerchief. If there was danger in the darkness, it would come at him now, before he had an opportunity to get his balance and look for cover.

Nothing.

He had lost the beacon seconds prior to touchdown as it was extinguished by his contact—or his enemies. He did not need it; the moonlight was sufficient for him to detect a slender figure, seemingly alone, approaching him across the stony ground. The shadow walker made no effort to conceal himself, but he was armed, the outline of a rifle barrel clearly visible above one shoulder.

"Far enough."

If he was Bolan's contact, he should certainly be able to converse in English. He would also know the recognition signal. If he wasn't, his lag time on the draw would see him dead before he had a chance to slip the rifle off his shoulder, swinging it around and into target acquisition.

"The quality of mercy..."

" . . . is not strained."

"I am Hafez Kasm."

"Mike Belasko."

The Arab's grasp was firm and dry.

Bolan tugged the helmet off and dropped his harness, reeling in the parachute until it foamed around his knees like surf. He was unfolding the collapsible entrenching tool when Kasm cleared his throat.

"A waste of time," the Arab said.

"How's that?"

"This ground is hard for digging. We will be here after sunrise."

"I can't leave this gear exposed."

"There is a better way."

Hafez Kasm helped to gather up the gear, then led the Executioner across the rocky landscape, climbing fifty feet or so as they traversed a hundred yards. The ridge was broken into stony shelves, with recessed niches underneath, and Kasm spent a moment with his flashlight, searching for a niche to meet his needs.

"No cobras here," he said. "If they come later, it is all the same to us." With no more explanation, he began to stuff the parachute and other gear beneath the rocky outcrop, Bolan helping once he saw what the man meant to do. The arid soil revealed no footprints when they finished, and the evidence of Bolan's midnight touchdown was invisible without determined scrutiny.

"We go."

"How far?"

"One day, if we are lucky. There is climbing to be done. Our road is upside all the way."

"Up*hill*," Bolan corrected.

The Arab grinned. "Okay."

Kasm had not exaggerated. It was uphill all the way, and Bolan's legs were aching by the time they put a mile behind them, winding in and out among huge stones, along a track that seemed to be reserved for mountain goats. There was a road nearby, but it was dangerous to travel in the open, even after nightfall, and Kasm refused to take the risk. In any case, the moon provided them with ample light for navigation, warning them of hooded cobras in their path on two occasions. The guide pelted them with stones until they slithered out of sight among the boulders.

The desert night was crisp and clear, the temperature belying latitude and longitude. By day, the barren land would bake beneath a brutal sun, but after nightfall, human flesh would chill if left exposed to the eternal, moaning wind. A land of contradictions and anomalies, where the love of Allah and mankind walked hand in hand with the concept of jihad—holy war against the infidel.

As Bolan climbed the rocky slope, he wondered at the motives of his guide. Hafez Kasm was from all appearances a native Syrian, presumably a follower of Islam, but he also drew a covert paycheck from the CIA. Without assistance from Kasm and others like him, Bolan's present mission would have been impossible.

He had a target and an enemy in mind; the rest was open, blank. He had no estimate of hostile numbers, arms, deployment. He was winging it, from touchdown onward, and he did not like the feeling. Not at all.

There were trees in the landscape now, stunted, ghostly shapes by moonlight, twisted shadow arms outstretched in supplication, knotty roots like serpents, writhing on the surface of the arid ground. They would provide no cover in a firefight, but their very presence told him that the worst part of the desert was behind them. If he looked closely, sprouts of brittle grass were visible between the jagged stones, around the crooked tree roots. After six or seven miles, they had already climbed a thousand feet above the desert floor. Meager rain would fall more often here, although it would not come with frequency sufficient to support abundant life. In five or six more miles, they would be truly in the mountains, reasonably safe from observation by pursuers on the flats.

Kasm had stopped ahead, a silhouette against the sky, which had gone pallid with approaching dawn. "We have the sunrise soon," he said. "Time now for us to rest."

"You have a camp in mind?"

"This way."

He trailed the Arab for another hundred yards, until they reached a cave concealed from aerial reconnaissance by trees and overhanging rocks. Inside, the guide had hidden his bedroll, water bags and a satchel filled with food.

"No fire," he said and pointed toward the sky. "The smoke may bring us uninvited visitors." Extracting dates, raisins and strips of cured beef from the food bag, he offered some to Bolan, who accepted, washing down the fruit and salty meat with water from one of his canteens.

"How far?" he asked, when he was finished.

"Twenty-five kilometers, approximate. If we begin this afternoon, we should arrive this evening, late."

"Is there a faster way?"

"If we had vehicles, perhaps, but on the highway..." Bolan's guide looked sorrowful and shook his head, as if the very thought of driving to their destination was abhorrent, perilous beyond imagining.

"I don't have lots of extra time."

"Rest now. We will continue when the sun begins to fall. Less heat, more shadows for the blanket."

"That's 'cover.' You've seen the target?"

Hafez nodded, frowning. "I have seen it, yes."

"Describe it for me."

"How does one describe a legend? I am not a story-teller."

"Take a shot."

The Arab shook his head. "To understand the enemy, you must know something of his past."

"I'm listening."

"The story has its roots in ancient Persia, many, many years ago...."

2

Mack Bolan's mission had its roots at Stony Man, among the Blue Ridge Mountains of Virginia, half a world away from the embattled Middle East. He seldom showed his face around the Farm these days, preferring to avoid the ghosts and memories that lingered there, but on occasion it was unavoidable. Some messages could not be trusted to a runner or the telephone; some briefings could not be postponed. And it was better now, he told himself. New faces, for the most part. New ideas. Fresh blood.

He had been winding up a brutal skirmish with some cocaine cowboys when his brother Johnny had relayed Hal Brognola's message from their San Diego Strongbase. It was not a summons—Hal had never worked that way with Bolan—but the Executioner had come to recognize his old friend's moods, his turn of phrase, and Hal's oppressive sense of urgency was obvious when Johnny rolled the tape.

"I need to see the man as soon as possible. We've got a situation here that needs some personal attention, soonest."

Only that, nothing more, but he could read between the lines, inferring volumes from the tension in Brognola's voice. Hal would not call unless he thought it was important; he would not request a face-to-face unless the situation needed swift attention to avert catastrophe. It was enough for Bolan; he had wrapped up his current mission in record time and headed to Stony Man without delay.

Arrival at the Farm by air had never failed to spark a sense of unreality in Bolan's mind. The setting was idyllic, overlooking the historic Shenandoah Valley, heavily forested with hardwoods and conifers, the ground cover broken by gently rolling meadows on the Blue Ridge crest. The Farm had been named for neighboring Stony Man Mountain, one of the highest peaks in the range, and its sprawling acreage was less than a hundred air miles from Washington, D.C.

The pilot made a single pass before he set the chopper down, and Bolan scanned the layout—clustered buildings, cultivated fields. It was a working farm, from all appearances, but anyone who found his way inside the razor-wire perimeter would be surprised by the reactions of the farmhands. All of them had learned to handle automatic weapons first, before they took a turn with tractors, rakes and hoes. Beyond the planted acreage, in the trees, a team of mounted sentries kept their watch around the clock. Intruders would be taken into custody alive, if possible, but at the first sign of resistance, there would be no hesitation in the use of deadly force. Invasion of restricted space could get you killed, and anyone who opted to ignore the posted warnings took his own life in his hands.

Standing off to one side of the helipad, a solitary figure waited for him, hands in pockets, eyes invisible behind dark glasses. A smile was tugging at the corners of Bolan's mouth, and he let it win as he deplaned.

"Good morning, Mack," Barbara Price said in greeting. "I've missed you."

He followed her inside the ranch house, through the dining hall and kitchen to the elevators, for a short ride down. They found Brognola pacing in the basement War Room, Aaron "The Bear" Kurtzman watching from his wheelchair.

"Greetings," said The Bear. His grip was solid, firm, and Bolan marveled once again that Kurtzman's spirit had survived his crippling wounds, apparently unscathed. If he was suffering, the Stony Man "librarian" had learned to keep it under wraps.

Brognola crossed the room to greet the new arrival; brand-new worry lines around the big Fed's mouth and eyes confirming that Bolan had not been invited for a social visit.

"Everything turn out okay?" Brognola asked. It was a measure of the man's anxiety that he had been reduced to making small talk.

"Fine."

"You need to freshen up or anything before we start?"

"I'd rather get to business."

"Right. Okay."

He took a seat, with Barbara beside him, while Brognola pulled a chair out on the far side of the conference table. Kurtzman, at the console, was already dimming lights and calling up the video display. Downrange, a six-foot television screen filled up with silent snow, then cleared to present a battle scene.

No, he had been mistaken. This was not a battle. Rather, it had been a massacre, the twisted bodies of civilians piled on top of one another, seeming awkward and uncomfortable in their death throes. Panning now, the camera caught more bodies, dozens of them.

"Orly International," Brognola told him simply, calling up the memories of screaming headlines that were not yet two days old. "Four gunmen, thirty-seven dead, another fifty wounded."

As they watched, the screen went blank for several seconds, coming back to life with yet another scene of bloody chaos. This one was a street scene, shrouded bodies lined up outside what seemed to be a synagogue. He counted fifteen pairs of feet before the camera made its way inside, examining the bullet-scarred interior, more bodies wedged between the pews, awaiting extrication and removal by the paramedics.

"Amsterdam. May. The Temple Beth Shalom. Two shooters, nineteen dead and twenty-seven wounded."

Cut to a nocturnal scene, illuminated by the pulsing strobe lights of emergency vehicles. Slick sidewalks, dark and wet. Policemen wearing yellow slickers in the drizzling rain. A double-decker bus was stalled with two wheels on the curb, its broad expanse of windshield starred with bullet holes. The silent camera moved inside, this time before the ambulance attendants had a chance to do their job, and Bolan had a close-up view of the dead and dying passengers, their bodies slumped in narrow seats or tangled in the aisle. One of them moved—a woman in her middle thirties, bloody hands outstretched in the direction of the cameraman, lips moving in a sluggish supplication.

"London, earlier this month. One man on the bus, two others in a crash car. Twelve dead, eighteen wounded."

And the giant screen revealed another street, this time by daylight. Gawking passersby surrounded the remains of what, presumably, had been a building. Now it was smoking rubble, with soldiers moving in the wreckage. Bolan recognized Israeli uniforms.

"Bene Beraq," Brognola said, "a few klicks south of Tel Aviv. What you're seeing used to be a school before a pair of terrorists went in with AK-47s and a satchel charge. Another fifty-seven dead, with roughly equal numbers injured."

Kurtzman killed the video and keyed a slide projector, throwing faces onto a screen that had descended from the War Room's ceiling. There were twelve in all, eleven young faces in their last repose, all similar in death, the twelfth still alive, glaring back at the camera with supreme defiance, managing a sneer despite swollen lips and other evidence of rugged handling.

"The shooters," the Fed explained, as Kurtzman left the last face on the screen. "Israelis captured this one at Bene Beraq, some kind of lookout for the two inside the school. He killed himself in custody—wedged his head between a drainpipe and the wall of his cell and broke his own neck, if you can believe that—but he did some talking first. Mossad can be persuasive."

Bolan knew a bit about persuasion. "And?"

"According to the horse's mouth, the shooters at Bene Beraq were members of a Shiite faction, the Ismailis, based in Syria. Normally a quiet group, as Shiites go...until the past couple months."

"I take it other members of the sect have been connected to the incidents you've shown us?"

"That's affirmative. It seems male converts must be branded, here—" a finger jabbed at his lapel "—above the heart. A star and crescent. We've been noticing the brands since Amsterdam, but no one knew exactly what to make of them until Mossad got lucky. All four gunners at the Orly shooting match were marked."

"That isn't much to go on."

"We've got more," Brognola said. "A little, anyway. The Company has ears in Syria, and they've been tuning in for anything and everything about this group. They claim to have a general fix on the Ismaili stronghold."

"That sounds like one for the Israeli air force."

"Oh, they're willing, bet on it...but we've got problems. When I say a fix, I'm speaking generally. It's nothing you could plan an air strike from, and anyway, its not confirmed. As much as Tel Aviv would like to fry the scum, they can't afford a fumble. Things are bad enough without their Phantoms taking out some rural mosque or orphanage by accident."

"They need an agent on the ground."

Brognola nodded. "Right. They've tried three times. So far, they've got an MIA and two men dead, for sure."

"I've heard of these Ismailis," Barbara interrupted. "Haven't I?"

Brognola frowned. "You might've, if you're up on your religious history. They date back to Mohammed's time, or thereabouts, but they were best known in the Middle Ages. They were known as the Assassins."

Bolan felt his stomach tighten.

Barbara Price leaned forward, arguing with Brognola. "There must be some mistake. The cult of the Assassins was suppressed more than a hundred years ago. Its members were annihilated, temples razed."

Brognola spread his hands. "They're back," he said, "or else someone is trading on their reputation. Hell, for all I know, it may be like the Klan. Each time you break one up, some pinhead takes the name and starts all over. Either way, we've got a situation on our hands, and we can count on more of what you've seen today, unless we take the bastards down."

"We'll need a better fix," the soldier said.

"I'm working on it," Brognola replied. "The Company's got a guide on tap. He's ready when we are."

"This wouldn't be the same guide the Israelis used?"

The big Fed made a sour face. "I understand that *he*'s no longer with us."

"It's a risky business."

"More so, all the time."

"When do I leave?"

Brognola looked both relieved and troubled. "Tomorrow morning...if you're sure."

"I'm sure."

"I ought to tell you that the Man has some misgivings."

"Oh?"

"He knows we need to do it, but he doesn't like the risks involved, the chances of exposure."

"We'll just have to be discreet."

"Exposure?" Barbara Price was livid. "Damn it, the Israelis should be doing this! Let *them* make the connection with this so-called guide."

Brognola kept his eyes on Bolan, trying to ignore the woman's outburst. "Word from Tel Aviv is that the operation's cost too much already. They're prepared to launch an air strike—random targets, if it comes to that—but they won't put another agent on the ground until they find out what became of number three."

"They figure he's alive?"

"They don't know what to think, but they're not buying any offers of assistance from a Syrian, regardless of his contacts with the Company."

"Can't say I blame them."

"Well..."

"Go on and set it up. I'll pick the necessary gear tonight. How are we penetrating?"

"Air drop."

"One request?"

"I'm way ahead of you. Grimaldi's standing by. He'll meet you in the morning."

"Fair enough."

"I've got a briefing back in Wonderland at two o'clock," Brognola said. "Unless you've got some other questions...?"

"No."

"Okay. The Company's arranged a recognition signal; you can pick it up before you leave. Beyond the drop—"

"I know—I'm on my own."

Brognola scowled. "I hate this job."

The soldier smiled. "I don't believe that for a minute."

"No? I tell you, sometimes...ah, the hell with it. Be careful, will you?"

"It's my middle name."

"And I'm the secret son of Howard Hughes. Just watch yourself, all right?"

"All right."

Brognola shook his hand and left them there, returning to the helipad for the short ride to Washington.

"Anybody up for lunch?"

The soldier's appetite was fading fast, but he would eat. Every ounce of strength and stamina would be required on touchdown in a hostile land, and once across the battle lines, he would not have the luxury of dining rooms and catered meals. Desire for food bore no relationship to the necessity of nourishment. It was a lot like life, that way.

"More than nine hundred years ago," Kasm began, "three young men met at a religious school in Nishapur, becoming friends and brothers of the blood. A pact was made, that each would help the others when and where he could, throughout the years to come. If any one should prosper, all would share in his good fortune."

Feeling rather like a character from *One Thousand and One Nights*, held captive by Scheherazade, Mack Bolan kept his peace and listened.

"Each of these young men had hopes of doing well in life, especially since the students of their school never failed to find power and fame. One of them was Omar Khayyám, a great poet, author of *The Rubáiyát*. The second, Nizam-ul-mulk, became the Grand Vizier—what you in the United States might call the president—and he went on to offer each of his friends a governorship. Omar Khayyám declined, believing that he was not destined for a life of civil service, so the vizier granted him a pension for life, permitting him to lead a carefree life at Nishapur, pursuing the studies of poetry, astronomy and mathematics.

"The third man's name was Hasan al-Sabbah. He, too, declined the vizier's offer, not because he feared responsibility, but rather because his heart and mind were set on greater things. A provincial governorship would have confined him to Persia, but he sought to visit Cairo—then the seat of Muslim power—and the court of the caliph. Nizam-ul-mulk, a loyal friend, used his influence to secure employment in the caliph's service for Hasan."

The Arab paused to study Bolan's face a moment, then forged on.

"Now, Hasan al-Sabbah was a pious Shiite from the north of Persia. As you may already know, the Shiites believe that Ali, son-in-law of the prophet Mohammed, was Mohammed's true successor, while the great majority followed the first caliph, Abu Bakr. Thus, Islam suffered its first great rift soon after the prophet's death, in the year 632, and the Ismailis—followers of Ismail, the sixth 'true leader' after Ali—broke away from Shia doctrines in their turn.

"Persecuted as heretics in the early years, the Ismailis became a secretive and fanatical cult, drawing thousands of members from other Islamic groups. They became highly organized, dedicated students of science and astronomy, couching their doctrines in seductive form. So successful were they, in the face of persecution, that ten million known Ismailis still exist today...but that is neither there nor here."

"That's 'here nor there.'"

The slender Arab shook his head and smiled. "We know that Hasan al-Sabbah spent three years at the caliph's court in Cairo, at a time when the Ismaili sect controlled the caliphate. Within that time, he made powerful enemies with his intrigues. He was deported, but the ship was lost at sea. Hasan survived, and traveled overland to Syria, collecting followers along the way with promises of paradise on Earth. Unable to control the whole Ismaili sect, he would create another faction, with himself as leader."

"Sounds like certain people I could name today."

"Indeed. The name of Allah has been much abused by men who lust for power." Kasm hesitated, eyes downcast, as if his own words had embarrassed him.

"You don't have any corner on the market," Bolan told him. "The United States was founded with religious liberty in mind, and churches have been fighting ever since."

"You understand, then, how Hasan al-Sabbah could recruit young men in Syria, Iraq, throughout the region, winning them with visions of adventure and intrigue, a heavenly reward on Earth for those who would perform their duty faithfully. Selecting the castle of Alamut, in the heart of these mountains, for his headquarters, Hasan acquired it using stealth and treachery. One of his missionaries smuggled Hasan and a number of his followers into the castle, where they took the ruling leaders hostage and persuaded them to sell."

"An offer they couldn't refuse?"

"Precisely. With the castle and adjacent valley in his hands, Hasan assumed the title of Sheikh al-Jebal—the Old Man of the Mountain—implying that he was an incarnation of the prophet. His new doctrine demanded the murder of his enemies as a sacred religious duty, and Hasan's disciples were quick to obey his orders. Many of them drew their courage from the use of hashish, and were known as Hashshashin, or what you call Assassins. Sheikh al-Jebal also used the drug to make his followers believe that he had shown them paradise on Earth, a garden of delights where every wish and fantasy was instantly fulfilled by lovely women, nubile boys, the finest food and wine. Disciples who were privileged to see the garden came away devoted to the master, having lost all fear of death."

"It sounds effective." Bolan had encountered various conditioning techniques before, most of them negative and very painful, but it sounded like the Old Man of the Mountain had employed the pleasure principle to build himself a dedicated cadre. "I imagine there was very little his disciples wouldn't do to keep the master's favor."

"There was *nothing* they would not attempt, upon his slightest whim. Assassination, arson, rape and pillage were committed with the blessings of the prophet, in the name of Allah. In the early days, Hasan used terror to eliminate his enemies and win new followers. As time went on, he launched a holy war against the Turks and killed the Turkish emir of Damascus. Soon, the rulers of surrounding kingdoms—even, it is said, the Britons' Richard Lionheart—were using members of the Old Man's sect to kill their enemies, avoiding guilt by hiring 'heathen savages' to carry out their crimes."

"An early Murder, Incorporated."

"I beg your pardon?"

"Never mind. Go on."

"Hasan al-Sabbah lived until the time of the Crusades, becoming ancient in his castle fortress, ordering the deaths of thousands in his time. One of his victims was an old friend, Nizam-ul-mulk, who knew the falsehood of the Old Man's claims to personal divinity. Hasan is also rumored to have killed his sons—one of them simply for consuming too much wine."

"A sweetheart."

"Truly. But his death did not abolish the Assassin cult. He was succeeded by another Old Man of the Mountain, and another after him. The reign of terror continued for 150 years, until Crusaders of the Christ invaded Syria and captured Alamut. It was believed the sect had been destroyed, but soldiers of the British empire found it active in Bombay as recently as 1850. I am told that some historians believe the Old Man's scattered followers may have adopted Kali as their goddess, so creating the Thuggee."

"And now they're back?" It was a lot to swallow, with a century and more between the Bombay trials and the attack on Orly International, but Bolan noticed that his contact was not smiling.

"The Eagle's Nest at Alamut is occupied once more, and killers with the mark of the Hashshashin have been slain or captured by authorities of several nations. It is not for me to say, but I believe the facts speech for themselves."

"That's 'speak.'"

"A thousand pardons."

"Skip it. The original Assassins... they were mercenaries?"

"So it has been written."

"And this latest bunch?"

"The same, if my accumulated information is correct."

"If the religion's back in business, it must have a leader."

"Yes. Another Old Man of the Mountain."

"Let me get this straight. The government of Syria allows this cult to operate, despite the risks involved?"

"Our government is dominated by the Ba'ath Arab Socialist Party, which in turn is dominated by the military. Above all else, the government of Syria is Muslim first. We are perpetually at war with Israel, momentarily hostile to Iraq and closer to the Shiite rulers of Iran. You are aware of the position that our government has taken on support of training camps for fedayeen, the liberation fighters?"

Bolan nodded. Anyone with the ability to read a headline knew of Syria's continuing support for Arab terrorists through maintenance of training centers and supply depots. It came as no surprise that remnants of the old Assassin cult should find their sanctuary in the country that had sheltered Carlos, gunners for the PFLP and the PLO, along with sundry other jackals from around the world. Aside from Libya, where coexistence with the egomaniac Khaddafi might have been impossible, the Executioner could think of no more fertile soil for a "religion" founded on the tenet of murder for hire.

"You are a Muslim?"

Bolan's contact nodded. "Yes. But 'Muslim' and 'murderer' are not the same. I have participated in the war against the Zionists, but as a soldier." Kasm pinned the soldier with his eyes. "Will you believe me when I say that I have never killed a woman or a child?"

"I have no reason not to."

"Ah. Some of your people see an Arab, and they need to see no more. They see Khaddafi, Arafat, no matter where they look."

"*My* people?"

"The Americans, the Europeans. It is much the same."

"Like Arabs?"

For the briefest moment, Bolan's contact frowned, and then he shook his head, a sheepish smile appearing on his face. "Your point is taken. I apologize."

"No need. We live and learn."

"Some live," Kasm replied, "but never learn."

"Which brings us back to the Assassins. How long have they been in operation this time?"

"It is difficult to say. Perhaps a year. My contacts in the government are frightened. When the leader's name is mentioned, they begin to roll their eyes."

"You know his name?"

"I know the one he uses, though it may not be the name his mother gave him. He calls himself Abdel al-Sabbah and claims to be a lineal descendant of Hasan, the founder of the sect. His followers revere him as Sheikh al-Jebal."

"The Old Man of the Mountain."

Kasm nodded grimly. "This one knows his history, if nothing else. His followers believe he is descended from

Hasan al-Sabbah, who in turn was thought to be descended from Mohammed. Thus, he is infallible, the voice of Allah.''

"That's incredible.''

The Arab shrugged. "Perhaps. But in America, do you not have the ministers who make a mockery of their religion, using Christ for selfish ends?''

"We do,'' the Executioner conceded, "but I have never heard of anyone who claimed he was the great-grandson of Jesus.''

"It is all a matter of degree. Another prophet has been looked for, by Ismailis in particular, and some of them believe that they have found him. It matters little if he calls on them to kill or sacrifice themselves. He makes a guarantee of paradise, and many such young men would join the fedayeen in any case. The promise of a perfect afterlife assures them they can do no wrong.''

"And while they die, the Old Man profits?''

"So it would appear. These days, he ventures rarely from the Eagle's Nest, but when he does, he travels, as you say, in fashion.''

"That's 'in style.' ''

"I have a problem with your idiots.''

"Try 'idioms.' '' The soldier grinned.

"Of course.'' Kasm responded with an easy smile. "It is apparent, from his scope of operations, that the sect is well-financed, supplied with weapons and explosives.''

"Government support?''

"Undoubtedly... but from *which* government?''

The Executioner was edging toward thin ice, but he was not about to turn back now. "You may not have to look too far from home.''

"It was my own first thought, but such is not the case. How can I make you understand? The military leaders of

Ba'ath are followers of Islam, as am I, but they are not such zealots as the Old Man of the Mountain and his followers. I think our leaders are afraid to trifle with the Hashshashin."

"The guns and money have to come from somewhere. Have you thought about Khaddafi?"

Kasm nodded slowly. "Once again, my sources claim uncertainty. As for myself, I think the Libyan is too—how would you say it in America—involved with Number One?"

"That's how we'd say it," Bolan answered. "If you're right, we've narrowed down the possibilities."

"Indeed. Despite their recent actions, I do not believe the sect is self-supporting. Weapons and explosives must be purchased, cash exchanged with willing vendors."

"Not if they're a gift, with strings attached."

The Arab's eyes were downcast. "I have pondered this. It grieves me, but I fear that you may be correct."

"The KGB?"

"I have no proof, but it is foolish to suggest the Russians are not active in my country. They are friendly with the fedayeen, although such friends, I think, are worse than enemies."

It played. Throughout certain parts of the world, agents of the KGB were known as sugar daddies of misguided revolution, doling out cash and arms like there was no tomorrow, giving weapons freely where recipients could not afford to pay. Kalashnikovs and Soviet grenades had turned up in the hands of terrorists from Bogotá to Belfast, from Venice to Vientiane. The Russians had a stake in chaos, an investment in the sordid world of terrorism, and they meant to get their money's worth.

The soldier changed his tack. "How long have you been working for the Company?"

"Almost three years. This strikes you as unusual?"

He nodded. "Frankly, yes."

"You must not think I am a traitor to my country. I am not a puppet who will dance whenever someone in the Agency pulls strings."

"I see."

The Arab hunched forward, elbows resting on his knees. "I still believe the Zionists were wrong to build their 'homeland' on the soil they stole from others, but the time for holy war is past. We cannot live on oil and hatred for all time." He paused. "This business with the Hashshashin is dangerous for Syria, my people. If we seem to sanction such extremities, we may become like Libya, a land apart. I have no wish to live in exile from the world."

"You've given this some thought."

"A man must choose his destiny," Kasm went on. "Allah may attempt to guide his footsteps through the holy word of the Koran, but in the end each one of us must stand alone."

"I would imagine that you're taking quite a chance."

"Opposing evil is a dangerous pursuit. I think you know that, from your own experience."

"I'm in a different situation. You have family here."

"A wife, two children. They know nothing of my business with the Company."

"I wonder if the General Intelligence Directorate would buy that?"

At his mention of the Syrian secret police, Kasm paled, but his jaw remained firm, and Bolan saw no tremor in his hands. "I pray about such things," the Arab said at last. "One day, the leaders of my country will be thankful that the Hashshashin were driven out. With Allah's guidance, they will understand the error of their ways."

"You place a lot of faith in God."

"What else do I have?"

The silence spun between them for a moment, Bolan realizing that the Arab had been speaking from his heart.

"When this is over," he suggested, "you might want to think about evacuating."

"No." Kasm shook his head in an emphatic negative. "My place is here. These times shall pass."

"How old are you?"

The Arab looked confused. "I will be twenty-eight next month," he said at last.

"This war was going on a dozen years before your birth. You really think you'll see the end of it?"

"I must believe. When Allah made this land, he did not plan for it to be a battlefield."

"Some plans just don't work out."

"Indeed. But *you* believe. I see it in your eyes. You would not be here, otherwise."

"Sometimes I wonder."

"Do you? I believe you know precisely what you have been fighting for."

"It's different," Bolan told him. "I don't mean to change the world. The best that I can hope for is to even out the odds a little, keep the jackals running. If you let them rest too long, they start to feed."

"They have been feeding here. Together, I have hopes that we may scatter them again."

"You wouldn't work with the Israelis?"

"No. They only care about *their* people, land they stole from others to create a sanctuary for themselves. I will not bring them here to trespass on my homeland."

"I'm a stranger here, as well."

"There is a difference. You have no desire to rule my country, or destroy it in the name of self-defense. The Hashshashin have jeopardized the safety of your people, as they jeopardize my own. We share a common interest, you and I. Together, with the help of Allah, we will find the Eagle's Nest and rid the world of many jackals.''

Bolan made no mention of the compact signaling device he carried in his pack, the Phantoms standing by to strike on cue. His mission and his life depended on the Arab's guidance, his cooperation, and the soldier's ears were ringing with a sour note.

"Did you say *find* the Eagle's Nest?''

"I did.''

"It was my understanding that you had the target spotted.''

Warily, his contact shrugged. "I know the mountains, the location, but in truth, I have not been to Alamut myself. Is this a difficulty?''

"You could say that.'' Alarm bells went off inside the warrior's skull, and he felt the short hairs rising on his neck. "Do you have aerials?''

"Again, please?''

"Photographs, from airplanes. They would show the layout, give us some idea of numbers. Do you have them?''

Kasm shook his head. "The government has made no aerial reconnaissance of Alamut. No photographs exist...or so I have been told.''

"All right, an estimate of numbers, then.''

"Sheikh al-Jebal has many followers. We know that much, but numbers are uncertain. It has never been considered wise to count the Hashshashin.''

"We're blind, then.''

"Not entirely. We have Alamut, we have our faith, we know our enemy by name.''

"I make it zero out of three,'' the Executioner replied. "We haven't found our target yet, I don't take anything on faith, and names don't mean a whole lot in this business. Give me numbers any day.''

"Would you have come in any case, if you had known?"

That stopped him for a moment, and he finally nodded. "Yes."

"And why?"

"To do the job."

"Precisely. We must do the job, regardless of the cost. The 'numbers,' as you call it, are irrelevant."

Perhaps. But they could get a soldier killed.

"We'd better get some rest."

"Indeed. Tomorrow—no, *today*—we have a march of several hours still ahead of us. The mountains give us shelter, but they also make us work to reach our destination."

Bolan thought about the march of "several hours," climaxed by a battle he could never hope to win. It had been foolish to accept the mission knowing he was cut off from supply lines and support. He had one man to back him up, and that one man was pinning all his hopes on an assist from Allah in the crunch.

Terrific.

Spreading out his bedroll at the far end of the cave, he lay down with the Makarov in hand, his AK-47 propped against the rocky wall, beside his head. If they were taken by surprise, he still might have an opportunity to make a showing for himself. It was the best that he could do. They had no place to run.

And sleep was coming. He could feel it tugging at his eyelids now, demanding unconditional surrender. Kasm was on first watch, so Bolan let the creeping sluggishness insinuate itself into his arteries and veins, the natural narcotic wafting him away.

As sleep moved in to claim him, Bolan prayed he would not dream.

4

He woke to the sensation of a strong hand on his shoulder and swung up the Makarov, the muzzle leveled on Kasm's face before the slender Arab could react. He eased the hammer down and checked his watch, surprised to find that he had slept undisturbed for seven hours.

"You were supposed to wake me when your shift was over."

"I had sleep last night, while you, I think, did not."

"The last thing I need is a groggy guide."

The Arab shook his head and grinned. "Americans. You think that I will not—how I say it?—go the length?"

"The distance."

"Ah."

"We're ready, then?"

"Almost."

The guide rummaged in a pack that had been waiting for them in the cave, producing linen robes Bolan recognized as caftans, favored by so many desert travelers in the Middle East. A *keffiyeh*—an Arab headdress—would complete the outfit perfectly.

"What's this?" he asked, although he had an inkling of Kasm's plan.

"Your uniform will do quite nicely for a meeting with Sheikh al-Jebal," the Syrian replied, "but in the meantime, we endeavor to be less conspicuous. The caftan will conceal a multitude of sins, as you might say." As Kasm spoke, he gestured toward the AK-47 that rested against the rocky wall near Bolan's bedroll.

"And you think the robe will help me pass for a native?"

"Possibly, if you resist the urge to speak in English for the benefit of strangers. When we reach the Eagle's Nest..."

He let the statement trail away, and his frown told Bolan that he was not certain what would happen once they made their destination. Bolan felt a measure of that same uncertainty, but he could not afford to let it grow.

"We'll manage."

"Yes." His contact did not sound convinced. "It would be better if we had a plan, I think."

"I'll have to play it by ear," Bolan told him. "If we find an in, I'll take it. If we don't..."

And there was nothing more to say. He took a moment to arrange the AK-47 on its shoulder strap so that it hung beneath his right arm, muzzle downward. The Makarov was shifted in its holster, from his right hip to the left, a cross-hand draw that sacrificed a fraction of a second, but that made more sense beneath the robe. He used the Tanto blade to slit his caftan on the right, from belted sash to armpit, granting quicker access to the folding-stock Kalashnikov. He tugged the *keffiyeh* into place, adjusted the headband for comfort and turned to face Hafez Kasm once again.

"I think that you will pass," his guide declared. Kasm had donned his traveling attire while Bolan dressed, his semiautomatic rifle casually slung across one shoulder. "But remember. I must do the talking if we meet with any strangers on the way. Until we reach our destination, you are deaf and mute from birth. Agreed?"

"Sounds good to me."

They shouldered packs and bedrolls, then left the cave once Bolan's guide had satisfied himself they would not be observed. Their den had been protected from the desert sun and was relatively cool, but now the baking heat struck Bolan like a fist, producing instant perspiration on his brow. The earth was simmering below them on the desert floor, but even altitude could not assure them total respite from the heat.

Kasm was pointing northeast. "Five more kilometers," he said, "until we reach a mountain spring where travelers are welcome. We can refresh ourselves there before continuing."

Five more kilometers. Bolan made it roughly three miles, give or take. It should have been an easy stroll, except the path they followed still led uphill all the way, negotiating goat tracks, blazing trails where mountain fauna had declined to go. The "highway," well below them, was a one-lane ribbon scarcely worthy of the name. No traffic passed as they were climbing, but Kasm kept glancing backward, toward the lowlands, like a fugitive expecting hot pursuit.

With mental time to kill, the soldier scrutinized his guide. The Arab seemed sincere enough, and he had spoken from the heart that morning; Bolan would have bet his life on it. He *was*, in fact, by trusting everything to someone he had met just hours earlier, but he was caught up in the kind of mission where you couldn't simply hit the beach, blitz everything in sight and fade back out again. Successful penetration of a hostile camp, inside a hostile country, made the buddy system mandatory, and if it was still too soon to fully trust Hafez Kasm, Bolan was prepared to grant a measure of that trust, provisionally.

He was a decent judge of character, all in all, and he assessed the Syrian as honest, even dedicated, in his way. If Hafez Kasm was a patriot, his loyalty to a homeland didn't blind him to the human frailties of the men in charge. He could revere the land of his birth and still resist the tide that swept so many of his countrymen toward chaos and destruction. Once a soldier, he could draw the line between combatants and civilians, terrorism and the conduct of a fighting man at war.

The choice to work with the CIA could not have been an easy one, all things considered. With a wife and family at risk, the very fact of his involvement with a foreign government spoke volumes for the Arab's courage, his determination to oppose the dark malignancy of terror that had fastened on his native land.

Would he succeed at last? Did he have any chance at all? Could one man—or a hundred—turn the running tide in Syria? In any country?

Bolan shrugged the questions off. Philosophy was not his field of expertise, and he would leave it to the thinkers in their ivory towers to debate the ultimate futility or worth of human sacrifice. He knew one dedicated man could make a difference—and he also knew that there were limitations on a single man's ability to shape the course of history. Each man on Earth was spinning out his days on borrowed time, engaged in fruitless games of beat the clock, and many never found a way to make their time count at all. Each man would face his private judgment day, regardless of his chosen role as poet, patriot or executioner.

Perhaps today.

Bolan marked a pair of vultures circling in the distance, mere specks against the shocking azure sky. They had no interest in him, their keen eyes focused on carrion below.

On level ground, the three-mile hike should have consumed an hour or less. Today, the rough terrain combined with heat and altitude to nearly double that, and Bolan's legs were aching when Kasm declared the first phase of their journey at an end.

"Wait here," he said, and Bolan noted that his contact's voice was lowered almost to a whisper. Crouching in the shade afforded by a stand of trees, he watched as his guide scaled a rocky outcrop then disappeared on the other side. He ticked off ninety seconds in his mind before the Syrian returned, a pained expression on his face.

"What is it?"

"We have company." He frowned. "Four men on foot, with rifles."

"Can we go on to the next spring?"

"There will be no other on our way," the Arab told him, shrugging resolutely. "We must have the water for our journey."

"We could wait them out." But even as he spoke, he knew that they couldn't afford to wait. The clock was running down on this mission, precious moments slipping through his hands.

Kasm could obviously read his companion's sense of urgency. The Arab shook his head and offered a cautious smile. "They may be ordinary travelers," he said. "Not all who pass through the mountains here are bandits. They should not feel threatened by a man alone, and I will offer nothing worth their effort for the taking."

As he spoke, he slipped the semi-auto rifle off his shoulder, passing it to Bolan. "From the point that I will show you, you will have a view of anything that happens. If there should be trouble..." He shrugged and left the final plea unspoken.

"You'll be covered," Bolan promised, "but you shouldn't go in empty-handed."

"Never fear." Kasm reached underneath his caftan and withdrew a vintage Webley revolver. He broke the weapon, checked its load and tucked it beneath his robe. "If you will follow me?"

Bolan's lookout post was roughly eighty feet above the point where native stone had been collected to create a basin for the flowing mountain stream. The spring, in turn, was roughly twenty feet above the level of the narrow highway, access granted by a footpath etched out of the mountainside. Four men in brightly colored caftans lounged around the spring, enjoying shade from the trees that overhung the small pool. From his perch, Bolan had a shot at all four, providing he didn't allow them time to scatter, if and when the fireworks started.

The rifle in his hands was a Czech Model 52, chambered in 7.62 mm, with a 10-round, double-staggered magazine attached. Similar in overall design to the M-1 Garand, the weapon was a virtual antique. The Executioner's expression as he looked it over brought a cautious smile from his companion.

"It is accurate," Kasm informed him. "I have seen to that."

"Okay."

The veteran sniper found himself a niche and settled in. Kasm began the combination hike and crawl downslope with their canteens, all dangerously close to empty now. The strangers heard him coming halfway down and broke off their conversation, all four men immediately on their feet with weapons pointed at the new arrival.

Bolan pressed his cheek against the worn stock of the borrowed rifle, praying that Kasm was right about its accuracy. There was no time to make the switch in any case. Whatever happened in the next few seconds, he was bound to play the game according to the rules the Syrian laid down. But he was not obliged to like it. Not at all.

HAFEZ KASM SCRAMBLED DOWN the last few yards of sloping, rocky ground, endeavoring to keep his hands in view without surrendering his balance completely. If he fell, the strangers would be bound to laugh at him, and honor would demand some form of satisfaction. In the circumstances, even with the American prepared to cover him, it was a risk he did not relish taking.

Feeling better with his feet on level ground, Kasm put on his most ingratiating smile. "Greetings, my brothers. Peace to you this day."

"I know my brothers when we meet," one of them growled. "Your face is strange to me."

"A weary traveler in need of water," Kasm replied, a knot of apprehension tightening around his heart. He held up the canteens, his free hand tugging the sash around his waist to loosen it and let his caftan gap in front. "I mean you no disturbance."

"You disturb me all the same," the leader sneered, and his companions chuckled. "How can I rest with magpies all around?"

Refusing to accept the insult, Kasm made a show of glancing at the sky, apparently bewildered. "I regret your rest has been disturbed by thoughtless birds," he said at last. "By some good fortune, it appears that I have frightened them away."

"One still remains."

"A coward, then. He will not show himself."

"He stands before me, crowing."

This time, Kasm scanned the ground around his feet, still smiling. "Surely there can be no magpie here."

"A mangy dog, then, baying at the moon."

"In daylight?"

"He is blind as well as stupid."

"Then I pity him. If I may have the water that I need, perhaps the thoughtless cur will follow me."

"This water?" Turning toward the spring, the gunman frowned, his rifle never straying far off target. "It belongs to me."

"Perhaps you are mistaken, brother."

"No. *You* are mistaken. You have twice confused me with your brother, and the second time since I attempted to correct your error. Those who fail to profit from mistakes are foolish."

"I must beg your pardon and rely on your generosity."

"You are presumptuous as well as ignorant."

"Again, I must apologize. I was informed this spring was free for travelers."

"Your information is mistaken, as are you."

"In that case, I will leave you to your rest."

It was a calculated risk to turn his back, but he had no choice. His robe was nearly hanging open now, the Webley in its holster, inches from his itching hand. Before he covered half a dozen paces, he was frozen by a voice behind him.

"Wait! I did not give you leave to go."

"I beg your pardon."

It was timing, plain and simple. As he turned, one hand was sliding underneath his caftan, circling the Webley's butt and sliding out again, his thumb already drawing back the hammer as he made his move. The gunmen were expecting meek compliance; they were unprepared for sudden thunder as the Webley roared to life, its heavy bullet toppling the leader in his tracks.

Kasm was diving for the precious cover of an outcrop as the second bandit took a rifle bullet in the face, his body twisting in an awkward pirouette before collapsing near his fallen comrade. Thirsty soil was drinking up their blood as number three collapsed, his hands clasped across a spouting chest wound. From the slopes above, the sound of rifle fire rolled down like summer thunder, echoing against the backdrop of the mountains.

Number four was moving, squeezing off a burst of automatic fire in the direction of the upper slope without a target firm in mind. Kasm used up a heartbeat as he aimed the Webley, firing once at twenty yards. The heavy slug ripped through his target's rib cage and dropped the gunman to his knees. Before Kasm had a chance to finished off the job, however, the American had launched another thunderbolt downslope, its lethal impact marked by spraying blood and brains.

An eerie, ringing silence settled on the killing ground. The Syrian emerged from cover, checking on the fallen enemy from habit rather than necessity. All four were dead—he knew that at a glance—but it was better to be certain.

The American was climbing down, the rifle slung across his shoulder to free his hands. Another moment, and he stood beside the Syrian, his face solemn, eyes like chips of flint.

"Let's get that water, shall we?"

"Yes."

Hafez bent, retrieved the canteens he had dropped and was moving toward the spring when he was frozen by a sudden, unexpected sound.

"What is it?"

"Listen!"

Now it was apparent the American could hear it, too, and there was no mistake—the sound of an approaching vehicle from the south, traveling along the narrow mountain road. And with the sudden clarity of one who sees his doom reflected in the stars, Hafez Kasm knew that there was nowhere left to run.

5

Securing the bodies was impossible, within the time allowed. Bolan and Kasm dragged the corpses to a stand of cedars, twenty feet beyond the running spring and rolled them down a rocky incline to the bottom of a small ravine. They would be clearly visible if someone wandered off in that direction to relieve himself or stretch his legs, and they would soon begin to ripen in the sun, emitting odors that would carry on the desert wind. But it was early yet for anyone to smell the dead, and with a little luck, they might be overlooked.

They spent another moment scuffing at the blood-stained sand with their boot heels. Before they finished, Bolan saw the vehicle approaching, which he recognized as a military jeep, the arrogant driver keeping to the middle of the narrow mountain road. There were three men, two of them dressed in military uniforms. Their passenger, sitting in back, was wearing light civilian khaki, with a *keffiyeh* on his head to shield him from the sun.

"Remember, you are deaf and dumb."

"Got it."

They had settled near the rocky basin of the spring, canteens still empty as they tried to strike the posture of two travelers at ease. The Executioner had hoped their visitors might pass them by, but running mountain springs appeared to be a mandatory stopping point. The jeep was slowing now, the driver braking to a halt below them at the bottom of the slope. His shotgun rider had them spotted, nudging his companion, and the soldiers both had hands on holstered pistols as they left the vehicle.

The civilian took his time about unloading, watching as his escorts made the first approach. Despite the *keffiyeh* and the shades, his face was familiar. Bolan set a portion of his mind to work trying to place the guy.

"Salaam alaikum."

Bolan caught that much of it, and then the rest was lost to him as Kasm and the soldiers spoke back and forth in Arabic. He didn't speak much of the language, but he trusted that his contact would provide some kind of danger signal if their butts were on the line. He knew that he could reach the Makarov before the soldiers drew, but whether he could take them both remained uncertain.

Still, it might not come to that. Their hands were off their pistols, and one man was smiling. He glanced at Bolan and said something to Kasm, provoking laughter from the guide. Some bit of humor at the Executioner's expense, no doubt. He didn't care what any of them said, as long as they were on their way within the next few minutes.

Scuffling sounds from the slope revealed that the civilian passenger was climbing up to join them. At close range, he was even more familiar, though the Executioner was certain they had never met. A photograph he'd once seen at Stony Man, perhaps, or something broadcast through the media. If he would only remove the shades . . .

"So what the bloody hell is goin' on?"

Suddenly Bolan had it. The Irish accent clinched it for him, and a mug shot flickered on his mental viewing screen. It was a face he might have seen on Wanted posters when he'd been in London or in Belfast, but it would not be familiar to the average stateside resident. The FBI would have that face on file, as would the CIA. And there was a rather bulky file at Stony Man.

The passenger was Bryan Harrigan, a triggerman and sometime spokesman for the Provisional IRA. According to the files, he had been active in the cause since adolescence, boasting that he killed a British solder—the first of many—at the tender age of seventeen. A virtuoso with explosives, he had been suspected in the murder of Mountbatten and had traveled widely in the intervening years, one step ahead of Interpol and British justice. Surfacing in the United States, he had secured cash and arms from Noraid; popping up in Moscow, he reportedly had forged a gentleman's agreement with the KGB. Along the way, a dozen cadres from the ETA and Baader-Meinhof to the Red Brigades had made him welcome, learning from the master, offering safe passage in return. There had been rumors—unconfirmed, as yet—of secret meetings with Khaddafi, to discuss the possibility of Libyan support for IRA campaigns in Northern Ireland. Be that as it may, the Ulsterman was here, in Syria, and Bolan had a notion as to why.

The driver had explained the situation to his passenger in broken English. Bolan caught the gist of it, his eyes on Harrigan. Kasm stood off to Bolan's right, endeavoring to look relaxed. He smiled too much, like someone who believed good-natured banter will disguise his guilt. The Arab had been cool enough in handling the bandits, but their plan had been considered in advance. He hoped Kasm would not do anything to botch the plan he had in mind.

The plan had sprung to life spontaneously, when he made the roving IRA ambassador. It was apparent from the escort, the direction of their travel, that the government was introducing Harrigan to the Assassins. Training camps for fedayeen and other terrorists were to the south, below

Damascus, but the Irishman was headed north. It didn't matter how he had persuaded members of the Ba'ath regime to set the meeting up; his topic of discussion with the Old Man of the Mountain, though predictable, was also momentarily irrelevant.

What mattered was that Bryan Harrigan must have a scheduled meeting, an appointment, with Sheikh al-Jebal. He had an *in*. And if the government believed an escort necessary, there were decent odds that Harrigan had never made the trip before. It was a gamble, but it was a good deal more than Bolan had to work with at the moment.

"Can we get a move on, then? I've got a schedule to keep, you know."

The Makarov was in his hand before the driver could respond, and Bolan never let him have the chance. Round one ripped through his temple at a range of twenty feet and dropped him in his tracks without a sound. His partner was off-balance, taken by surprise, and was clawing for his weapon when another head shot sent him sprawling, wet brains glistening in the dust.

Kasm and Harrigan were staring at him, open-mouthed, each equally surprised. Bolan kept the IRA man covered, putting no faith in the fact that he appeared to be unarmed, and nodded toward the fallen driver as he passed the Syrian.

"He looks about your size. We'll need that uniform."

"You're not a wog at all!" Surprise was giving way to curiosity as Harrigan removed his sunglasses, examined his enemy more closely. He didn't seem to be afraid. "American?"

"That's right."

"Small world, eh?"

"Getting smaller all the time."

"I know the feeling. Bloody countries like a bunch of postage stamps, all sand and stone."

"You're not on a vacation, I take it."

"Well, I'm not at liberty to say."

"Too bad." He raised the Makarov and sighted on the sole survivor of the party.

"Is this the part where I'm supposed to piss myself? You're wasting time, you know. I've seen it all before."

He could have killed the terrorist at once, but Bolan tried a different tack. "Okay," he said, "you're right. Suppose I do the talking?"

"It appears that I have nowhere else to go, just now."

"All right, let's start with introductions, Mr. Harrigan. The sun's a little hotter here than in Belfast, isn't it?"

The Ulsterman was unruffled. "It appears you have me at a disadvantage, sir. You mentioned introductions?"

"Call me Belasko. You're en route to meet Sheikh al-Jebal, at Alamut. I'll have to wing it on the topic of discussion. An assassination, possibly? A second front in London?"

"Just my bloody luck. I travel halfway round the world and run into the bleeding CIA."

"Not even close."

"Oh, no? You've piqued my interest, I'll give you that. Who am I talking to?"

"Let's say we have a similar idea. I'd like to meet the sheikh myself, but invitations are in short supply."

"And you'd be after taking mine."

"That's it."

"I don't appear to have much choice."

"No choice at all."

"I reckon you know where you're going, then?"

"We'll manage."

"Ah. I've never seen the place, but I've been told its deuced difficult to locate."

"Nothing ventured—"

"Nothing gained. I understand. You're sure you haven't got a mite of Irish blood, besides?"

"You never know."

"Aye, that's a fact." The Irish terrorist was eyeing him with interest. "You could use a guide, I'm thinking."

"Got one, thanks. Besides, you've never seen the place, remember?"

"It was worth a try. I really wouldn't trust the wogs if I were you. Look what it did to me."

"You pick your side and take your chances."

"Aye, I've always been one for that."

He took his chances then, without a flicker of an eye for warning, digging for the shoulder holster beneath his open jacket as he sidestepped, dodging to his left.

And it was almost good enough. Almost. He had a pistol in his hand as Bolan let the Makarov take over, round one catching Harrigan off-center, splintering his collarbone without inflicting mortal damage. Driven to his knees, blood soaking through his tunic, Bolan's adversary was returning fire when he was toppled by a rifle shot, heels drumming on the sand for several seconds as his death throes ran their course.

Hafez Kasm glanced from Bolan to the fallen Irishman and back again. His face looked haggard, weary, and there was confusion in his eyes.

"Why have we killed these men?" he asked. "I understood the other ones, but these?"

Bolan pointed to the latest casualty. "This one is known in Europe as a murderer of women, children. Bombing theaters and markets was his specialty. The soldiers were his escort."

"He is bound for Alamut?"

"He *was*. We're going in his place."

"I see."

The Arab's eyes spoke volumes, but he kept his apprehension to himself. He set down his rifle and went back to stripping the late driver of his uniform. Bolan used the time to drag the other bodies out of sight, depositing them with the bandits, then moving back to help Kasm when he had finished dressing. After topping off the canteens, they made a final sweep for blatant evidence of what had transpired, then prepared to leave.

"There may be recognition signals we are not aware of."

Bolan had considered that and saw no viable alternatives. He put the problem out of mind.

"We'll wing it. Military inefficiency. Somebody botched the password. Harrigan's a stranger to these people, and unless they're holding photographs, we ought to be all right."

"And if they have such photographs?"

Bolan shrugged. "We'll get a chance to do some thinking on our feet."

"You Americans are impetuous."

"We have our moments."

"Are you also indestructible?"

"We're working on it," Bolan said. "There are still a few bugs to be ironed out."

"Too bad."

"We'll see."

The soldier shed his caftan, kept the *keffiyeh* on for shade. His own fatigues would do as well as Harrigan's, and his companion made a perfect soldier, baggy uniform and all. Kasm deposited his rifle and revolver in the jeep, encumbered with the dead man's automatic now. A pair of Uzi submachine guns, stacked against a leather satchel in the rear, appeared to lift his spirits slightly.

Bolan sprang the satchel's latch and found it stuffed with Syrian pound notes, a small fortune in paper. Kasm whistled softly.

"Praise Allah."

"Praise Harrigan. This is the IRA's greeting card."

"We are in business?"

"We might be, Hafez. We might be."

It would take more than cash, Bolan knew, to deceive the Assassins, but it was a point for their side, all the same. He could speak with a greater degree of authority now, and command more respect while he sought out a chink in his enemy's armor. With luck, it just might be enough.

Then again, it might not.

If they fumbled a password, or Sheikh al-Jebal had a snapshot of Harrigan, they were in trouble. If two men arrived, and the Old Man was looking for three, they were dead.

Bolan knew all the risks, and he still had no choice.

He was there. He was forging ahead.

To the end of the line.

6

A set of wheels made all the difference in the world. Their risks were multiplied tenfold by sticking to the highway, but it would improve their time, potentially by hours, and the ache in Bolan's legs was fading rapidly. If nothing else, he would be able to conserve some energy, confront the enemy more swiftly, if and when the ambush came.

He rode the shotgun seat, the AK-47 muzzle-up between his knees. Kasm was driving with an Uzi in his lap, the other stuttergun between them on the floorboards. Given half a chance, they were prepared to answer a surprise attack with concentrated firepower, but a shoot-out on the highway was not Bolan's goal. He had not come this far and risked so much to throw his life away in futile confrontation with a gang of roving bandits. He was looking forward to a meeting with the Old Man of the Mountain, and from that point on he would have to play the cards as they were dealt.

Kasm was nervous, checking out the rearview mirror frequently, examining the wooded slopes on both sides of the road. His hands were steady on the wheel, but he was rigid, like a mannequin—or like a man expecting unseen enemies to take his head off any moment. Bolan would have offered to relieve him, but the Arab knew their destination, and it made no sense to spell him. Besides, if trouble came, the soldier wanted both hands free.

The countryside bore no resemblance to a desert now. As the Syrian took them higher, the straggling cedars grew thicker, becoming a forest of sorts. When it rained, upper slopes took the brunt of the water, and life was abundant here, birds and small animals streaking for cover at the sound of the jeep. Bolan was reminded, vaguely, of the Colorado Rockies, but the Elburz range rode lower on the skyline, and there was no trace of snow. A glance down at the weapon braced between his knees reminded Bolan that he was not bound for Vail or Aspen. He was in search of a resort whose clientele was more exclusive, where the dues were paid in blood.

"How long?"

Kasm was startled by his voice, a sheepish grin replacing momentary fright. "I beg your pardon?"

"How much longer?"

"Possibly an hour on the road. From there, we must walk again."

"The Old Man doesn't have a driveway?" Bolan grinned.

"There is a road that leads to Alamut, but it has no connection with the highway."

"Makes it hard for anyone to take him by surprise."

"I should imagine a surprise would be impossible."

"There's no such word."

"I'm sure there must be."

"No, I mean . . . forget it." Bolan tried another tack. "Their guns and ammunition have to get there somehow. Have you got a handle on supply lines?"

"I suspect they are supplied by air, although I have no proof."

"And food?"

"The Eagle's Nest commands a fertile valley. Farmers there have fed the rulers of the castle for a thousand years."

It played. A fortress, virtually self-contained except for arms and ammunition, which were readily available by airdrop. Mother Russia was a short five hundred miles by air, and night flights under radar would be simple for the KGB to orchestrate. If it came down to that, a seaplane, from the west, could cut that time dramatically, the in-and-out as simple as Grimaldi's own incursion eighteen hours earlier.

The thought of Jack reminded Bolan he was running out of time. The best part of a day was gone, with one remaining, and he meant to meet that deadline if it was within his power. If he blew it, failed to make connections somehow, Jack would have no target and the scheduled strike would not proceed. The Old Man of the Mountain would be safe inside his lair, protected by the ancient walls of stone and modern government indifference to humanity.

He shrugged the morbid thoughts away and concentrated on the road ahead. They had been climbing steadily for half an hour, and the air, if not precisely cool, was at least better than the hell draft of the flats they had left behind. The winds below would bake a man and make him old before his time; up here, while falling short of a caress, the breeze was softer, less inclined to claim its pound of flesh.

For all his mental preparation, his belief that he could not be taken wholly by surprise, the horsemen were an unexpected touch. Four of them filled the road, their mounts deployed at alternating angles, compact submachine guns leveled at the windshield of the jeep. The bearded faces were serene, almost lethargic, as they closed the trap.

Immediately Bolan ran the short list of his options. They could try to ram the living roadblock, batter through the flesh of animals and men, but they would be exposed to concentrated automatic fire, and there was almost certainly a backup team, prepared to hit them with a broadside if they tried a rush. Retreat was tantamount to suicide; Kasm would have his hands full backing down the mountain at the best of times, and bullets crashing through the windshield, through the engine block, would not improve his chances.

"Bandits?"

Bolan's driver tried a shrug and settled for a jerky movement of his shoulders. "I don't know. I'm sorry."

"Never mind. We'll find out soon enough."

As if in answer to his words, the rider on their starboard flank immediately broke formation, urging his mount toward the jeep. He stopped abreast of Bolan, glancing at their weapons, frowning to himself as he addressed Kasm in Arabic.

"They are Ismaili," Bolan's driver told him. "And they were expecting three."

"Last-minute change of plans."

Kasm relayed the message, and they waited while the rider thought it over, staring deeply into Bolan's eyes as if he sought to probe the warrior's soul. As Bolan met his gaze and held it, their interrogator seemed to make his mind up, swiveling around and barking orders toward the wooded slope on Bolan's left. Another trio of Assassins clattered into view, the new arrivals leading horses that were saddled, but without riders.

Three fresh horses, for the visitors whom the Ismailis were expecting.

The extra weapons in the jeep might prove embarrassing, but Bolan was prepared to make himself seem paranoid, if necessary, to explain the surplus hardware. If their contact was suspicious, he concealed his feelings well—a trait that, Bolan reasoned, the professional Assassins would be forced to cultivate.

Had they already been marked as impostors? Was their fate already sealed? And if they had been marked for death on sight, why were they still alive?

No time for questions. The leader of the escort team was barking orders, and a gesture from his submachine gun made his meaning plain before Kasm had time to translate.

"They will take the vehicle from here."

"I gathered that."

"We are to leave our weapons."

Bolan stiffened. Giving up the jeep was one thing; handing over their hardware might be suicidal. Bolan took a chance and tried to put himself inside the mind of Bryan Harrigan.

"Hold on a second. Tell him I said honest friends should not attempt to leave their comrades naked and defenseless in a hostile world. I give my gun to no man."

Kasm stared at Bolan for a moment, as if pondering his sanity.

"Go on."

Reluctantly his contact passed the word, and Bolan watched the members of their escort stiffen, fingers tightening on triggers. If he pushed too far, too fast, they were as good as dead.

The leader eyed him coldly for a moment, chewing on his indignation, finally snapping out a comment to the Syrian.

"He says that you may keep a pistol, for the ride to Alamut. Beyond those gates, no man goes armed without permission of Sheikh al-Jebal."

"That's fair enough." Bolan put a touch of arrogance behind the smile and left his AK-47 in the jeep as he climbed down. The holstered Makarov would scarcely measure up to seven submachine guns, but it beat the thought of unarmed combat all to hell. If they were marked for execution where they stood, at least he might have time and opportunity to take a couple of the bastards with him.

Reaching back to fetch the loaded satchel, Bolan felt the gunners watching him, alert to any trick. He let them see the bag, approached the point man's mount and held it open, waiting while he probed inside to check for any weapons hidden underneath the bundled cash. When he was satisfied, the gunman nodded, waving Bolan off.

As they retreated from the jeep, the leader of their escort barked an order to his team. One of the riders hastily dismounted, passed his reins to a companion and went on to take his place behind the steering wheel. The roadblock parted as he put the jeep in motion, his companion trailing at a distance, with the driver's mount in tow. Another moment, and the jeep had disappeared around the next sharp curve, its engine noises swallowed by the mountains.

Bolan took his cue from the commander of the troops and chose a mount, Kasm proceeding to the next horse in line. Bolan used the saddle's ornate horn for purchase, mounting on the left and settling in, his boots a snug fit in the stirrups. At his side, unused to horseback riding, Kasm made it on the second try.

They left the road immediately, two Ismailis leading, Bolan and his native contact in the middle and three more armed Assassins bringing up the rear. Bolan saw that it was an adequate arrangement, covering the possibilities in case he had a change of heart and tried to bolt. He might be able to eliminate the point men, if he did not spook his mount with sudden gunfire, but the three men at his back would bring him down before he had a chance to turn around. And if he attempted to reverse directions suddenly, he would be trapped and pinned before he could complete the move. A break to either side was simply not an option, as he saw once they were off the road.

Their path, at first, led up a rocky slope. Bolan could hear Hafez Kasm cursing underneath his breath, absorbing each new jolt as if it were a personal affront, eyes tightly closed until their mounts reached something that approximated level ground. The slope behind them, Bolan's contact risked a shaky smile, embarrassed by his momentary fright. The Arab pride was showing through again, but he was still a little green around the gills.

They found the footpath Bolan and Kasm had taken from the LZ to their confrontation at the mountain spring, and followed it for half a mile or so before the leader took them up another wooded hillside, branches whipping in their faces, snagging at their clothing as they climbed. The horses negotiated the terrain easily, as if they had pursued the course a hundred times before, but Bolan found it rugged going, and his contact had the worst of it, face pallid as they galloped on a path that seemed invisible to human eyes. A drooping branch ripped off his *keffiyeh* at one point, but a member of the tail crew caught it, spurring up the slope to catch Kasm and hand it back, all mocking smiles. The Arab clutched it tightly in his fist, refusing to release the saddle horn or reins to put it on again.

Time blurred. They might have ridden through the forest for an hour or a day, but Bolan's watch informed him that it was, in fact, two hours from their starting point until they cleared the tree line, perched atop the ridge that overlooked a narrow, winding road. This thoroughfare had not been paved; and ruts etched deep by wagon wheels were visible from where they sat. A few klicks farther on, the road spilled out into a verdant, cultivated valley flanked by stony peaks on every side. From Bolan's vantage point, he picked out orchards, vineyards, scattered hovels—and he knew that they had found the source of food for tenants of the Eagle's Nest.

The fortress of his enemies was not yet visible, but Bolan had his hands full at the moment, as the leader of his escort started down the final slope at a near full gallop. Bolan had to stand in his stirrups and lean back across the heaving flanks. Behind him, bitter exhortations from the Syrian told him that his guide was hanging in, however tenuously, and he gave the Arab points for courage. Once on level ground, the leader slowed his pace, and Kasm let his pent-up breath escape, allowed himself to breathe again.

It took the better part of three more hours to traverse the valley at a combination trot and walk that gave their mounts an opportunity to rest. True dusk was falling now, exaggerated by the line of rugged western peaks that screened the setting sun. They passed small groups of peasant farmers, homeward bound from labor in the fields and orchards, but the men on foot refused to meet his gaze. Instead, they kept their eyes downcast, heads lowered, as if death might be the consequence of a direct glance at the riders filing past.

And, Bolan thought, it just might be.

For all his mental preparation, Bolan's first view of the castle took him by surprise. The orchards had obscured his view for most of forty minutes, and the fortress was before them when they cleared the trees, its battlements carved out of living rock, rising a hundred feet or more above the valley floor. A human fly would be hard-pressed to climb the walls; the passage of perhaps a thousand years since their erection had, apparently, done nothing to erode their strength or offer handholds to potential prowlers. He could pick out tiny figures pacing off their beats on the parapets, a squad of sentries on patrol.

The single, narrow road to Alamut climbed steeply from the valley's floor, although the grade seemed modest in comparison with some of the uncharted tracks that they had followed in their journey from the highway. A few more moments brought them to the looming gates, which had already opened to receive them.

Halting, Bolan's escort formed a line across the open gate. The leader stared at Bolan, confident, not bothering to train his weapon on the tall American. Instead, he thrust out an open hand, snapping orders that were dutifully translated by Kasm.

"He wants your pistol now."

Bolan's show of stubbornness had served its purpose, and he drew the Makarov, delivered it butt-first and saw it tucked away inside the gunner's caftan. Satisfied, the horsemen turned in tight formation and trotted through the gate. Mack Bolan felt the short hairs rising on his neck as they passed inside, the portals tightly closed and barred behind them.

They were in the center of a courtyard, roughly three times the size of a football field, surrounded by sixty-foot walls. In addition to height, Bolan saw that the walls were about twenty feet thick at their base, with apartments for sentries and storerooms for weapons or food that were chiseled out of the stone. At the near end, the courtyard was L-shaped, retreating toward stables that housed as many as twenty-five horses. At the far end, the earth had been paved for a heliport.

Frowning, he knew that Hafez had been right on the mark. When supplies came to Alamut, they would most likely be coming by air. With a heliport right in the courtyard, a drop was superfluous; anyone welcome could touch down in style, bearing gifts for the Old Man or coming to bargain for one more atrocity.

Bolan dismounted on cue from the chief of their escorts, and other Ismailis were waiting to handle the horses, conveying them back to the stable for rubdowns and oats. Bolan followed their guide, with Kasm at his heels, as they moved toward the heart of the keep.

Stony towers thrust up from the earth in the midst of the courtyard, abutting the peak of which they were a part. Bolan guessed that the rooms of the castle might wander for miles underground, hand-carved chambers immune to the light of the sun. Windows facing the courtyard were well above ground, so that hard-core defenders could fight on, in spite of a breach in the great outer wall.

There were guards on the door, submachine guns and scimitars mingling the old and the new, East and West, but they passed through, unchallenged. Inside, Bolan thought that he might have stepped into a fantasy: tapestries covered the walls, scenes of battle and triumph handwoven by artists in centuries past. Polished marble was smooth underfoot, and the numerous wall-mounted lamps had the look of real gold. Bolan noted the lamps were electric, their cables concealed by the various tapestries. That meant a power plant somewhere inside, an addition the builders had never imagined, and where there was power there also was weakness, a pressure point ready for use in a crisis.

He stopped himself short of disabling the plant in his mind. He was getting ahead of himself, allowing his mind to roam free when he needed to focus on the task at hand. They were passing more sentries, who were decked out in turbans and vests with fine stitchery and holding their Uzis like pros. He had counted thirty-three gunners so far— thirty-five with the two who were stashing the jeep—and he guessed that he might not have seen one in four of the cultists on hand. They were facing an army, unarmed, and he still had to meet the CO.

Double doors twice the height of a man whispered open, and Bolan fell in behind their guide, noting the handwoven carpets that muffled their footsteps. The receiving room may have been fifty feet square, but the mirrored walls amplified spatial dimensions, creating an agorophobe's nightmare. Glancing off to either side, the soldier saw himself in triplicate, quadruplicate, his image dwindled and repeated to infinity. Above them, crystal chandeliers lit up the room like starbursts.

At the center of the chamber, mounted on a dais, stood the Old Man of the Mountain's throne. It was not occupied at present; rather, as they stopped before the elevated platform, Bolan's escort kneeling, he observed a slender, turbaned man emerging from *behind* the massive chair. He stood beside it for a moment, scrutinizing Bolan, studying this infidel who did not kneel and finally sat down.

The Old Man had a timeless face, like weathered parchment, wisps of iron-gray hair still visible beneath his turban. He wore flawless silk, with handmade sandals on his feet, his throat and hands adorned with gold. The left side of his nose was pierced, a ruby winking from the outside of his nostril like an errant drop of blood.

"I bid you welcome, Mr. Harrigan," he said in perfect English.

"Thank you." Conscious of his limitations, Bolan made no effort to affect an Irish accent. If he fumbled it, a misplaced burr could get him killed, and it was easier to justify the absence of an accent than to fake a realistic one.

"You have something for me?"

The Old Man's eyes were fastened on the satchel that Bolan carried. Bolan passed it to his escort, waiting while the gunner fairly crept toward the throne on hands and knees. Sheikh al-Jebal spent several seconds studying the contents of the bag, then set it on the floor beside his chair.

"A small down payment," Bolan said, before the Old Man had an opportunity to speak. "I like to think of it as an investment in the future."

"Ah." The Old Man's face was deadpan, but there was a glimmer in his eyes. "I will look forward to our conversation on the subject. First, however, I believe that you and your companion might enjoy some small refreshment, possibly a bath and change of clothes, before we meet again. A banquet has been readied for tonight, in honor of our guests. You will enjoy it more, I think, once you have washed away the dust of travel."

"Thank you, very much."

"Amal will show you to your rooms. If any comfort has been overlooked, please be so kind as to inform him of the oversight at once."

"I will."

The Executioner had turned to leave, but he was halted by the Old Man's voice.

"One thing, before you leave us, Mr. Harrigan."

"Yes?"

"We were expecting three. Perhaps you can explain why there are only two of you?"

"I can, indeed. My other baby-sitter had a hungry eye. He got a bit too cozy with your money, and I was forced to blow his brains out."

"I appreciate your candor... and your interest in my property."

"No worries. If you think about it, I was looking out for Number One. What kind of idiot would I be, showing up without the full amount that we agreed?"

"A dead one, Mr. Harrigan."

"Precisely. I intend to go on living for a while, yet. I've got things to do."

The Old Man smiled. "Enjoy your rest. Amal will call for you when it is time."

"I'm looking forward to it," Bolan told him, meaning every word.

He was inside, and if appearances were trusted, he had passed the first inspection by his enemy. Before he started celebrating, though, there was a great deal more to be accomplished.

And so precious little time.

7

Kasm and Bolan were assigned to separate suites, which were luxury incarnate; Persian rugs and tapestries, elaborate hand-carved furniture, a massive bed that would accommodate four bodies easily.

It took a moment for the Executioner to realize that he was in a suite of rooms devoid of windows. Shrugging off a twinge of claustrophobia, he took the information in, assimilated it and realized that he was somewhere on the cliff side of the castle. He could not observe the courtyard, could not leave his room by means of any exit other than the door. On impulse, Bolan tried it, found it open. He might not be trusted, but the Old Man of the Mountain did not fear him, either.

And why should he?

Bolan was unarmed, surrounded by a private army that might easily exceed one hundred soldiers. He could not escape, and empty-handed, he could do no crucial damage to their operation. Friend or foe, he had been neutralized, effectively and simply.

They had bargained, though, without the homer.

Smaller than a pocket calculator, the device emitted silent signals that would span a distance of 150 miles. It relied on a battery—its life was limited—and it could not broadcast through walls of solid stone. But Bolan was not ready to employ his secret ace. Not yet. He had to get a feel for the Ismaili operation, first, discover what the Old Man had in mind for Northern Ireland and as many other targets as he could unveil. He had to do it all within a day, and plant the homer somewhere in the courtyard, where it would be safe and unobserved before the air strike. On the side, it would be helpful if the Executioner could find a way to save himself and his companion from the rain of hellfire that Grimaldi and his backup would release on cue.

Kasm would not be counting on the air strike. He had already made it clear that he would not cooperate with the Israelis. Bolan felt a momentary pang of guilt at the deception, but it vanished swiftly. Countless lives were hanging in the balance, and he would use every means available to neutralize the threat of the Assassins. If Hafez Kasm felt betrayed and wound up hating Bolan as a consequence, it was a burden he could live with. In the meantime, there was work to do.

But first, the bath their host had promised. Situated in one corner of a smaller, barren room, the shower was a primitive contraption, with its pipes exposed. Its spray was steaming hot, however, as the Executioner discovered when he stood beneath the nozzle, grimacing in momentary pain. His skin was lobster red when he emerged to find a steam cloud overhead, the sweat of condensation leaving wet tracks on the hand-hewn walls. He found a towel and dried himself, examining the single closet of his suite for some alternative to putting on the sweaty uniform again.

A dozen caftans were arranged on wooden hangers, and he chose the first in line. Leather sandals were supplied in several sizes, and he found a pair that fit him well enough. The robe was loose enough to hide a weapon, but the Executioner had nothing to conceal.

Except the homer.

He couldn't afford to have his only means of contact with the outside world discovered by the enemy. Without the miniature transmitter, he was isolated, absolutely on his own, and its discovery would irredeemably destroy his cover. Bryan Harrigan had come to deal, and he would have no use for homing devices or other electronic gadgetry. Just as the transmitter was his lifeline, the cover was his life, and he couldn't part with either at the moment.

Bolan studied his surroundings, passing on the obvious—the bed, the closet—searching for a place where the transmitter would be safe from prying eyes. He finally chose a tapestry that hung beside the bed, concealing more electric wires, and clipped the homer to the rich material. It scarcely weighed an ounce, and did not cause a wrinkle in the fabric; as well it was thin enough to let the tapestry hang flat against the wall, without a telltale bulge.

When he was satisfied with his selection of a hiding place, the Executioner stretched out across the king-size bed, relaxing with an effort. He didn't feel the need for sleep, but he would not resist it. There was nothing more that he could do before his scheduled dinner with Sheikh al-Jebal, and he had learned to take advantage of the opportunities for rest as they arose.

In fact, his mind was too alert for sleep to come, the crucial questions keeping his nerves on edge. Would there be time to plant the homer? Would he be allowed outside? If he succeeded, could he find an exit from the Eagle's Nest before the doomsday numbers ran out?

It was a relatively simple mission, in conception. Bolan merely had to find the home of the Assassins, mark it for the air strike and withdraw. His chance encounter by a mountain spring had made the first part easy... as it might have made the other parts impossible.

The soldier closed his eyes, deliberately made his mind a blank. It was a talent he had acquired in Vietnam, permitting him to let accumulated tensions melt away and leave him totally relaxed. His problems would be waiting for him when he chose to surface; in the meantime, he needed rest, and in his quiet state he might surprise himself with some solutions.

He was wakened forty minutes later by a knocking at his door.

"Come in."

Amal, the leader of his escort from the highway, entered with Hafez Kasm on his heels. The slender Syrian was also wearing a caftan, had sandals on his feet and a turban coiled atop his head. He seemed to mesh with their surroundings, but there was a nervous quality about him that betrayed the fact that he was an outsider. As Bolan rose, he hoped the Arab's agitation would not be apparent to Amal or to their host.

Amal was speaking now, and Bolan waited for Kasm to translate.

"We are summoned to the banquet chamber."

"Good. I was about to ring room service for a snack."

They trailed Amal through corridors of stone, electric bulbs in wire cages overhead providing illumination. Bolan realized immediately that the fortress, with its tunnels through the mountainside, was more extensive than he had at first imagined. Twice, they passed by stairways chiseled out of rock, one leading to a level overhead, the other leading downward. To the dungeons? Storerooms? Bolan made a mental note to check it out, if possible, before he called in the air strike.

The banquet chamber was a hundred feet in length and half as wide, with vaulted ceilings and a floor of polished granite. Two men occupied the room. Amal led the newcomers to the single table, which was situated at the far end of the room, their footsteps ringing hollowly as they closed the gap.

Sheikh al-Jebal was seated at the place of honor, at the middle of the banquet table, and watched their approach without the vestige of a smile. Beside him, on his right, a younger Arab with a mustache and goatee made no attempt to mask his frank suspicion of the new arrivals. The man was dressed less sumptuously than his master, but his restless hands were bright with gold and diamonds.

Bolan stood his ground while Amal bowed deeply before the Old Man of the Mountain. Kasm, accustomed to the Eastern forms of courtesy, compromised with a simple bow from the waist. The sheikh's companion studied Bolan closely, and the Executioner returned his gaze, unflinching, reading hidden fear and overt cruelty in the other's soul.

"I trust you have refreshed yourselves?"

"I'm feeling better by the minute."

"Excellent." The sheikh turned to introduce his aide. "Tahir Arrani, my right hand. Our guest is Bryan Harrigan, an Irishman in need of some assistance."

"You are Irish? From your voice, I would have guessed American."

"It took a while to lose the accent," Bolan told him, smiling thinly. "It was either that or lose my head. The walls have ears, you know? These days, I get around much easier."

"So we have heard." Arrani's smile was cold, reptilian. "You were involved with Lord Mountbatten's execution, I believe?"

"Let's say I know who was, and let it go at that. I didn't come this far to talk about old times."

"Be seated, please." The chief of the Assassins gestured grandly to a pair of straight-backed chairs positioned on his left. When they were seated, Arrani raised a silver bell and struck it sharply with his knife blade, which produced a single, mellow tone.

The servers instantly appeared with bowls and baskets, bottles and tureens. The plates they set before Mack Bolan were of fine bone china, filigreed with gold. The silverware was polished sterling, and the beverage that accompanied the meal was served in goblets forged, if he was not mistaken, out of solid gold. Whatever his beginnings or his link to the original Assassins, this particular Old Man was living out his days in style.

The menu ranged from beef and steaming rice with herbs to sauteed vegetables, grapes and other fruits. The sheikh seemed disinclined to broach the subject of their business over dinner, and as they dug in after small talk, Bolan was suddenly reminded that he had been on short rations for the best part of the day.

When they were done, Arrani struck the silver bell again, and the servants reappeared to cart off the remnants of the feast. Restraint had kept the Executioner from overeating, and he now felt satisfied, instead of groggy from the meal. Kasm, beside him, had relaxed enough to work his way through double portions all around, and he was clearly feeling the effects.

The warrior prepared to deal with business now, or fake it to the best of his ability, but as he tried to formulate an opener, Arrani raised his silver bell again and struck it twice. The court musicians entered through a side door, lining up along one wall with flutes and mandolins, a sitar, drums resembling a set of bongos. A pair of muscular men entered on their heels, naked but for breechcloths and the scimitars they carried in their hands.

"I trust you will enjoy our humble entertainment."

Bolan smiled and waited, while the swordsmen bowed before their master, foreheads pressed against the granite. They retreated, facing each other as the band struck up a lively tune. On cue, the mock combatants circled, closed, their weapons flashing, curved blades ringing out like cymbals as they clashed. As one man ducked a swift, potentially decapitating swing, he countered with a sweep at ankle-height that made his adversary leap for safety. Back and forth it went, the flashing weapons missing naked flesh by fractions of an inch, the swordsmen glistening with perspiration.

The war of make-believe went on for several moments, neither athlete showing any sign of tiring, slowing down. From what the Executioner could see, they might have battled through the night without a break, but now Arrani had his silver bell in hand, its ringing note the signal for cessation of hostilities.

The swordsmen stepped apart, bowed deeply once again, and took their leave. No sooner had they cleared the doorway than a dozen women clad in harem costumes took their place. Their faces were veiled, but otherwise their gossamer apparel left little to the imagination. They formed a circle, waited for the lilting music to begin and then exploded into twirling, undulating steps that obviously had been practiced to perfection. Supple bodies moved hypnotically in rhythm with the music, dipping, swaying, teasing.

Bolan was surprised to see a pair of blondes among the troupe. He wondered where the sheikh acquired his dancers, cutting off that train of thought as it swung southwest, toward the slave marts of Algiers. He had attempted once to close the markets down, but they were doing business at the same old stand these days, and they were not alone. It was ironic that the Middle East and many parts of Africa still tolerated secret slavery in the shadow of the Third World's angry dedication to assorted "liberation movements." And the more things changed, it seemed, the more they stayed the same.

These women might be Syrians, of course—except the blondes—and Bolan had no way of knowing how they came to join the Old Man's stable. He had not anticipated women in the hostile camp, but there was little he could do to help them. It would be hard enough to extricate himself and save Hafez Kasm in the bargain. A mass escape was hopeless, tantamount to suicide. There was a chance the dancers would survive the air strike, and if not . . .

At first, he thought the meeting of their eyes was accidental, mere coincidence, but then he caught the brunette staring at him, studying his face as she went through her moves. It was a pleasure to return her gaze, although he could not force himself to concentrate entirely on her eyes. She had the body of an athlete, trim and shapely, but without the muscularity of one who emphasizes pumping iron. Her flesh was alabaster, lightly kissed by desert sunshine, and her hair was gleaming. Her eyes were touched with fire.

He glanced away, and found Tahir Arrani watching him, a curious expression on his face. As Bolan turned to face him, the Assassin swept the dancers with a brooding glare, apparently found nothing out of place. Unsettled by the warrior's stare, Arrani felt compelled to speak.

"I trust you find our women pleasing to the eye?"

"They'll do." He took a chance. "I've never encountered an Arab blonde before."

The sheikh ignored his statement, but Arrani smiled, the same disturbing viper's grimace.

"Our performers come from many backgrounds, many walks of life," he answered. "They are honored to fulfill their destinies as servants of Sheikh al-Jebal."

"Who wouldn't be?"

Arrani searched his face for hints of disrespect, looked sullen when he came up empty. "As you say. It is an honor for us all."

The airy music was approaching its crescendo, and the dancers came together, moving in a tight formation that reminded Bolan of a sensuous aerobics video. They dipped and swayed in perfect time to drum and flute, all facing inward, the silk and sequins of their harem costumes whispering.

On cue, the music died as if it had been cut off by a saber stroke. The dancers folded, knees in toward the center of their circle, arms and flowing hair outflung like petals of a rare, exotic flower. Prone, they held the pose until Arrani struck a sharp note on his bell.

Bolan watched the dancers rise and bow their way out of the banquet chamber, followed by the members of the tiny orchestra. Was it a figment of imagination or had the brunette delayed her exit long enough to shoot him one more searching glance?

He couldn't say, but Bolan made a special effort to conceal his own reaction, just in case. There was no point in giving anything away before he knew precisely what the hell was going on.

They were alone, the hall deserted by servants, dancers and musicians. Bolan turned to face the Old Man of the Mountain, smiling thinly. "That was quite a show," he said. "Can we get down to business now?"

"Tomorrow," the sheikh replied. "A good night's sleep will clear our minds of sweet distractions. In the morning you will see our fortress and present your proposition."

"No time like the present," Bolan pressed.

"Tomorrow, Mr. Harrigan."

The sheikh rose to leave, and Bolan followed suit, Arrani and Kasm already on their feet in gestures of respect.

"Tomorrow," he told the sheikh, his disappointment only partly feigned.

Arrani hung back for a moment, staring Bolan in the eye. "Sheikh al-Jebal may not be hurried."

"Well, you never know until you try."

Amal had turned up on the sidelines, with his usual scowl in place, and Bolan trailed him back through winding tunnels to his suite. This time the door *was* locked, perhaps because the guard force was reduced by night, and Bolan did not bother working on the latch. He had nowhere to go, and the idea of roaming aimlessly through stony corridors did not appeal to him this evening.

He would see the sheikh's operation in the morning, and they would discuss the deal that Harrigan had come to make. Potential problems there. If Ulster's traveling ambassador of death had briefed his contacts on the subject of his visit, Bolan would be rapidly exposed as an impostor. He had no idea of any items on the IRA agenda, but if Harrigan had kept the crucial information to himself—which seemed entirely probably, all things considered—Bolan should be able to conduct a bluff with fair results.

The late and unlamented Irishman would have assassination on his mind, or else why would he visit the Assassins, bearing gifts of cash? A sensitive assignment, certainly; one vital to the IRA, but "hot" enough that they could not afford to claim the credit publicly. Outsiders were required, fanatics from the East to carry out a special mission, bear the heat and keep their mouths shut afterward. The shooters would be sacrificed, of course. As for the men who pulled their strings . . . well, there would be no rash exposures or admissions by the Old Man of the Mountain or his handpicked team.

Tomorrow, then. There would be time enough to formulate a story, time enough to think about the woman. She was already on his mind, her dark, disturbing eyes still with him as he stretched out on the king-size bed and waited for the day to fade.

His first day on the ground, in hostile territory.

One day left to go.

Tomorrow, he would have to plant the homer surreptitiously, with time to spare before Grimaldi made his offshore pass. If Bolan missed his deadline, Jack was under orders to abort the mission, scrub it clean and take himself back home to Stony Man. There would not be a second chance, with so much riding on the value of surprise. If Bolan missed his contact, it would mean that he was dead or otherwise debilitated, and the stateside crew would write him off. He would become another casualty of everlasting war.

At the moment he was not inclined to think in terms of death or failure. He was still alive, and while he lived there was a chance for victory.

Bolan closed his eyes and focused on the darkness, merging with it and becoming one, allowing it to carry him away.

8

Breakfast was a replay of the evening meal, without the benefit of swordsmen, dancers and musicians. They convened within the banquet hall, and servants flourished trays of gold and silver, bearing delicacies for the four men who assembled at the single table. There were grapes and citrus fruits, stuffed grape leaves, loaves of rich, dark bread still hot enough to melt the butter Bolan lathered onto every slice. He did not ask about the eggs, which came hard-boiled and seemed a trifle larger than the average, but he had seen nothing in the courtyard to suggest that there were chickens in the Eagle's Nest. Unsettled by potential explanations, Bolan ate the eggs and kept his questions to himself, content to wash the whole meal down with strong black coffee of a Turkish blend.

"I could get used to this," he said, and meant it. Luxury was rare enough for any soldier waging endless war. The lavish meals, the women—they were staple items from a warrior's fantasy, and he had shared the dream with comrades in the Asian hellgrounds, dreaming of a day when there would be no need for arms and bloodshed. Dreaming of a day that had not yet arrived, and that appeared to have no prospect of arriving.

Remembering the eggs deliberately to break his drifting train of thought, he rose as servants helped Sheikh al-Jebal out of his chair. The Old Man was not frail, by any means, but he was treated almost like an invalid, presumably a token of respect. This time he waved his lackeys off and sent them packing.

"There is much for you to see before we speak of business," he informed the Executioner. "Amal will show your driver to his room while we are occupied."

"Is he a prisoner?"

The sheikh made a stab at looking hurt. "By no means," he replied. "There are, of course, some portions of the castle where a stranger is not welcome . . . without escort. I am sure you understand."

"Hafez?"

"Of course." If anything, the slender Arab seemed relieved to be excluded from the tour of Assassin Central.

"All right, then."

Arrani snapped his fingers, and Amal did his appearing act, approaching from their flank on silent feet. As he led Hafez Kasm through a side door, Bolan followed his hosts as they struck off across the broad expanse of marble floor.

The many guards they passed bowed deeply at the sheikh's approach, their turbans grazing stone. The soldier made a mental note of their abject reaction, realizing that if worse came down to worst, the sheikh himself might serve as cover and a way of exiting the fortress. Granting, always, that the Old Man valued life enough to try to save his own.

It was an open question, one Bolan could not hope to answer on his own, before the crisis moment had arrived. In Nam, he had known men who thrived on death the way an infant thrives on mother's milk, addicted to the act of spilling human blood. In time, it had not mattered to them if the blood was spilled from friend or foe. Most of them were dead now, victims of the private search for bigger, bloodier encounters with the enemy.

If Bolan's host was a fanatic cultist, he would likely be immune to threats of violence. On the other hand, if he was strictly mercenary, looking out for Number One, he would be vulnerable in a pinch.

The sunlight in the courtyard was a momentary shock to Bolan's eyes. He made a show of squinting as he scanned the yard to left and right, in search of a secure place in which to plant his homer. He was not carrying the small transmitter, for the hour was early yet, and if he set it now, the battery would be long dead before Grimaldi made his midnight pass. This was a scouting trip; if Bolan found a likely place to hide the homer, he would mark it in his mind, return with darkness and put the wheels in motion then.

"This fortress was erected by the sultan of the Seljuq dynasty," the Old Man said, "almost one thousand years ago. My ancestor, Hasan al-Sabbah, won the castle from its stewards, and my family has held it ever since...with minor interruptions from the jackals in Damascus. Here, my father's father forged the heart of an empire that I, in my humble way, endeavor to maintain."

"I'd say you've done all right."

"There have been obstacles, of course. Despite their pose as followers of Allah, men who claim to rule this country have the hearts of infidels. There have been certain pressures, efforts to prevent us from fulfilling our holy mission. But we shall prevail."

They were passing the stables, a smith's forge where horseshoes were made and repaired. Sentries on the wall above kept pace, with automatic weapons at the ready. As they toured the courtyard, Bolan was aware of hostile glances from Tahir Arrani. For whatever reason, the sheikh's assistant had apparently mistrusted "Bryan Harrigan" on sight, and Bolan knew that it would do no good to try to curry favor with him. An honest enemy was preferable to a phony comrade, any day.

"How many soldiers do you keep on hand?"

"Disciples," the Old Man corrected him. "Remember, Mr. Harrigan, that we are a religious order, not an army."

"As you like it."

"Numbers are a fragile thing, is it not so? A man is born, he dies, and in the meantime, who can say his influence is that of but a single man? Each of my disciples has the dedication of a hundred men."

"That's very nice, I'm sure, but can each one stand off a hundred men in case of an attack?"

"I have no fear of being overrun by enemies without or traitors from within. The force on hand is adequate for my defensive needs, and every man among them has been tested for his loyalty to Allah."

"And to you?"

The Old Man smiled. "I am the voice of Allah."

"Makes it nice, eh?" Bolan caught Arrani's eyes and winked, eliciting a scowl. "Your boys are primed to go the limit, then?"

"They do not fear the afterlife," his host replied. "If Allah calls them home, they are prepared."

"I ask because the mission that my people have in mind is...touchy, shall we say? The shooter isn't likely to be coming home again."

"As I have said—"

"Yes, sir, but as *we* say, the eyes don't lie."

"Impertinence!" Arrani's face was flushing crimson, and the change in color was accelerated by another mocking smile from Bolan.

"You desire a demonstration?"

"If it isn't too much trouble for you."

"A simple matter, easily arranged. If you will follow me?"

"Of course."

They climbed a flight of steps that had been carved into the wall, ascending to the parapets and passing lookouts who were bowing. At a word from Bolan's host and guide, one of the gunners scrambled to his feet and fell in step behind them, trotting to keep up as they continued on their way.

Outside the fortress walls, the ground had fallen off increasingly, until they stood above a chasm several hundred feet in depth. From Bolan's vantage point, he saw the castle's hidden strength: its manner of construction, hewn out of the mountain peak itself, prevented enemies from flanking the defenders. It would take a troop of dedicated mountain climbers to assault the fortress from the rear, and they would be exposed to hostile fire, like insects climbing on a windowpane.

They reached the point where human handiwork and native stone became inseparable, and they could proceed no farther. Bolan, peering cautiously beyond the ledge, experienced a moment's vertigo as he beheld the tiny boulders of a rugged river canyon, some four hundred feet below. That first step was a killer, and he moved back from the edge with a sensation of relief.

Sheikh al-Jebal was speaking to the sentry who had joined their party, issuing commands in Arabic. The gunner nodded once and passed his rifle to Tahir Arrani, bowing deeply to the master with a beatific smile upon his face. From all appearances, he might just have been touched by God.

"The demonstration you requested, Mr. Harrigan."

The sentry had removed his cartridge belt and placed it at Arrani's feet, immediately dropping to his knees before the sheikh and speaking rapidly. Although his words were lost on Bolan, it didn't appear that he was begging off of his assignment; rather, if his face and tone were any indicators, he was offering sincerest thanks for what appeared to be a golden opportunity.

The sheikh reached down to pat his chosen gunner on the head, a faithful pet rewarded for its show of fealty. As if on cue, the sentry rose, retreated toward the wall and climbed on the parapet, his turbaned figure standing out in stark relief against the crystal sky. He spread his arms, addressed himself to Allah in a ringing voice—and jumped.

It took a heartbeat for the Executioner to realize what he had seen, a heartbeat more before he found the strength to draw breath. He didn't need to check the falling body's progress, felt no urge to scrutinize the bright graffiti on the rocks below. It was no trick, no sham. There was no ledge or net to catch the sentry, no trapeze to save him at the final instant.

He was gone.

In truth the Executioner felt nothing for the fallen sentry. If the man was not a killer yet, it was by accident. He had aligned himself with the Assassin cult and served its master with his final act of twisted courage, praised him with his final breath. Whatever sudden nausea the soldier felt was brought on by the knowledge of the power that Sheikh al-Jebal commanded from his various disciples. They were ready to sacrifice themselves on his behalf, and that meant they were primed to slaughter others on command. The evidence from Orly, all the other strikes, was falling into place.

"You are surprised?" There was a trace of condescension in the master's voice.

"It's different," he conceded. "I assume your men have no more qualms about eliminating others?"

"They will do as they are ordered by the voice of Allah."

"I'll admit I'm curious. We've got our dedicated lads in Ulster, mind you—we proved that in H Block with the hunger strike—but what you've shown me here is something else. I wonder how you can command that kind of blind obedience."

"Allah commands. I am the vessel."

"Of course, I understand. But there must be some motivating factor."

"They have seen the future. Each of my disciples has implicit faith in paradise, because they have already seen it for themselves."

"Now *that*'s some trick."

"The members of our order are initiated in the garden of delights, an earthly recreation of the afterlife that Allah promises to all his loyal servants. Having sampled their reward, they have no fear of death in battle."

"So I see. Your garden must be more than roses and petunias."

"Would you care to see it for yourself?"

The soldier shrugged. "Why not? I've always wondered what it's like in paradise, and this might be my only chance."

HAFEZ KASM COUNTED OFF five minutes in his mind before he tried the door. It had been left unlocked, but he delayed another moment, giving any watchers ample opportunity to show themselves. When he leaned out to scan the corridor, he found himself alone. He slipped out, immediately wishing that he had a weapon in case he met the grim Amal or one of his associates.

They had been promised freedom, of a sort, but watchful guards were everywhere, and it would be a challenge for Kasm to move among them unobserved. But to what end? He had no firm objective in his mind, no destination, goal or object of desire. What was he looking for? How would he know when it was found?

He chose the right-hand path, because he had not gone that way before and had no inkling of what might lie in that direction. If his calculations were correct—a dangerous assumption in the circumstances—then the corridor ran east to west, across the mountain's face. He would be moving in the general direction of the stables, and he wondered if there might be some connecting door, another means of exit from the castle.

Thus far he had marked the single entrance, noted windows that would be of little use without a ladder, and he knew the castle was secure. If he should find another door, it would be guarded, would it not? Unless, perhaps, it was an entryway considered otherwise secure.

Doors opened off the stony corridor on either side, but all were closed, and he was not inclined to test them. If there were vital secrets hidden in the rooms he passed, Kasm would have to seek them out another time. At this moment his mind was focused on the problem of escape, and intuition told him that he had no time to waste.

The tall American might have a plan in mind, but if he did, Kasm had not been briefed on its details. He thought the soldier probably was faking it, as the Americans would say, or "playing it by ear." And if his supposition was correct, the end might come at any moment, their disguises penetrated by the Old Man of the Mountain or his grim attendant with the cobra's eyes. In that event their one chance in a million of survival would depend entirely on their access to an exit. If they had a way to slip out of the castle, they could—

What? Steal horses from the stable, gallop to the gates and find them barred? Perhaps a magic carpet would be waiting for them, or a genie with three wishes who would spirit them across the fortress walls.

He froze. A magic carpet might not be available, but he had seen the heliport and recognized its bottom-line significance. There had not been a helicopter on the pad when they arrived, but one might be there *now* or else expected soon. It might be waiting when they were compelled to flee the Eagle's Nest, a means of scaling walls and leaving the Assassins far behind.

As quickly as the inspiration came into his mind, it withered. Was the tall American a pilot? If he could not fly, it made no difference *what* was sitting on the helipad; the Syrian knew nothing of the airship's handling, and they could never hope to find a willing pilot in the ranks of the Ismailis. This much he knew: the Old Man's followers would rather kill themselves en masse than help an enemy escape.

Kasm shrugged off the morbid train of thought. He had not found the exit yet, much less a helicopter, and he had them dead already in his mind.

Lighting in the corridor consisted of electric bulbs spaced twenty feet apart. Connecting cables ran along the ceiling, and he thought that with an insulated tool of some sort he could plunge the tunnel into darkness with a moment's effort. It was something to consider, possibly a means of slowing down pursuit, but would they not have flashlights? Lanterns?

Never mind. It was enough that he had struck upon the vestige of a plan, the first step in the formulation of escape procedures. The pursuit would still continue, even with the tunnels cast in darkness, but at least the aim of marksmen would be ruined, and they would not be shot down so easily, like stray dogs on the public street. It was a start, and at the moment he was thankful for the inspiration.

Moving on, he reached an intersecting corridor that ran—
he thought—from north to south. A right-hand turn would
take him toward the courtyard and escape...unless, of
course, he was mistaken. If he chose the wrong direction, he
would never find an exit from the halls of Alamut.

Electing to continue with the corridor he recognized,
Kasm took time to glance in each direction, satisfied that
there were no sentries in the tunnels. He crossed the open
space with hurried strides, aware that he was terribly exposed, a sitting target if he ran into a member of the killer
cult. Was the Old Man sincere in stating that they were not
prisoners, and had his troops been so informed? Were the
Assassins all on notice that the strangers should not be mo-
lested? Or had one or two of them, perhaps, been overlooked when the instructions were relayed?

He moved along the corridor, exaggerated strides designed to minimize the echo of his boot heels on the granite
floor. Kasm glanced over his shoulder frequently, afraid of
what he might discover creeping up behind him, conscious
of the image his skulking progress would present to hostile
eyes. He looked like what he was—a prowler, a spy on hostile ground.

If interrupted, and assuming that he was not shot on
sight, he planned to say that he was seeking the latrine, disoriented by the labyrinth of tunnels. It was thin, at best, but
he was good at playing dumb, and there was still a chance
that he might pull it off.

Some twenty yards farther on, the tunnel terminated in a
heavy wooden door. From its location, he was certain that
it offered access to the outside world, and he suppressed an
urge to shout his joy out loud.

He tried the handle cautiously and was surprised to feel
it turn without a sound. He checked the corridor behind him
one more time and tugged against the heavy door until it

gave an inch, then two. The fragrance of manure struck his nostrils, and he heard the horses stamping in their stalls.

The stable.

He had been correct.

Another fraction of an inch, and he could peer around the corner, scanning equine faces that regarded him impassively. He took a chance and poked his head out, drew it back immediately at the sight of stable hands, their naked backs turned momentarily, no more than fifteen feet away. Would they have sounded the alarm if they had seen him? He could see no point in taking chances. Kasm had found his exit from the fortress proper; testing it for usefulness would have to wait.

He didn't have a watch, but knew instinctively that he had used up his allotted time. He didn't think Amal would check his room, but there was still no point in courting danger any more than absolutely necessary. For the moment, he had managed the impossible, and in his mind, he was already working on a plan: it might be possible to kill the lights in their corridor, proceeding swiftly through the darkness to the stable door, and from there, if they were not anticipated, trapped, they would have access to the courtyard, possibly the helipad.

They would still be easy targets for the marksmen on the walls. They still might find no helicopter on the pad, and if there *was* one, they might have no way of lifting off. They might be dead before they cleared the stable's outer doors, their bodies riddled, so much useless garbage to be hauled away.

He forced the bloody image out of mind and closed the door securely, moving back along the tunnel toward his suite. It was ironic, he decided, that the plush accommodations he had dreamed about since childhood proved to be a prison, possibly the chamber where he would be put to death. Perhaps, in spite of everything, he had been fortunate in poverty.

He thought about his wife and children, waiting for him, unaware of where he was and what had brought him to that place. What would become of them if he did not return? There was the money he had hidden, saved through years of scrimping, for the day when Mara might be left alone. A letter, which she left unopened by agreement, would direct her to the cash, would provide her with names of contacts in the CIA who might agree to find her passage out of Syria. Each time he left their home "on business," without an explanation to the ones he loved, they had agreed upon a deadline for the letter to be opened. Thus far, he had always made it home in time....

His suite revealed no evidence of prowlers having entered in his absence, and he stretched out on the bed, attempting to relax. His plan was weak. It needed work. And he would have to find a way to speak with the American, alone, communicate his findings so that they could synchronize their plans regarding possible escape.

A little rest, and he would check the suite where Mike Belasko had been lodged. The soldier might be back from his excursion with the sheikh and his aide. If not he would have to wait and wonder how much time remained for staying in the dragon's lair.

9

"Are you aware of how we got our name?"

"Ismailis?"

They were back inside the castle proper, moving through an unfamiliar tunnel, bearing northwest.

"There is another."

"Ah."

"In certain quarters, we are called Assassins. You must know this. Otherwise, you would not be here."

"Yes."

"Perhaps you also know the vulgarism is derived from yet another name: Hashshashin—users of hashish."

"So I've heard."

"You disapprove?"

The soldier shrugged. "Your business. We've got our religious quirks in Ulster, too."

Arrani shot a burning glance at Bolan, who responded with a mocking smile. He didn't trust the sheikh's aide de camp, and saw no point in trying to make friends where it was neither possible nor necessary.

"Of course," the sheikh went on, "your war against the British. We will speak of that, in time. Hashish is more than a diversion for the members of our sect, however. It allows us to commune with Allah on a level unattained by other men of faith. It grants us insight, broadens our horizons."

Bolan's host was sounding like a sixties-style guru, intent on selling flower power and the Church of the Expanding Mind. It almost seemed that he could yank the Old Man's turban off, remove his beard and find Timothy Leary hiding underneath. Except that the Ismailis had been practicing their lethal brand of mind-altering worship for the better part of a millennium.

"I should imagine that it also helps you keep the troops in line," he offered, half expecting a reaction from the sheikh, receiving the expected grimace from Arrani.

"So it does. A few of our disciples are impetuous, and most grow restless over time. Hashish has powers to calm them, and it also makes them more receptive to the word of Allah."

"And the afterlife?"

"Through careful study of the holy word, my ancestors created an approximation of paradise on Earth—a garden of delights. I have revived the custom. Warriors who are certain of their heavenly reward, and who have sampled it beforehand, fear no enemy in battle."

"And hashish enhances their appreciation."

"Certainly."

The corridor was sloping downward, finally terminating at a heavy wooden door with armed Ismaili cultists standing guard. Before the sheikh had an opportunity to speak, the guards were on their knees. He left them there and turned to face the Executioner.

"Beyond this door, the dreams and fantasies of every man are perfectly fulfilled. In normal practice, those selected for a mission are, how shall we say—sedated—and they wake to find themselves in Paradise. Of course, your entry to the garden is unorthodox, but I am confident you will be satisfied with the experience. If you would like a little hashish, first—"

"No, thanks. I figure this could be my only look at Heaven, and I wouldn't want to miss a thing."

"Of course."

The master clapped his hands and brought the sentries to their feet. One stood at stiff attention while his comrade drew the door back, offering a wedge-shaped view of ferns and undergrowth beyond.

"Enjoy."

As Bolan stepped across the threshold, heard the heavy door swing shut behind him, he was struck immediately by the scent of flowers and the sound of running water. All around him trees and shrubs were brilliantly in bloom, the sweet aroma of their blossoms lying heavy on the air.

He spent a moment scanning his surroundings. He was in a garden, true enough, its rampant flora cultivated on a terrace carved out of the mountainside. The trees obscured his view, but Bolan knew that it would be surrounded by protecting walls of stone. The usual visitors, already high on hashish and sedated for the trip, would scarcely notice, but he knew the Old Man of the Mountain would not leave his back door open to the world, with just a pair of sentries to secure it.

On a whim, the soldier drifted to his left, along the cliff face that was overgrown with vines and creepers, following the sounds of flowing water. After several moments, he reached a point where sparkling water trickled from a fissure in the stone. A mountain spring, or some device prepared by men who built the Eagle's Nest in ages past? It scarcely mattered now; the presence of what seemed to be a never-ending water source would almost be enough itself to make a drugged-out desert cultist think that he had found Paradise.

A pair of brightly colored birds were trilling at him from the treetops, but he heard another sound audible above the avian salute, above the constant rippling of the spring.

The sound of voices. Laughter.

Bolan moved as quietly as possible, covering nearly fifty yards before he reached the tree line, hesitating while he still had cover. Just ahead, the mountain stream spilled out into a basin which, if not man-made, had certainly been modified by human hands. The pit, which might have been a simple crater some time in the past, was smooth and oval, with sand and polished stones along its banks. It had become a swimming pool, of sorts, and it was occupied.

There were two young women, and he wondered where the other dancers from the banquet hall were being kept this morning. Granted, two were plenty, and he spent a moment watching them as they cavorted in the water. Neither was wearing anything but sunshine and the beauty she was born with.

Bolan recognized the dancer who had stared at him with such intensity the night before. Despite the fact that she had earlier been veiled—and clothed—he knew her instantly. Her eyes had been the giveaway, and there was no mistaking them.

Bolan felt himself responding to the scene and the supple bodies of the forest nymphs. If he emerged from hiding, would he startle them? Or had they been instructed by the master of the castle to expect a guest? Their presence here was clearly not an accident; rather, it smacked of a performance, carefully rehearsed and polished over time. And there could be no harm, then, in another player taking part.

He stepped into the open and stood unnoticed by the women. Finally the nearer of the two spotted him and gave a little gasp, retreating so that just her head and shoulders could be seen above the surface while she spoke rapidly to her friend in Arabic. The other seemed to take his entrance in stride, and Bolan thought the shy one must have been more startled than embarrassed, for a moment later she was on the bank, her body sleek and glistening.

The other woman joined her, and they whispered for a moment. The dark-eyed dancer seemed to win the toss to serve as spokesperson. Stepping forward and making no attempt to hide herself from Bolan's gaze, she spoke to him directly, and despite the view, he found he had no problem concentrating on her deep, almost hypnotic eyes.

"I'm sorry, I don't understand."

"Then, you speak English?"

"Yes."

She had an accent, but he could not place it. Bolan thought the riddle's answer might have been important, but at the moment it didn't seem to matter.

"My companion, Alia, does not speak your language, but if you have any questions, any needs, I will be pleased to serve as your interpreter."

"Sounds good to me."

"My name is Shari."

"Pleased to meet you."

Shari took his hand and led him toward the pool, and before he knew precisely what she had in mind, his caftan fell to the ground. The water in the pool came up to Bolan's waist, and it surprised him with its warmth. It did not have the normal bite of a mountain spring to it, and the soldier let himself relax a little as the woman joined him in the water, circling him slowly, counterclockwise, soft hands reaching out to stroke him.

Within a moment, he was ready, eager, but the garden nymph wasn't prepared to hurry her performance. Her hands grew more demanding, more inquisitive, and Bolan fought the urge to close his eyes, surrender to the moment.

All movement abruptly halted, and Bolan found himself face-to-face with Shari. He could lose himself in those eyes, he thought, but she was doing something with her hands, her hips, that broke his train of thought. Her lips brushed his lightly, and she trailed a string of teasing kisses down his throat, across his chest, descending. In a moment, she was submerged, her dark hair fanned out on the surface as she caught him. He felt the moment stretch into infinity, aware that she must soon take oxygen, amazed that she could hold her breath so long.

When Shari broke the surface, she was like a graceful dolphin surfacing, head thrown back and dark hair streaming down her spine. She locked her arms around his neck and clamped her thighs around his waist, accommodating Bolan with a single, practiced thrust. He clutched her urgently. It seemed impossible, the strength and depth of the sensation that he felt, and Bolan knew the moment was too powerful to be maintained. A gasp, a shudder, and he was aboard the old, familiar roller coaster—only this time, he was plunging from a height he had never known before, and he was taking Shari with him, racing toward their mutual release.

They separated, aeons later, and Shari and the other woman, Alia, bathed him tenderly, rejuvenating energy through the selective laying of hands. Incredibly the soldier felt himself responding, and he made no protest as they led him from the pool area, toward quilted blankets that were spread out on the grass. He saw that silver platters heaped with fruit and other refreshments were waiting for him there.

"Your every fantasy come true," the dark-eyed dancer told him, as she stepped aside and let Alia take his hand.

So this is paradise, he thought, and realized how an impressionable young disciple of the sheikh, already flying high on hashish and assorted other drugs, might think that he had died and gone to heaven. As a thought-control technique, it seemed a damned sight more effective—not to mention more enjoyable—than narco-hypnotism or aversion therapy. If he had been a loyal disciple of the master, and he knew that *this* was waiting for him on the other side of death, he might have volunteered to take that long, last dive himself.

The sheikh had made his point, and Bolan knew he could expect no quarter from the soldiers at al-Sabbah's beck and call. While they existed, they were clearly a danger to the world at large, a suicidal force of mercenary killers who would welcome death on orders from their master, welcoming the reaper with a lover's open arms. It was imperative that they should be destroyed.

But first, Bolan thought wryly, he had to finish off his tour of paradise. The Old Man of the Mountain was expecting it, and Bolan could not afford to blow his cover. He was obligated to pursue his mission to the limits of his personal endurance, and he would not flinch from that commitment.

TAHIR ARRANI WATCHED the stranger from his hiding place without a flicker of desire. The harlots did not move him, though he realized that other men must find them beautiful, alluring. Unconsciously he offered thanks to Allah that his flesh was strong, his heart committed to the holy war that lay ahead.

Jihad. The final war against the infidel. It was a concept that had captured his imagination years before, when he had fought beside the fedayeen, against the Zionists of Israel, and a grim succession of defeats had failed to quench his thirst for blood. The Old Man of the Mountain had attracted him with visions of a world in flames, the true believers riding down their enemies like Death incarnate, and it mattered little that the sheikh had lost direction in the meantime, giving in to the temptations of the flesh. No matter that the holy quest had been diverted, briefly, into mercenary channels, serving men instead of Allah. There was ample time to bring the mission back on target, and his time was coming. Soon.

Meanwhile, it served Arrani's purposes to help Sheikh al-Jebal spread violence and chaos in the West. If the accursed infidels were bent upon destroying one another, was it not the duty of a dedicated true believer to assist them? If the fools were anxious to employ the agents of their own destruction, who was he, Tahir Arrani, to prevent them?

It amused him to imagine members of the Red Brigades, the Baader-Meinhof faction or the South Moluccan network doling out their cash in the belief that they were moving toward an epic victory. In fact, disruption of the several governments they hated served the purposes of the Jihad perfectly, and each dead infidel was one less who would stand against the faithful on the coming day of reckoning.

At the moment, his mind was on the Irish and the man called Harrigan. Of course, the name was false—or so he had convinced himself—and radio communication with assorted contacts on the outside had done nothing to relieve his first suspicion of the stranger. The missing accent had been troublesome, but logically explained. The vanishing tattoo was something else entirely.

In his youth, according to Arrani's sources, Bryan Harrigan had shown the ultimate contempt for queen and country by acquiring a tattoo—the British Union Jack—across his buttocks. He had never been arrested, and the information was not in his file maintained by the authorities in London, but it was a fact well-known to fellow members of the IRA, along with certain of their sympathizers. It had been a standing—or rather a sitting—joke among the Ulster partisans for more than twenty years.

An accent might be lost, with practice and determination. Surgery could change a face so that it went unrecognized by parents, wives and lovers. As well, a tattoo could be removed, but there would be a scar, some vestige of the human canvas having changed his mind too late.

The buttocks of this man, clearly visible from where Arrani stood, were unblemished.

It was enough to prove his case, but not, perhaps, enough to satisfy the master. Money had changed hands, with more to come, and these days it would not surprise him to discover that the sheikh was more devoted to his private income than the holy mission. He might accept the fact that Harrigan was an imposter and continue doing business with the man in any case. Through greed and negligence, he might destroy them all.

It would be different if some further proof of treachery existed. If Arrani could convince the sheikh that "Harrigan" was not a simple stand-in for their scheduled contact but a hostile agent sent to do them harm, the Old Man would be forced to put his personal venality aside and take decisive action.

Proof.

He could interrogate the weasel who had brought this stranger to them, use his talents to extract each hidden grain of knowledge while a trace of sanity remained, but such a breach of hospitality might lead to questions from the master that he was not yet prepared to answer. With the proof in hand, he would be free to move against their enemies without restriction, but he must acquire the evidence beforehand, to protect himself.

He examined the warrior's body with its several scars of battle. This man was no stranger to the moment of the kill.

It would be difficult, perhaps, to take him by surprise, but he was hopelessly outnumbered here and without a weapon to defend himself. If one or two of the disciples should be lost in bringing him to heel, it was a trifling price to pay. They were prepared to die, in any case, to win what the impostor was sampling now.

Arrani turned away and left the stranger to his pleasure, moving through the garden like the shadow of a thought. No man observed his passing, and no sentry watched the secret entrance he used to make his way inside the castle. Unknown even to the master, it had been discovered by Arrani, quite by accident, some months before, and he had used it sparingly. He had no business in the garden ordinarily, and did not take his pleasure with the harlots who were kept sequestered there. His own belief in paradise, the ultimate reward of Allah, had no need of artificial reinforcement through the flesh.

Tahir Arrani was a true believer, dedicated to Allah and the destruction of the infidels who made a mockery of his sacred word. He was devoted to Jihad, the cleansing holy war, above all else, and in that cause he had accepted the assistance of the Russians, in his master's name. The Communists believed they owned him now, but there were more surprises still in store for them. Jihad, when it began in earnest, would not be confined to nations that revered the Christ. There would be time enough to deal with godless Bolsheviks, as well.

But first, the lone imposter. And the proof.

Tahir Arrani left the garden of delights behind him, entering the mountain's heart where secrets could be nurtured in the dark, away from prying eyes. He still had work to do this morning, and there was no time to waste.

10

Shari scrubbed herself with energetic strokes, as if she could eradicate her memories, all traces of the stranger's touch, with soap and water. It had never worked before, but she observed the ritual in any case, unwilling to forsake the futile gesture of defiance.

As a member of the sheikh's harem, Shari was expected to perform upon command, with anyone selected by her master. Personal initiative and individuality were not encouraged by Sheikh al-Jebal; if demonstrated publicly, they might be punished in the dungeons, and she knew from grim experience that no one made a return trip.

For the past seven months she had done her job without complaint, the perfect model of submission. Oh, there had been feeble protests in the early days, but those were mandatory, absolutely necessary to convince the Old Man and his toady that they had another ordinary slave girl on their hands. In truth, the sheikh had found her anything but ordinary in their various prolonged encounters. His assorted gifts had marked her as a favorite in the harem, but he still did not possess the slightest notion of her true identity, the mission that had placed her voluntarily within his grasp.

When she was finished drying off Shari slipped into her costume of gossamer and silk. She felt ridiculous, avoided mirrors when she could, but she knew that there was power in her body, in the face that men found beautiful. Their own lust to possess her would betray them in the end, and so she wore the harem costume as she wore her lot in life, without complaint.

From the beginning, she had accepted the mission with her eyes wide open. There was no point in contending that she had been deceived by her controllers or misled by anyone, in any way. The choice had been her own, and she would live with it—assuming that she lived.

In her present situation survival was by no means certain. Over seven months, the number of her harem "sisters" had been whittled down from sixteen to an even dozen. Of the missing, three had simply disappeared without a trace, a circumstance veteran members of the master's stable seemed to take in stride. The fourth had fallen victim to "an accident"; one of the sheikh's commandos-in-the-making had erupted from sedation in a violent rage and locked his fingers around the nearest throat. He had crushed the life out of a young woman from Damascus by the time he'd been bludgeoned into unconsciousness. The sheikh had been solicitous, a minor miracle considering the victim's sex and rank, but life—and death—went on at Alamut, and Shari's task remained the same.

In fact, her mission could not be so easily defined. Having taken on the job, she was instructed to observe, disrupt whenever possible, and to remain in place, above all else. Her presence in the Eagle's Nest was critical. When it was time for her to leave, the order would somehow be passed along, and she would find her own way from the fortress.

Shari had some thoughts on that already, but her exit plans were in the embryonic stage. Thus far, she knew how women were stolen from the streets, how they were forced into a life of servitude, how the Assassins were prepared for war. But none of that concerned her government. She needed targets and agendas, names, dates and places for impending raids—the better to prevent them from occurring.

How could she accomplish this? She was a prisoner, a slave, deprived of all communication with the outside world. Her cover had demanded that she go in "clean," without equipment or an established contact in the outside world. The word would come, she had been told, and when it came, she would escape with all the vital knowledge she had gathered from her enemies.

But in the meantime, there was something she could do right now, today. The ice-eyed stranger could be stopped before he made his deal with the Assassins, carrying the torch of terrorism back to Europe or America, wherever he had come from. She could stop *this* enemy on her own, and with a bit of luck, she might escape detection.

She had begun to think of home more frequently, had dreamed of it on two occasions in the past ten days. Her vital mission had begun to pale, when held up against the cost it exacted on a daily basis. On the upside, Shari did not feel humiliated or degraded by the acts she was obliged to perform. The sex meant no more to her than killing had in other situations where she had been called upon to do her duty. She felt nothing with her enemies; they never touched her soul.

Shari knew the stranger must be an important guest. His visit to the garden had been hastily arranged, with orders for every wish to be fulfilled. He had not been especially demanding, but he had been pleased with his reception; that much had been plain to see. He had been vigorous, which was surprising, considering the fact that he had obviously shunned the normal drugs and stimulants that were available. His body had been scarred by war, but there had been a certain softness in his eyes.

Shari knew her duty, realized that she could never hope to learn the stranger's business, make her getaway and carry the report to her superiors in time. The tall man would be gone, his devil's work complete before she had a chance to intervene, unless . . .

It would require precision timing, a degree of privacy, but Shari thought that she could pull it off. The stranger had been pleased with her today, she knew that much beyond the shadow of a doubt, and he would doubtless be agreeable to further encounters, should the opportunity arise. Sex would be the weapon of his ultimate destruction, and if she was careful, planning every move precisely, she would have him at her mercy. Who would suspect a harem girl, a slave, of staging an assassination in the heart of the Ismaili stronghold?

She had armed herself with a long knife from the kitchen shortly after her arrival, but as yet there had been no occasion to remove the weapon from its hiding place behind a loose stone in the floor of her sleeping chamber. She could hide it underneath her costume with a bit of difficulty, and the tall man would be in for a surprise. His last.

Shari would have liked to know his name, his mission, but it didn't matter. His obvious association with the Old Man of the Mountain was enough to seal his fate, and any plans she disrupted would spare the lives of innocents abroad. Those who dealt with the Assassins were themselves beyond the pale, fair game for any who would strike on the behalf of peace and justice.

Taking out the tall man would be her gift to future victims yet unborn. It was her duty.

"WHAT REASON HAVE YOU to suspect our guest?"

Tahir Arrani spread his hands, eyes downcast in a semblance of humility. "I have no proof, Your Highness, but you have been generous enough to trust my intuition in the past. I am convinced that evidence can be obtained."

"And if you are correct," Sheikh al-Jebal inquired, "who is this man who poses as our Irish comrade?"

"Once again, I cannot say. If my suspicions prove correct, and I can demonstrate that Bryan Harrigan is not among us, time and patience will supply the answers that you seek."

"Why would a stranger wish to pose as Harrigan?" He knew the answer in advance, but he was interested in Arrani's own assessment of the situation.

"To destroy us." The response was given without a trace of hesitation. "To subvert your rule and crush the faith before our destiny is realized."

"And whom do you suspect of plotting this offensive?"

"Israel."

"Does our Mr. Harrigan resemble an Israeli in your eyes?"

"A mercenary, then." Arrani was not shaken by the sheikh's facetious tone. "Your messengers of death have traveled widely, O Enlightened One. Your enemies are legion in the West."

That much, at least, was true. The British, the Italians and the French would all be pleased to see him dead, his followers annihilated. The Americans, as well, bore watching. The CIA was not above assassination if it was considered necessary "in the national interest." Still, the Israelis were the best bet, with their late attempts to infiltrate his stronghold. He had destroyed the agents sent against him, punishing the traitors who had helped them come so far, and Tel Aviv might be prepared to use a mercenary warrior this time out.

Then again, Arrani might be wrong. Their guest might be precisely who he claimed to be, with endless sums of ready cash to supplement the offering he had made upon arrival at the Eagle's Nest. He might be one more in the string of "terrorists" and freedom fighters who solicited the Old Man of the Mountain for assistance in these times of trial. The sheikh had lucrative arrangements with the Basques, with certain factions in West Germany and Italy; why should he be surprised at honest overtures from Northern Ireland? Members of the IRA were too well-known these days to carry off a major-league assassination anywhere within a thousand miles of Belfast. Local boys were fine for sniping soldiers, dropping gasoline bombs on armored cars from darkened rooftops, but precision murder of celebrities in public would require fresh faces, someone Scotland Yard and SAS would never spare a second glance.

He did not know the details of the IRA's request, could not surmise whether the target would be royalty, a ranking politician, or perhaps Parliament itself. Whichever, his disciples would be equal to the task. Provided, always, that his guest was who he claimed to be.

"What is it that you wish?" he asked Arrani, careful to betray no indecision of his own.

"Permission to conduct a search for evidence... outside."

"Where would you go?"

"Not far. If your guest is an impostor, then he must have intercepted Harrigan along the highway from Damascus. If the Irishman had turned up missing earlier, our contacts in the government would certainly have warned us."

"I agree. Go with my blessings and return with all due haste to make your findings known."

"To hear is to obey."

"Arrani."

"Yes, Your Highness?"

"Do not speak of this to Mr. Harrigan or his companion. If your intuition proves correct, I will have questions of my own for him to answer. If you are mistaken, I will have no shadows cast upon our hospitality."

"As you desire, my lord."

Alone once more, the master of the Eagle's Nest considered all that he had heard, the suppositions and suspicions that had moved Arrani to request permission for an expedition to the world outside. He hoped his second-in-command was wrong, for varied reasons. A mistake would keep Arrani in his place, for one thing, and an error in judgment would be infinitely preferable to the infiltration of his stronghold by an agent of his enemies. He did not fear the man called Harrigan, but where one spy slipped through, another might someday succeed in circumventing the security of Alamut. The isolated and impenetrable fortress was his strength, his trump card, and it would not do for infidels to learn that there were loopholes in his personal defenses.

Abdel al-Sabbah had waited much too long, worked much too hard, to gain the title of Sheikh al-Jebal. No traitor from the West could stop him now; no overly ambitious member of his entourage could dazzle him with words of "wisdom" and provoke a rash response to manufactured crises. If the man called Harrigan was shown to be a spy, he would be dealt with as the Hashshashin had dealt with enemies for centuries untold. If he was who he claimed to be, their business would proceed without disturbance, and the Irishman would never know how close his brush with agonizing death had been.

Whichever way Arrani's search for evidence might end, the master of the Eagle's Nest was ready to respond with swift, decisive action. He would not be made a fool by the infidels, nor would his course of action be dictated by presumptuous subordinates.

He was the voice of Allah, and his word was law.

HAFEZ KASM WAS UNEASY. Even in the absence of a wristwatch, he was painfully aware of passing time. He thought that hours must have passed since Mike Belasko left to make his tour with the Old Man of the Mountain and the ferret named Arrani. Should they have returned by now? Or was he merely growing paranoid, the product of confinement under stress?

No, he was certain of it; Belasko should have finished with his tour of the castle long ago. Or had he? In his personal anxiety, Kasm had thought his contact would immediately summon him upon returning, or at least drop by his sleeping chamber to describe what he had seen. But what if Belasko had returned directly to his suite? Was it not logical? He might need rest, an opportunity to think in peace and solitude before he hatched a battle plan.

If so, should not he permit him to enjoy his privacy? What did he have to offer, other than the information on an exit through the stables?

Startled by his own astounding ignorance, the slender Arab sat bolt upright on his bed. Of course! The exit. Belasko must be told at once, in case the information might affect his final plan. And if the American had retreated to his room, Hafez would find him there; he would apologize for the intrusion, recount his findings and depart.

Relieved by his decision, conscious of the rumbling in his stomach now that breakfast lay some hours behind them, the Syrian crossed the room and hesitated, listening at the door. There were no sounds outside, which could mean anything, so he went through the humiliating ritual of peeking through a crack at first, then checking out the corridor, like a child about to cross the street. He was alone, from all appearances, with no one to observe him as he closed the door behind him and moved silently along the corridor.

Two other suites, whose doors were closed, stood between his own and Belasko's. He passed each door with hurried strides, afraid that one of the Assassins might suddenly emerge from the room to take him by surprise. He stood now before Belasko's door, almost afraid to knock in case the sound drew attention from the minions of their host. Embarrassed by his reticence, which smacked of fear, Kasm rapped lightly on the panel.

Nothing.

Again, this time a little louder, just in case the American was drowsing.

No response.

He knew the door would not be locked. His own—and so, by inference, the others, had no inside latching mechanisms. Tenants of the Old Man's guest wing could be locked up in their rooms, but they could never lock themselves inside. If someone wanted them, at noon or midnight, they would be available to anyone who held the key.

He slipped inside, calling out, knowing there would be no answer. Kasm checked the small connecting bathroom to satisfy himself that no one else was lurking in the shadows, waiting for his comrade to return. He was, incontrovertibly, alone.

What now? He could retrace his steps and wait for Belasko in his own room, or he could remain exactly where he was. There were advantages and disadvantages to both ideas. If the American should go looking for him on completion of his tour, the empty suite of rooms might cause him some alarm. In contrast, if the American was suspected, even broken in the dungeons, the Assassins would come looking for him in his own room, first, allowing him a momentary respite from the fire.

On balance, Kasm felt safer where he was, and so he settled into an uncomfortable wooden chair, prepared to wait. His mind was racing with alternative reactions, to be implemented if his worst suspicions bore fruit. The stable exit was his best hope for an escape, but if the Assassins came for him, he would be forced to pass them in the corridor. Unarmed, his hopes of taking out a crack Ismaili squad were nil; his only hope for ultimate survival lay in stealth, and even then, his options would be limited.

His enemy would have the numbers on their side, and they were all familiar with the tunnels of the Eagle's Nest, while he had managed to explore one section of a single corridor. It still might be enough, however, if Kasm could find a hiding place and let the manhunt pass him by. If he could reach the stable exit, then the courtyard—

And again, the vision came of marksmen on the parapets, their automatic weapons spitting flame directly in his face. With a disguise, he might just have a chance, but there was still the gate, the valley just beyond.

Depressed, he shook his head to clear away the morbid thoughts. Before he panicked, he would hear what Belasko had to say about their situation. There was still a chance his contact had discovered something, possibly another exit from the castle, which would see them through the coming hours, alive and relatively whole.

He still was not precisely sure what Belasko meant to do about their enemies, and the uncertainty did not increase his confidence. What was the man's plan? Did he *have* a plan? Their entry to the castle, with the American posing as an Irish terrorist, had been completely unexpected, a surprise to all concerned.

He was not convinced, by any means, that they *could* manage an escape, but Belasko might have something in the nature of a plan. If not, their efforts and their sacrifice would all have been in vain, and the Assassins would continue as before, a living disgrace to the people of Syria.

If things went badly for them, he might reach Sheikh al-Jebal before they killed him. It would only take a moment, time enough to lock his hands around the Old Man's throat and squeeze...

But that would be a last resort. He had not come this far to throw his life away on suicidal gestures. First, he had to speak with Mike Belasko, find out what the tall American had seen and done this day. From there, they would be better able to devise a plan.

And some time later, even as his mind continued grappling with the problems that surrounded him, Kasm slept.

11

"You are refreshed by your experience?"

"I wouldn't say refreshed, exactly."

If the truth was known, he felt a good deal closer to exhaustion. Reluctantly he pushed all thoughts of willing flesh aside and concentrated on Sheikh al-Jebal. The old man was alone, the first time Bolan had observed him without his shadow, Arrani, and the Executioner experienced a mixture of suspicion and relief. Where was Arrani? What was he doing? Was the sheikh less difficult to deal with on his own?

"I think perhaps you understand the workings of our garden of delights."

"I'd say it works just fine."

"Indeed. The great majority of my disciples have been drawn from simple peasant stock. They lust for greatness, heroism, even death in battle if it grants them one bright, shining moment in the sun. You understand?"

"I've met the type."

"Of course, there are the normal fears to overcome, and Allah offers us a blueprint in His holy scripture. As the fields of Paradise have been described in the Koran, so I have recreated them on Earth. A simple 'vision,' easily arranged, and my disciples wake to the assurance of their heavenly reward. Their fears are washed away."

"It beats a pep talk on the night before a raid, I'll give you that. But can your shooters follow orders?"

"You are well aware of our successes in the recent past or you would not be here."

"That's true, but spraying lead around a crowded room is rather different from the job we have in mind. Our project would require precision accuracy and split-second timing."

"Perhaps you would like to observe how my warriors are trained?"

Bolan swallowed the new urge to smile. Any training with weapons would be conducted outside, in the courtyard or valley below. One more chance with the homer.

"Yes, I would." Bolan hoped he did not sound too eager. "But I should get cleaned up a little, before—"

"As you say. It is noon, now." He saw that the old man did not wear a watch. "Shall we say, in two hours?"

"That's fine."

"Food and drink will be brought to your chamber."

"Thanks, again. Now, regarding our business..."

"Tonight. We have time."

"As you say."

Bolan was escorted back to his room by a sentry who carried an Uzi and scimitar, one of the crack palace guards. They were shorter than average height, these disciples of death, but their bodies were trim and athletic, their weapons borne effectively, lacking the posture and show displayed by amateurs playing soldier. The high-dive, that morning, had shown him the cultists had no fear of death, and he knew that fanatics died harder than most.

At his door, Bolan's escort turned back and was gone in an instant, devoured by the tunnels. He waited a moment more, thought of proceeding to meet with Hafez and decided to shower first. Food was expected, and he must be there when it arrived if he wished to avoid stirring up more suspicion. He thought of Arrani, again wondered where the sheikh's right hand had gone. He opened the door—

And he froze.

For a heartbeat, the soldier believed that he had been betrayed, marked for death by the sheikh or Arrani. Why else would a turbaned Assassin be waiting inside his room, crouching to spring from a chair near the door?

A heartbeat, and then he relaxed, as he saw that the man was not crouching, but dozing, chin on his chest. It was not an Assassin at all, but Hafez, wearing robes and a turban that the sheikh had provided. Before he could reach out and touch the slim Arab, Hafez sprang awake, the embarrassment bright in his cheeks.

"I apologize."

"No need. You been waiting long?"

"I do not believe so. Half an hour, perhaps."

"I got sidetracked awhile." Avoiding the prurient details, he filled in Hafez on his trip to the garden, the cliff diver, all that the Old Man had told him. He thought he detected the ghost of a smile on the Syrian's face when the garden was mentioned, and then it was gone, as his contact absorbed every word.

"You saw no other way of escape from the garden?"

"No time," Bolan answered. "There must be another way, possibly several, but we could be dead by the time we came up with an exit."

"Indeed. I have found one . . . as far as the courtyard, at least."

"Lay it out."

Kasm cocked a thumb over his shoulder, eastward. "The corridor runs for a distance without deviation. This morning, no guards were on duty that I could observe. At the end of the tunnel, a door opens into the stables. This door, like the tunnel itself, was unguarded."

"How far?"

The Arab thought about it for a moment. "Possibly 350 meters."

Bolan frowned. "That works out to a long, straight run, with the Ismailis on our heels."

Kasm had thought it through. "The corridor is lighted by electric bulbs," he said. "The cable runs along the ceiling, and it is exposed. If it was cut or broken, somehow..."

Bolan's frown became a cautious smile. "It might work—and I emphasize the 'might.' Before we start escaping, though, we have to do the job we came for."

It was now Hafez Kasm's turn to frown. "We have no weapons," he reminded Bolan, "and we are outnumbered. I see nothing left to do."

"I came to blow their house down," Bolan answered, "and I mean to do exactly that."

"But how?"

The Executioner was running out of options. He had managed to conceal the grim specifics of his mission from the Syrian to this point, but the time had come to lay his cards on the table. He could only guess the man's reaction, knew he might resist, but Bolan would be braced for anything, prepared to take decisive action if it sadly came to that.

He found the homer, in its place behind the tapestry, and showed it to Kasm. "We're not as isolated as we seem," he said.

"What is it?"

"A transmitter, miniaturized and designed to emit a directional beacon for tracking. In this case, an air strike."

"An air strike?" the Syrian echoed. A long moment passed before full understanding was clear in his eyes. "The Israelis!"

"No choice. They're in range, and they're capable. Washington won't lift a finger without provocation. The French and Italians are too busy counting their dead."

"I was told the Israelis would not be involved."

"Not by me."

"By my contacts, then."

Bolan could feel for the guy, but the numbers were falling, and he had no time to play watchdog or wet nurse. "You're all they had left," he said gruffly. "Last chance. You might just be the last chance for Syria, too."

Kasm thought about that for a moment, his mind mulling over the limited options. Aborting their mission meant further attacks by the Old Man's disciples, on unknown targets. If the raids were directed at Israel again—and they would be, in time—a reaction was certain. Without an identified target, the strike force might unleash its fire on Damascus or some other kill zone selected at random. If war should result, the Israelis were ready, the Syrians poorly prepared.

"Could I stop you?" Kasm asked at last.

Bolan held him with eyes that were stony. "I doubt that. I hope you won't try."

"I am, how do you say it, between a rock and a hard-on."

"A hard *place*," the soldier corrected him, grinning in spite of himself. "I'm sorry."

"No matter. You speak the truth. As long as Sheikh al-Jebal rules in this valley, my country will never be safe from her enemies. So, tell me what must be done."

Bolan opened his mouth, but the words never came. In their place came a knock at the door.

SHE HAD NOT BROUGHT the knife with her. It would be foolish to attack the stranger in his room when it was known to all that she had volunteered to take him food and drink. She would not make a move against him now, did not intend to speak if she was given any choice. She had concealed a note beneath the goblet. He could not miss it when he drank.

She had not spoken English since she joined the Old Man's harem, had not written it for months before that, but she thought the note would serve. Her language was deliberately ambiguous, enticing. She had offered nothing, but expressed a personal desire to meet him privately. He would inevitably draw his own conclusions, and if he reported her—a circumstance she regarded as improbable—the worst she could be charged with was excessive physical attraction toward a handsome man. She might be whipped, but if the guest was an important one—as he appeared to be—her zeal in seeing to his happiness might even be rewarded.

If he kept the rendezvous, she would kill him. It would be easy when his pants were down, his mind on sex instead of raw survival. She would take him then, leave no trace of herself, and if the unsigned note was found—if he did not destroy it, as requested—there would still be no connection for the sheikh to draw.

The door was opened at her knock, and she was thankful that she had not planned to kill him in his room, for he was not alone. The man who occupied a chair behind the low-slung coffee table was a stranger, but she knew that he was not Ismaili. There was nothing of the holy warrior in his eyes, his bearing; if she had been asked to name his chief emotion at the moment, Shari would have called it trepidation, even fear. Disciples of Sheikh al-Jebal had no fear left inside, as they had no compassion, pity, love for anything outside their sect.

She held the silver platter out, an explanation of her presence in itself. The tall man, her intended target, stood aside and pointed toward the coffee table, where his slim companion sat. He recognized her from the garden, there could be no doubt of that, and she had seen the spark within his eyes that signaled interest. He was only human, after all. The flesh was weak, and it would kill him in the end.

She set the tray down, bending at the waist, allowing him an unobstructed view of her behind through flimsy harem trousers. Turning to face him as she took her leave, she bowed—a bit of cleavage couldn't hurt—and when he thanked her, there was more than simple gratitude behind his words.

With the door closed firmly at her back, she hurried down the empty corridor, not anxious to be present if he found the note at once. Another summons to his room was not a part of Shari's plan. He would obey the note's instructions, or he would report her to the sheikh; there was no third alternative.

And when they met again, she meant to be prepared. The man who came to Alamut to purchase death for others would have found his own, instead. It was poetic justice, and she was delighted, finally, to have some goal beyond the passive role of eyes and ears inside the Old Man's harem.

Within the hour, she would strike a blow that would be long remembered by her enemies. And, as an added bonus, there was still a chance she might survive.

"ONE OF THE WOMEN from the garden?"

Bolan nodded, putting on a rueful smile.

"By Allah's beard! No wonder the Assassins all look forward to the afterlife with such enthusiasm."

Bolan chuckled, but Kasm was instantly suffused with guilt. His wife might not possess the charms of that one, but her beauty shone within, and it was honest, pure. He was ashamed of having looked upon the woman with desire.

"Something to drink?"

The warrior shook his head and helped himself to fruit from the elaborate arrangement on the platter. "Not for me."

Kasm picked up the heavy goblet, raised it to his lips . . . and saw the folded slip of paper lying on the platter, where it had been concealed. He set the chalice down, picked up the paper and unfolded it. A glance was all it took before he knew the message had been meant for his companion.

"Here. For you."

Bolan read it several times, his forehead lined with concentration. Finally he passed the message back and asked, "What do you make of that?"

The Arab read through the message, which had been printed in square block letters, like a sample from an English textbook.

Meet me at the entrance to the garden in an hour's time. The door will not be guarded. Come alone. Destroy this note when you have finished reading it.

The cryptic letter was not signed. Kasm was frowning as he passed it back. "Do you think it is a message from the girl?"

"Who else?"

He shrugged. "If I were you, I would ignore it."

"Just like that?"

"It is a trap. Or possibly a test."

"Explain."

"The Old Man—or that piece of camel's dung, Arrani—may be questioning your loyalty. If you are lured by this note, they might have further cause to doubt you. Who can say what they might do?''

Bolan considered it, but finally shook his head. ''I don't believe that. If you ask me why, I couldn't tell you. It just *feels* wrong.''

''Then, a trap. Why else would anyone desire to meet you in the garden when they could as easily approach you here? The girl was here just now, and she said nothing. Why delay your meeting for an hour?''

''Maybe she's the bashful type.''

''A bashful whore?'' Kasm made no attempt to hide his scorn. ''I know you do not hear my words, but on my life I beg you. Do away with this.'' He pointed at the note disdainfully. ''Forget you ever saw it.''

''Sorry. Can't.''

''Americans. Is this not what you call bullheaded?''

Bolan smiled. ''You may be right. Let's say I can't resist a mystery.''

Kasm could feel the color rising in his cheeks. ''And your appointed mission? What becomes of that, of Syria, if you are killed before your work is done?''

''It shouldn't matter. I'm invited to assassin's school this afternoon. With any luck, I should have this installed and functioning before we meet for dinner.'' As he spoke, the warrior brushed one hand against a pocket of his caftan, where he had concealed the miniature transmitter when the woman arrived.

''And that is all?''

''It's self-contained. The strike force makes its pass at the appointed hour, finds the beacon, and they're home. It would be nice if we were somewhere else just then, but either way, it's show time.''

''And the Eagle's Nest will be destroyed?''

"I wouldn't want to write the Old Man any home-insurance policies right now."

"If we are still inside . . ."

"The curtain comes down, either way. There's no abort procedure once the strike force has that beacon."

"And the scheduled time of their arrival?"

"Midnight."

"But the transmitter must be in place."

"That's right."

"In that case, I suggest your visit with the harlot should not be prolonged."

Bolan smiled. "Believe me, I don't have the energy for anything but conversation."

"You will please be careful?"

"Yes."

"I do not ask this for myself, but for my people. If this bloody business must be done, then let us do it properly."

He rose to leave, and Bolan stopped him with a hand upon his arm.

"If anything goes wrong," he said, "if they come looking for you and its obvious I'm out of it, do everything you can to get away. The stable route has possibilities. Outside, if you can make connections with your contacts, pass along coordinates. The raid can be rescheduled for another time."

"I will not leave you here."

"Get real. If they come looking for you, and I'm not around, it means I won't be coming back. In that case, you'll know you were right, and you might still have time to save yourself."

"It is a shameful thing to run away."

"You've got it wrong. The shame is giving up your life for no good reason, when you have a chance to make it count."

"I will consider this."

"You do that. And with any luck at all, I'll see you when we meet for dinner."

In the corridor outside, Kasm moved slowly toward his room, pondering the American's words. Before he reached his own door, he had made his mind up. He would not run away, no matter how Belasko might wish it. If the enemy should turn on him, if the summons from the whore turned out to be an ambush, Kasm would try to help his comrade with the means at his disposal. If he failed, and if he spent his life in the attempt, at least he would have died a man. But running? Never.

They would leave the Eagle's Nest together, or they would not leave at all.

BOLAN THOUGHT ABOUT THE NOTE while he was shredding it and moving toward the tiny bathroom, where he flushed its tattered remnants down the toilet. He had listened to Hafez Kasm, realized the common sense behind the Arab's words. It made no sense that anyone inside the castle—least of all Shari—would attempt to seek a private audience with Bryan Harrigan outside his chambers. Not unless they planned to do him harm or somehow test his loyalty to the cause he claimed to represent.

Forewarned, however, Bolan felt that he could not afford to let the moment pass. If there was unknown danger here he would be better off to meet the threat head-on, instead of leaving enemies at large to choose their time and place. If he was being tested by the sheikh or his associate, Tahir Arrani, Bolan thought that he could play his part convincingly enough to put their minds at ease.

What form would an attempted buy-off take, if that turned out to be the game? He had already sampled everything the woman had to offer, and the prospect of financial pay-offs from a slave were slim, indeed. Of course, if the

Old Man and his right arm were setting up an ambush, then the woman would merely be a gofer, carrying the message and, perhaps, remaining at the rendezvous to mark him with the Judas kiss. The killers would be members of the standing army Sheikh al-Jebal maintained for such emergencies, his own disciples, dedicated to the faith.

Unarmed, would he have any chance at all? No matter. Knowledge of an enemy in waiting could be half the battle. If he missed the meeting, left the hunters to decide upon another place and time, he would be granting them the critical advantage of surprise. At least, if Bolan knew that an attack was coming, he could take some measures to defend himself.

For openers, he wore his desert camo uniform beneath his caftan. It had been returned that morning, cleaned and pressed, along with his combat boots. His side arm and the AK-47 had *not* been returned, but he had not expected them. For now it was enough that he possessed the other gear. As Bolan counted down the final moments to his garden rendezvous, he pulled one of the plastic canteens from its canvas sheath, dipping anxious fingers inside, smiling with relief as he discovered that his hosts had missed the secret pocket there.

Withdrawing the Tekna "Security Card" from its hiding place, Bolan palmed it, ran his thumb across its plastic outer surface. Manufactured to the general dimensions of a credit card, the Tekna was, in fact, a compact skinning knife. The blade, when manually extended from its high-impact plastic sheath, was just over two inches long, an inch and a quarter across at its base. The cutting edge was razor-sharp and could produce appalling wounds in close encounters of the lethal kind. He thought about the woman once more and stopped himself before he had a chance to visualize her face, her supple body, opened by the blade.

And Bolan knew that he would do whatever his survival and the mission might require. If he was forced to make a choice, the mission would, of course, come first. There were innumerable lives at stake outside of Syria, and Bolan's death, when it arrived, could hardly be considered an untimely one, in any case.

He had already crammed more action, more success and failure, into one lifetime than most men ever dreamed of. Since his youth, in Asia, Bolan had been waiting for the Reaper, and it mattered little, in the final scheme of things, if he should meet death here or somewhere down the road.

The Tekna in one pocket, his directional transmitter safe inside another, Bolan knew that he was ready. He would keep his date with Shari in the garden, and if he was able, afterward, he would go on to join the Old Man of the Mountain for a tour of the assassin's school. Along the way he would secrete the homer, key its signal and begin the countdown toward destruction of the vipers' lair.

12

As she waited in the garden, Shari wondered if the tall man would succumb to curiosity and keep their rendezvous. She might have overplayed her hand, been too mysterious. There was the possibility that he had smelled a trap and shied away, preferring to remain secure inside his room.

He would not be secure, of course, but it would be more difficult to reach him there, more dangerous for anyone who tried to make the kill and cover up his tracks. *Her* tracks. If he ignored her message, an attempt to take him in his room would find the man on his guard against her, his suspicion already aroused.

Shari knew his name, now. It had come to her as information always traveled through the castle, carried on a tide of furtive whispers. He was Bryan Harrigan, an Irish name, and while the field of Western European politics was not her strong point, Shari knew the sort of Irishman who would have business with the Old Man of the Mountain. Bryan Harrigan had come to Alamut with bloody hands, no doubt, and he was there to strike a bargain with the devil, trading cash for lives.

In other circumstances Shari might have let him go, dismissed him as a minor character of no importance to her mission. In her seven months of silent watching, though, frustration had been mounting, urging her to take action that would provide some feeling of accomplishment, a sense that she was *doing* something.

She would have her chance today.

No guards were posted on the entrance to the garden as her harem sisters had been called away to other duties in the castle. Shari, for her part, had been assigned to work the laundry, but her friends would cover for her while she kept her tryst. It had been easy to convince them that the man sought her company, that he had offered gifts she could not refuse. Security was not as tight around the women now that they were seasoned in their duties, and an hour lost would likely go unnoticed.

The blow she struck this afternoon would shake the Old Man's confidence, allowing paranoia's voice to whisper in his ear and undermine his smug self-satisfaction. If nothing else, he would be damaged by the understanding that his fortress was not sacrosanct, his cherished privacy was not inviolate.

The temperature was mild, but Shari's palms were damp with perspiration. Nervously she rubbed her hands together, reached behind her back to make another readjustment to the long knife tucked inside the waistband of her harem pants. Its blade was cool against her skin, the sharp tip pricking at her buttocks as she paced.

She knew precisely what to do, had practiced and rehearsed the moment in her mind, until she was convinced no possibility for error remained. Seduction was her specialty, and Bryan Harrigan undoubtedly possessed the same male ego that would urge him to accept her story, lead him to believe a woman could desire his touch so ardently that she would risk her life for stolen moments in his arms. He would believe, because where their gonads were concerned, most men were fools.

She would not give him time to scrutinize the glaring flaws inherent in her tale of irresistible desire. Before cold logic had a chance to master flattery, she would have slit his throat from ear to ear and left him leaking blood on the garden path. It would be hours before his lifeless body was discovered and a search for his murderer mounted in the castle.

A sound beyond the heavy door made Shari hold her breath. The silence of the garden was oppressive, stifling, and she worried that her heartbeat might be audible, hammering, as it was, like a kettledrum. If anyone but Bryan Harrigan should find her here . . .

The door swung open silently on well-oiled hinges, admitting the Irishman. When it was firmly shut behind him, and Shari had confirmed he had come alone, she emerged from the leafy undergrowth.

"It pleases me that you have come."

"Your message sounded urgent, and I never could resist a damsel in distress."

She wore her most seductive smile. "There is no danger here. I simply wished to . . . see you."

"Funny thing. I had a similar idea, myself."

"I please you, then?" She was within arm's reach, but Harrigan made no attempt to touch her.

"I've got no complaints," he said.

She stepped into his arms, submission giving way to simulated ardor, one hand slipping down to fondle him, the other easing back in the direction of her weapon. Now she had it, was prepared to make her move—

And in a sudden, dizzy instant, she was airborne, tumbling through space. Her shoulders struck the ground with force enough to empty her lungs, and for a moment she was blinded by her loss of equilibrium, the rush of blood that sent a thousand colored asteroids to cloud her field of vision.

As she got her eyesight back, remembered how to breathe at last, she found the Irishman sitting astride her. Both arms were stretched above her head, her wrists secured by one of Harrigan's large hands. He held a knife blade tight against her throat, the keen edge dimpling her skin.

"So much for hearts and flowers," he declared. "Let's try a new game—like the truth."

"I DO NOT UNDERSTAND."

"Wrong answer." Bolan let the Tekna's stubby blade caress her jawline, sliding down to tease the skin where a pronounced and rapid pulse revealed the jugular. "I haven't got all day," he told her, "and I've got no sympathy for people who try to kill me. Even pretty ones."

She tried to bluff it out. "You will not do this."

"No? I guess you're right. I ought to let the sheikh take care of his employees."

Sudden terror in the woman's eyes told Bolan that his hunch had been on target. She had not been sent to kill him by the master of the Eagle's Nest.

He stood and backed away, retrieving Shari's fallen knife and pocketing the Tekna. "On your feet."

She rose on shaky legs, considered running for it, and finally decided that she wouldn't have a chance. "The master will be angry," Shari said at last. "I will be punished."

"I'd think so."

"Have you seen the way he punishes his concubines?"

"I must have missed it."

"If a woman laughs while in his presence, he commands Amal to pierce her tongue with heated iron. Two months ago, a sister of the harem was discovered with a sentry. They were making love without permission from the master. Her companion was chastised with twenty lashes. She was boiled alive.''

"You should have thought it through beforehand.''

"Is there nothing I can offer for your silence?''

She was already reaching for the buttons of her filmy vest when Bolan stopped her with a scowl. "We've been that route," he snapped. "The only thing I want from you is information.''

Shari hesitated, dropped her hands back to her sides. "What is it that you wish to know?''

"For openers, I'm interested in who you are and why you felt the urge to whittle me a second smile.''

She stiffened, then shook her head. "If you must kill me or betray me to the master, do it.''

Bolan hesitated, played a hunch. From the reaction of his captive, he was certain that the sheikh had not prompted her attempt to slit his throat. If she was operating on her own, it raised a host of possibilities he was anxious to explore.

"You know my name?''

"I know you, Mr. Harrigan.''

"And you decided you should take me out?''

This time, the woman held her tongue.

"Would it make any difference to you if I *wasn't* Bryan Harrigan?''

She looked confused, but hid it cunningly behind a mask of skepticism. "Oh? And if not Harrigan, who *are* you?''

"Names don't count for anything," he answered. "But I'm no more IRA than you are. I was sent here for a purpose, and unless I miss my guess, we have that much in common.''

"You confuse me.''

"Do I? Would it clear things up if I was sent to shut this operation down?''

"You speak in riddles.''

Bolan shrugged. "You can't expect me to reveal the details. I don't even know your name."

"I told you—"

"And I don't believe you. Fair enough?"

She nodded, still reluctant. "Sarah. Sarah Yariv."

"Israeli?"

"Now you know my secret." There was new defiance in her eyes.

"You're on assignment?"

Sarah nodded. "And you are?"

"American. Mike Belasko." Bolan's cards were on the table now, his cover well and truly blown, but he believed the woman, thought that he could understand her actions if he read them in the light of her affiliation with Mossad. "I'm in communication with your people."

"*You* were sent from Tel Aviv?"

"Let's say they know I'm here. They've got a little something lined up for the Old Man's entertainment at midnight."

Sarah's brow was furrowed with concern. "Explain."

"A little housewarming. Right down to the ground."

She understood him, and she was stunned. "I have been working seven months to gather information here," she fumed, "and now you tell me it was all for nothing?"

"I have no idea what's on your boss's mind. I know that midnight brings the house down, if I get my act in gear."

"All this for nothing." There was bitterness behind her words.

"Who knows? You might be listed MIA. I know your people have been losing agents right and left the past few months."

"But you are here."

"I had some luck along the way."

"How can you summon help?"

He told her, briefly, of the small transmitter and his plan to hide it in the courtyard, where its beacon would attract the Phantoms like a homing call to lethal birds of prey.

"But why not here?" she asked, when he was finished. "In the garden."

Bolan scanned the shrubbery, the open sky above, and wondered why he had not thought of such an option sooner. If the strike force got this far, the fortress would be clearly visible; a few yards wouldn't matter, either way. It would be easier to hide the homer in the garden, and he doubted that the place would see much traffic in the next twelve hours. If there was a drawback to the plan, it would be Sarah, and the level of his trust for her on short acquaintance.

Bolan had already made his mind up that she was not working for the sheikh. A female killer did not fit the Old Man's scheme of things, the holy order that he had decreed for his disciples. Women were reserved for pleasure and the menial pursuits of work around the castle. Given all of that, her tale made perfect sense, and Bolan was inclined to bet the odds this time.

Her bitterness could be a problem. From appearances, her mission had been scrubbed without the lady's knowledge, and it made her angry. Worse, she knew about the air strike now, and from a stranger. And she realized that her own initial warning would have been the shriek of Phantoms overhead, the stunning impact of their bombs and rockets.

Bolan could not blame her for being out of sorts, but he didn't believe that her emotions would propel her into any kind of foolish action. It was yet another hunch, but he had learned to trust them through the years, and Bolan was more often right than wrong.

He checked his wristwatch, found that it was nearly one o'clock. He was running out of time, his scheduled meeting with the Old Man of the Mountain fast approaching. He could place the homer now, but with the maximum duration of its battery, he could not activate its signal prior to 4:00 p.m. His chances of returning to the garden in three hours, unobserved, were close to nil.

It was time to gamble with his mission. With his life.

"Do you have access to the garden all the time?" he asked.

Sarah responded with a frown and a nod. "Yes, unless the guards are posted. Then we are inside and may not leave until our...demonstration...is completed."

"So, it wouldn't be a problem for you to come back in, say, three hours' time?"

"I can be here," she told him, "but the sheikh forbids us to possess a timepiece, so I may not be precise."

He slipped the anodized Omega off his wrist and handed it to her. "Four o'clock," he told her, "at the earliest. It doesn't matter if you're late, as long as you come back before, let's say, ten-thirty."

"Late for what?"

"To activate the homer."

Bolan let her have a close-up of the small transmitter, showed her how to turn the beacon on with the manipulation of a single switch.

"The battery will last eight hours, give or take, and if it dies before the cavalry arrives, we've got no backup plan. You follow?"

"Yes. I understand."

"How good are you at climbing trees?"

"I manage."

"Fine."

He chose a sturdy cedar, scrambled halfway up the trunk, until the limbs began to thin, and chose a slender branch that met his specs. With loving care, he clipped the homer to its perch, the small transmitter wedged between two branches. It was readily accessible to anybody standing on the branch that now supported Bolan's weight. He glanced down between his feet and saw that Sarah was memorizing his position.

She was quick, he had to give her that. If only she was stable under fire...

He dropped to earth and faced her once again, prepared to leave. "All right, it's set to go. Remember: four o'clock or later, and the Phantoms will be waiting at eleven, more or less."

"It will be done. Have you any plan for getting out before the air strike?"

"I'm still working on it," Bolan answered. "I might have a better angle on it once I've seen the sheikh's school for killers.

Her eyes lit with sudden trepidation. "And if there is a way, may I—?"

"You're welcome," Bolan said. "How do I get in touch with you again?"

"You can request a woman later, after you have finished with your tour of the castle. Ask for Sharl. Tell the sheikh that you were pleased with her performance in the garden."

"It's refreshing when I get a chance to tell the truth."

The woman dropped her eyes, and Bolan could have sworn the faintest trace of blush had crept into her cheek. Imagination, probably. She was a pro, beyond embarrassment, immune to flattery. He had already staked his mission and his life on that belief, and he could not afford the luxury of second thoughts.

"Until we meet again."

He left her then, aware that everything he had was riding on the woman, her ability to activate the homer in a given time frame. Simple, right? Unless her other duties kept her from the garden or she was observed in transit, held by sentries for interrogation at the Old Man's leisure. Bolan would not know if she had pulled it off, with any certainty, until the bombs began to fall.

And if they didn't... well, then it would simply be too late. For all concerned.

He shrugged the morbid thoughts away and concentrated on his destination as he left the garden, following his own steps back in the direction of the banquet chamber and his room. The Old Man's runners would come looking for him there, no doubt, and Bolan did not wish to keep them waiting, or to cause the smallest of suspicions.

He hoped the absence of his watch wouldn't become a problem, finally deciding that his own internal clock would have to serve. In Vietnam, and afterward, the Executioner had learned to gauge time's passage with his mind, his other senses. It was not precise, in terms of seconds won or lost, but it had served him thus far, and it was the only option that remained.

He knew that he would recognize the stroke of midnight when it came, and he would do his best to be prepared with an escape plan. Failing that, it would be every man—and woman—for himself, and Bolan would devote his dying energies to making sure the Old Man of the Mountain did not slip away in the confusion. If it came to that, it was the very least that he could do.

13

Sheikh al-Jebal was waiting for them in the courtyard with a pair of bodyguards, a groom and four horses, freshly saddled. There was no sign of Tahir Arrani, and Bolan felt uneasy at the second-in-command's protracted absence.

"Are we going for a ride?"

The Old Man's smile was polished, as impregnable as stone. "A great deal of our training is conducted there—" he pointed in the general direction of the gates "—beyond the walls. If you would witness the disciples at their best, a journey of some minor distance will be necessary."

"Fine with me." He nodded toward the bodyguards and raised an eyebrow. "Won't you need a little more protection?"

The chief Assassin's grinning face became more animated. "We enjoy an understanding with the people of the valley," he explained. "They grant us anything we wish, and we, in turn, permit them to exist."

"Sounds fair enough."

He mounted and settled in the saddle while his host was helped aboard by bodyguards and groom. The massive gates were opened for them by a team of armed attendants, gunners on the wall and in the courtyard bowing low before their master as he passed. The mounted riflemen hung back, bringing up the rear, and Bolan realized their presence was a mere formality, more of an honor guard than any serious concession to the dictates of security. Sheikh al-Jebal could probably be overpowered, killed, by any group of decent size and strength, but he displayed no fear of a potential ambush. He was clearly confident that no one in the valley dared to lift a hand against him.

That was power of a sort, submission won by application of selective terror. Bolan thought about the people of the valley, generations raised up in the shadow of the Eagle's Nest. A thousand years of tyranny, whose interruption— briefly, by the Turks, and later by the British—must have seemed like chaos rather than deliverance. How long could captive people live in thrall before their spirits were completely broken, crushed beyond repair?

There must have been *some* rebels through the years, but it would not be difficult to catalog their fates. A few—the early ones—would try to stand alone against the cult, and they would disappear, or possibly be executed in public as a warning to the others. More would follow the example of the martyrs, seeking strength in numbers and associations, but their strategies were poor, their weapons nonexistent, and their life span could be measured out in hours, days at most. These days, he thought, the malcontents and rebels would be bent on getting out, escaping from the valley that had been converted to a scenic prison camp. Discreet inquiries in Damascus would convince them that the government was not concerned with what went on at Alamut as long as the Ba'ath regime was not endangered and the holy war with Israel ground along on schedule. Finally the fugitives would face a range of choices: they could emigrate, they could adapt or they could burrow in and work against the cancer, as Hafez Kasm had elected. Hiding in the bushes to attack the master of the Eagle's Nest was simply not an option open to consideration.

For the better part of twenty minutes, Bolan recognized their track from his approach. Had it been only yesterday? The atmosphere of Alamut was stifling, disorienting, and he felt as if he might have been inside the fortress for a week. In fact, he realized, it was his second day.

His *last* day.

Soon, the Old Man of the Mountain led them off the beaten track and along a narrow, winding road that wriggled through the foothills like an adder. In minutes, Alamut was lost to sight, the trees around them closing in, their branches interwoven, filtering the sunlight. It was perfect for an ambush, but they passed on unopposed, with Bolan following the sheikh and their escort bringing up the rear.

They spent the better part of half an hour climbing through the trees and finally emerged into a level clearing. With a second glance, the soldier recognized that they were perched on a plateau, the southern end of which had been defoliated to facilitate erection of a training camp. The compound came complete with a Ranger-style obstacle course, rappelling towers and a firing range equipped to handle point-blank combat simulations as well as sniping exercises at two hundred yards. A three-story clapboard house stood off to one side of the firing range, its door ajar, the vacant windows watching Bolan with a consummate disinterest.

About twenty disciples of the cult were waiting for them, forming ranks and snapping to attention at their first glimpse of the sheikh. Amal was not among them, having recently delivered Bolan to the castle courtyard, but the thug in charge might easily have been his twin. Upon command, the double rank of cultists knelt before their master, foreheads pressed against the earth.

"Arise!"

The trainees scrambled nimbly to their feet and waited while the sheikh dismounted, with assistance from his bodyguards. The Executioner climbed down without a helping hand and joined his host in an inspection of the troops.

"Our standards are the highest, Mr. Harrigan. For every man who stands before you, three have been rejected on the basis of deficiencies that make them unacceptable to Allah. One in four of these will not survive the final stages of their training."

He realized the Old Man's words were meant to be accepted literally. "That must be some graduation exercise," he said.

"In training warriors, realism is of critical importance. Blanks and wooden swords are for beginners. Soldiers of jihad must be prepared to risk their lives at any moment of the day or night, upon command."

"I see."

"You will, in time. But first, a demonstration of the stamina and physical agility that sets these men apart." He turned to the instructor with a narrow, mirthless smile and said, "Begin."

Upon a curt command from their instructor, half of the trainees broke ranks and sprinted toward the obstacle course, throwing themselves into the exercise without restraint. As Bolan watched, they hurdled moats and scrambled over barricades, climbed ropes and swung across monkey bars hand-over-hand, slithered through makeshift tunnels and crossed a log bridge without breaking stride. The final phase demanded that they crawl beneath a maze of razor wire, across fifty yards of ground, while their instructor and the sheikh's two bodyguards filled the air with automatic fire, their patterns interlocking at a height of barely eighteen inches off the ground.

It was an adequate performance, but the Executioner had witnessed tougher training in the Special Forces, and he wondered how the sheikh's disciples would perform when they were flying high on hashish, primed to kill—or die, if necessary—on the orders of their lord and master. Based on the survival record from their recent missions, Bolan thought the training in evasion and escape was merely sham, designed to bolster confidence in warriors who had come to terms with death. The reality was that the executioners dispatched from Alamut were not expected to return.

Before the last man had completed his negotiation of the course, the leaders were en route to the rappelling tower, scrambling up a ladder fixed to one side of the wooden structure, hesitating on the platform only long enough to choose a rope before they started down, the hard way. Bolan watched them, human spiders dangling on webs of hemp, the rocky earth below them ready to receive their bodies as a human sacrifice. They wore no gloves, no special shoes or climbing gear, and they revealed no trace of hesitation as they automatically went through their paces, anxious for the sheikh's approval.

When all had run the course and scaled the tower, their instructor herded them in the direction of the firing range. The Old Man of the Mountain followed, Bolan trailing, conscious of the fact that fully half of the trainees had still done nothing. The twelve men stood stiffly at attention, their eyes fixed on the distant mountains that were the boundary of their world. He wondered if they had a function in the present exercise, deciding that the sheikh would play his hand when he was ready.

Each man displayed his prowess on the firing range with pistol, submachine gun and rifle, cutting decent groups in targets stationed at a distance from twenty feet to one hundred yards. The distance work appeared to be reserved for half a dozen of the gunmen who were being trained as snipers. Standing, crouching, prone, they popped off head and heart shots with an easy off-hand style that made it look deceptively easy. Bolan gave them credit for technique, but wondered once again how the consumption of hashish might tamper with their aim.

Thus far none of the raids conducted by Ismaili hit teams had involved long-distance sniping, and it struck him that the special training, like the mock evasion drills, were being utilized to make the cultists see themselves in military terms. For all of their devotion to the cause, their resignation to the "afterlife," devotion might begin to waver if the one-way, suicidal nature of their mission was discussed in frank and open terms. While the illusion of survival lingered, the disciples of Sheikh al-Jebal could function free of apprehension, nagging second thoughts. They were a step removed from kamikazes, fighting for a holy cause and still persuaded that survival was a possibility.

The rolling echoes of their gunfire died away, and Bolan waited while the final targets were reeled in for his inspection, designated shooters standing down and handing off their weapons to the backup members of their team.

"I'll grant you, they seem capable enough." He nodded toward the second dozen, still awaiting orders. "What's their story?"

"I have saved them for a special demonstration," Bolan's host replied, his smile unsettling the soldier. "It is no great feat to run the hurdles or to shoot at paper targets. Even unarmed-combat practice has its built-in limitations. You agree?"

"I'd say so, yes."

"For training to have any value, there must be a taste of realism to it. For a buyer to be satisfied, he must experience the product for himself, firsthand."

"You've lost me, now." In fact, he knew precisely where the sheikh was going, and he didn't like it. Not at all. But he could not afford to show the slightest trace of fear or apprehension.

"This—" the Old Man cocked a thumb in the direction of the clapboard house "—is also used for training purposes. A graduation exercise, as you might say. Selected members of our order are conveyed inside and left with one instruction—make their way back out again."

"I take it that they're not alone?"

"Precisely. They must cope with opposition from their classmates, former graduates and so forth. We consider it a challenge."

"I imagine so."

"I realize that you have not been trained as my disciples have, but you are still a military man, is that not so?"

"I served my time. It's been a while."

"Effective training lingers, in the mind and in the hand. A lazy man may lose his strength, but he will not forget the lessons he has learned. And I do not believe you are a lazy man."

"I take it I'm invited to participate?"

"My humble servants would be pleased to have the benefit of your experience."

He thought it over, knew the consequences of refusal might be dire. It was a test, apparently designed to separate potential customers from the vicarious poseurs who hung around the fringes of the underground. If he declined, his cover might be blown; at best, he would be treated with reserve, perhaps suspicion, while the sheikh debated tactful ways to send him packing.

"I believe it might be interesting, at that."

The Old Man of the Mountain seemed delighted. "Excellent."

"Is this a death match?" Bolan tried to make the question casual, but there was still a trace of latent tension in his voice.

"By no means." For an instant Bolan's host seemed wounded by the mere suggestion. "Under normal circumstances, the opposing force is armed with dirks and sabers, while the trainee has his choice of weapons, short of firearms. On this occasion, I have chosen kendo sticks for all concerned . . . if you approve?"

Bolan's dozen fresh opponents were already in possession of the wooden simulated swords employed in martial arts displays, some working through the pattern of aggressive thrusts, others chopping heavily, two-handed, at the empty air.

"Of course."

He took the weapon that was offered to him, weighed it in his hands and tried to recollect how long ago his training with the kendo stick had been. Too long, for damn sure, but he still recalled the basics, and he seemed to have no options left, in any case.

"All right, then, what's the drill?"

"Quite simply, you will be escorted to the top floor, a room with exits on three sides. Your adversaries will take up positions in surrounding rooms and on the lower floors. A signal will be sounded when they are in place. From there, your sole objective is to exit through the only door available."

"I understand." It sounded clean and simple, but he knew at least a dozen reasons why the exercise could turn into a free-for-all. "If I make it?"

"We are ready to discuss the business that has brought you here."

"And suppose I don't?"

The Old Man's smile remained in place, but any hint of human warmth was gone. "It is my custom to deal only with the worthy men, on whom I can depend."

Bolan swung the kendo stick across one shoulder, forced a smile. "Let's get this over with."

The bearded drill instructor led him through the open door and up a flight of wooden stairs, positioned in the center of the structure like an elevator shaft. They climbed four flights to reach the third and topmost floor, with Bolan counting doors along the way. The ground floor boasted four rooms, besides the entry hall, with doors for eight each on the next two floors. Scratch one room for himself, and that left nineteen places for a dozen warriors to conceal themselves. Connecting doors would give the enemy mobility and make an estimate of their deployment virtually worthless.

As promised, Bolan's room had exits on three sides: the door through which he entered and connecting doors with two adjacent rooms. There was no window in the outside wall. When he was left alone, the Executioner stood absolutely still and listened to the sounds in the house. He could hear his guide descending, others passing by him on the stairs. A step below the final landing creaked, and shuffling noises in the room immediately to his left told Bolan one of his opponents, at the very least, was planning to abbreviate their close encounter. He would have to watch himself when he left the room.

All things considered, he would have to watch himself the whole way down.

The room on Bolan's right was slightly smaller than the one in which he started. It was also vacant, and the cautious shift had put some combat stretch between himself and his assailant in the adjoining room on his left. It was enough, for now, and Bolan waited for the signal to begin his passage through the gauntlet.

To the Executioner's surprise, it was an air horn, of the sort employed by fans at stateside football games. The single note was strident, piercing, and he had no doubt that each of his opponents was alert and ready to begin the simulated dance of death.

And would they pull their punches? Could they? Was the whole routine a ruse to take him down outside the castle proper? Why go through the motions when a simple bullet in the head would do the job?

No time for answers now, he was on the move. A glance around the landing, and he eased through the door, immediately conscious of a thrashing in the room where he had started. Moving swiftly, he was halfway to the stairs before his would-be adversary struck, an angry blur of motion driving from his left, the makeshift wooden saber poised to strike.

Bolan went low and inside the swing, using his own kendo stick like a riot baton, the blunt tip driving deep beneath the slim Ismaili's sternum, emptying his lungs and briefly robbing him of power to inhale. The guy was struggling for breath when Bolan seized his collar, dragged him to the rail and tipped him over. He paused long enough to watch the man drop two floors.

He was at the stairs when number two erupted from another door along the landing, narrowing the gap between them with a cautious, mincing stride that mimicked something from a silent movie. Bolan saw the roundhouse coming, blocked it with his staff and then reversed, delivering a backhand smash across his adversary's face before the young Assassin could regain his balance. Teeth and cartilage were shattered by the stunning impact, and his opposition dropped without a sound, his breath a ragged whisper in the silent house.

Bolan overstepped the squeaky riser, simultaneously watching front and back as he descended toward the second floor. In spite of this precaution, Bolan nearly missed his third attacker, warned by fabric whispering across the banister as the Assassin poised to leap. Another heartbeat, and the man was dropping on him like a shadow of destruction.

A hasty backstep did the trick, and Bolan swung his stick, delivering a solid blow to feet that had been meant to strike his head and shoulders. Knowing that it could have been a fatal blow, he felt no vestige of remorse when his assailant smashed his head into the banister as he toppled to the floor. It might have been the woodwork or his neck that made the ugly snapping sound, but either way, Bolan's opposition made no further moves as he stepped across the prostrate body continuing his descent.

Three men chose to rush him on the second floor, with two more in reserve. He stopped the first man with a boot between the thighs, immediately followed by a crushing blow across the windpipe, but the effort left him open, and he was rewarded with a solid crack across his shoulders. Dodging, taking other hits along his flank, his thighs, he tried to parry with the wooden saber, feinting, buying time.

The Assassins were convinced they had him now, and two of them retreated, yielding to their comrade. Bolan let him close, then cut the slugger's ankles out from under him, delivering a solid jab behind one ear to keep him down. Before the others could recover, Bolan was among them, kicking, slashing with his elbows and his cudgel, opening one's scalp and flattening another's nose in record time. They got their licks in, raising welts across his back and belly, staggering him once, but weeks of training could not match the killer instinct that a veteran brings to combat, and they fell before him, one by one. He thought a couple of them might be seriously injured, even dying, but it made no difference. He could kill them now, or the Israeli bombs could kill them later. Either way, the result would be the same.

One floor remained, and another four Ismailis to be dealt with. Bolan took his time descending, conscious of the shadows moving out to greet him, saw them clustered at the bottom of the stairs. He scanned their young-old faces, saw determination there, with just a trace of doubt behind the eyes of one or two. And he could almost see the wheels in motion. If the infidel had conquered eight of their companions, what could four achieve?

But they would not be moved. Bolan seized the moment to launch himself into a flying kick, directly toward the central figure of the group. The tough guy didn't move, and by the time he raised his cudgel it was too late to save himself, with Bolan's boot heels planted on his chest. The man hit the wall and rebounded in a daze directly into Bolan's crushing backhand as the soldier scrambled to his feet. A second man tried to scramble out of range, and Bolan broke his staff across the back of that one's head, immediately stooping to retrieve a fallen kendo stick.

The nearer of his last two adversaries took a swing at Bolan's head, and it almost connected. Almost. His cudgel whispered past the soldier's face, and he was instantly repaid with an annihilating blow across the forehead, folding like a rag doll at the tall man's feet. His comrade snarled in rage and made his move—an awkward, headlong rush that set him up for Bolan's final swing. The impact knocked his jaw around behind one ear and put his lights out in a heartbeat, his flaccid body sprawling across the stairs.

Twelve up, twelve down.

Bolan's body was a tapestry of welts and bruises, and blood was leaking from a ragged cut above one eye, but he was mobile, and his battered ribs had not been broken. Bolan used his cudgel like a cane until he reached the open doorway, then discarded it and made the exit on his own.

From all appearances, the sheikh had been expecting someone else. The expression on his face might not be disappointment—not precisely—but it was readily apparent that the Old Man was not happy. His stormy eyes told Bolan that the twelve trainees were in for trouble, if and when they came around.

"Are those the best you have?"

"Trainees. A man of your experience is better matched, I think, against more seasoned troops."

"Another time, perhaps. We still have business to discuss."

"Tonight," the Old Man told him stiffly, turning with a flourish toward the waiting horses.

Bolan smiled and followed, suddenly unmindful of the pain. If nothing else, the sheikh's smug self-satisfaction had been shaken to the core, and for the moment, that was victory enough. The Executioner would have another opportunity to break his host.

Tonight.

14

Tahir Arrani put his faith in Allah and in vultures. Allah had provided him with the intelligence to see through "Bryan Harrigan." In time, the vultures would provide him with the evidence of treachery he needed to convince Sheikh al-Jebal that they had been deceived.

It was a point of fitting irony, Arrani thought, that he should use the traitor's jeep to search for evidence that would, eventually, cost the man his head. Cooped up at Alamut for weeks or months on end, compelled to ride on horseback when he left the castle for a tour of the surrounding countryside, he viewed the jeep ride as a luxury of sorts, despite the glaring sun and winding mountain road, which sometimes made his stomach queasy as his driver rushed the curves.

"Slow down," he spit, rewarded by immediate deceleration of the vehicle. When "Harrigan" was dead, Arrani thought that he might claim the jeep. It was perfect for outings, and with certain minor changes it could be of use in helping to keep the valley folk in line. The horses left Arrani saddle-sore, and he was terrified of flight—a weakness he managed to conceal, with difficulty, on occasions when the helicopter was his only means of transportation. Allah gave him strength at such times, and he had not shamed himself—yet.

A mile ahead of them, a single vulture rode the silent currents of the sky, describing lazy circles like a giant leaf compelled to travel on the winds. The other members of the flock had already descended to their feast, which might be anything from goatflesh to a jackal's pathetic leavings.

Or a man.

"Speed up," he ordered, generous enough to overlook his driver's wry expression at the sudden change of orders. They were close. He could feel it like a lover's touch upon his skin.

At half a mile, the scent of death became apparent, carried on a gentle mountain breeze. This was no camel. To anyone who dealt in death, who trafficked in annihilation, the aromas of corruption were distinct and separate: the sharp, metallic smell of blood; the barnyard reek of bowels that emptied at the impact of a bullet or a blade. No man who sampled the perfume of human flesh gone sour would confuse it with the smell of rotting sheep or bullock.

This had been a human kill, and if Tahir Arrani had not found his man, at least he had found *someone*, something that might be of interest on a sultry afternoon.

He recognized the turnout, saw the mountain spring, a vulture perched upon its rocky lip, its curved beak wet and glistening. No travelers were stopping here, just now, but some *had* been, and the odor in his nostrils told Arrani that they had not traveled far beyond the small roadside oasis.

Arrani's driver held a submachine gun in his lap, a minimal concession to the fact that they were miles from Alamut, in territory where a passing mention of Sheikh al-Jebal might not be adequate to cow the infidels they met along their way. Arrani had refused a larger escort, trusting in his fearsome reputation and his knowledge that concerted efforts by the government and the Assassins had been whittling the ranks of independent outlaws in the mountains, thinning out their numbers much as evolution weeds out weaker species, dooming them to ultimate extinction. Any highwaymen they met on this excursion would be rogues, alone or traveling in motley bands of two or three, living off the land. If they attempted to molest him, they would die.

Someone had died, already, at the turnout. From the powerful smell, he could count on several bodies, and they had to have been lying here, exposed to elements and predators alike, for better than a day. Despite the scorching sun, it took that long to raise a stench like the one that drew Arrani from his jeep, toward a gully set behind the mountain spring.

At his approach, the nearest vulture left its perch and flapped away to find another roost among the rocks. Arrani clapped his hands and whistled shrilly, putting the other birds to flight—perhaps a dozen in all. One of them was on a hard collision course with the intruder, veering off to starboard when Arrani clapped his hands again. The Arab noted that the vulture had been carrying a streamer of intestine in its beak.

The gully had become a slaughterhouse, or, more precisely, a communal grave. Six bodies had been dumped there—hastily, from all appearances—and all of them had died by violence. By the gun. As was their normal style, the vultures had been drawn primarily to open wounds, enlarging cuts and gashes, eating outward from the points where blood had freely flowed. Of six men in the gully, five had died from head wounds, scalps and faces long since peeled of flesh by hungry scavengers. Their mothers would have been hard-pressed to identify them.

It was a blessing, the Assassin thought, that he had not come out in search of faces. Bryan Harrigan could pass him on the street, might stop and speak to him, and they would still be strangers. He was searching for a different point of recognition, and Arrani had a fair idea of where to start.

Of the six men in the gully, three wore bloody caftans, one was dressed in standard military uniform and two had been stripped down to boots and underwear. With so much flesh exposed, the vultures had been busy, and Arrani breathed through his mouth as he descended the rocky slope, nearly losing his balance at one point, catching himself before he plunged facefirst into the grotesque carcasses.

One of the mutilated bodies was an Arab's, and the other was a European's. Sun and scavengers could not disguise the pallid flesh—or rather, what was left of it—from the Assassin's expert eye. This man had lived in cities, temperate climates, and he had habitually dressed accordingly. Long sleeves, perhaps with collar buttoned and a neatly knotted tie in place. His hands were tanned, but only from the wrists to fingertips. His face...well, that was anybody's guess, but from his nape down to the callused soles of singularly ugly feet, he had been pale, inclined to burn instead of tan.

The man had been well-fed, perhaps a trifle soft, and so the vultures had attacked him with a vengeance, but they had not reached the part Tahir Arrani longed to see. Suppressing an involuntary grimace of distaste, he rolled the faceless man onto his stomach, hooked his fingers in the waistband of the corpse's shorts and dragged them down.

Even the postmortem settling of blood in fatty tissues of the back and buttocks could not obscure the jaunty Union Jack. The visitor to Alamut was not Bryan Harrigan. The IRA ambassador was vulture food, his mission terminated by a bullet in the face.

And who was the impostor? How had he discovered the location of the Eagle's Nest? How had he known that Harrigan was coming to discuss a proposition with the sheikh? Was his associate affiliated with the government in some way, acting under secret orders? Why would Damascus turn against them now, when they were so successful, with the future bright ahead? What was the mission of the man who posed as Bryan Harrigan?

These and other questions would be answered when he brought the news to Alamut. Sheikh al-Jebal could not refuse to hear him now, dared not ignore the evidence of treachery by a man he had welcomed in his fortress home.

An order sent his driver scrambling for the camera Arrani had been clever enough to bring along. It was a small blackmarket Polaroid, producing snapshots that developed on the spot. They also faded, over time, but he was not preparing keepsakes for a scrapbook. As he focused on the buttocks of the bloated corpse, his mind was fixed on clarity instead of art.

The only prize he sought would be the pleasure of interrogating "Harrigan" for hours, days, whatever length of time might be required to learn the truth. The impostor's death would be a celebration of his own success in sniffing traitors out and running them to earth. Before he finished with the stranger, he would be aware of secrets the man himself had long forgotten. Finally, when he was finished, he would give the man called Harrigan a terrible, slow death.

First, however, there was still the matter of a conference with the sheikh. A mere formality, with evidence in hand, but he had learned from grim experience that logic did not always rule the Old Man's mind. The photographs were proof, but deft persuasion might be necessary to convey his message, win the proper answer from his lord. He would be humble, self-effacing, as he laid the evidence before the man whose word was law. And when approval had been granted, he would close the trap around his enemies.

Soon, now.

He scrambled up the slope, ignored the driver's outstretched, helping hand and shook his robes as if he could divorce himself from death's stench with a simple gesture. He would have the caftan cleaned, but even so, the smell might linger in the fabric, haunting, like a preview of the grave. On impulse, he decided to discard the garment when he reached his destination. Never mind the laundry; it was useless, anyway.

But for the moment, he was satisfied to travel with the smell of death around him. Let it be a warning to his enemies, all those who schemed against him, striving daily to prevent him from ascending the throne. In time, when he became the reigning Old Man of the Mountain, he would grind them beneath his heel.

In time.

He had a special enemy to deal with, and Arrani was already looking forward to it. With a passion.

ABDEL AL-SABBAH SURVEYED the kneeling men and scowled. They had dishonored him and shown themselves unworthy of their mission. Twelve on one, they should have had no problem dealing with the Irishman, but they had failed. Resoundingly. Their scandalous performance might have jeopardized his deal with Harrigan—the tall man still had doubts, which had to be allayed—but at the moment, Harrigan was simply laughing.

Laughing at Sheikh al-Jebal.

It was intolerable, but he could not blame his guest. The men who knelt before him now *were* laughable, impersonating warriors of the cause when they could not defeat a single man who had been outnumbered, virtually unarmed. They were a joke, and he would not be made the butt of foolish humor for an infidel's amusement.

Slowly, anger darkening his face like thunder clouds, he moved along the line. He stared at the ten "warriors," pitiful survivors of a bungled exercise that had rebounded to his detriment. One man had died inside the house; another had been comatose when he was carried out, and euthanasia had been ordered at the scene. These ten had managed to survive, although they sported cuts and bruises, blackened eyes, a shattered jaw. If they had died in combat, some small measure of their honor might have been redeemed, but as it was, they left a yawning debt to be repaid.

Beginning now.

He reached the end of the line, turned back to watch them as he snapped his fingers, nodding to Amal. The bearded warrior drew his scimitar, approached the nearest man in line and barked an order. On command, the penitent bent forward at the waist, head bowed, eyes closed, the brown curve of his neck exposed.

Amal delayed for half a heartbeat, studying his target, then the blade descended, whispering, until its voice was silenced in a sheath of flesh. The young man's blood erupted in a scarlet fountain, spattering the walls and floor. At liberty, his severed head had come to rest ten feet away, the eyes still open, staring sightlessly at what had been its body.

Amal moved down the line with terse commands and flashing blade, dispatching two, three more in swift succession. Now, his scimitar was slick with gore, his caftan decorated with the fanlike patterns of arterial explosions. Crimson droplets glistened in his beard, and he was smiling, that rarest of expressions he wore uneasily and only at the most peculiar times.

The fifth man's jaw had been so badly broken, twisted, that he could not bow his head. Amal was flexible. The horizontal progress of the curving blade was so meticulously smooth that it appeared he might have missed, then red tendrils overran the dead man's collar, and his head fell forward, bouncing on the tiles before his body followed, almost gracefully in pursuit.

The sixth man had begun to weep, a final insult to his master and to all Ismailis. At Amal's approach, he tried to rise, but he lost traction in the spreading slick of blood and fell on hands and knees. The scimitar swept upward, down again, and there would be no second chance to run away. Amal spit on the twitching body of the coward, moving on to number seven with his dripping blade.

The Old Man of the Mountain watched it all, and when Amal had finished, he was satisfied. Almost. He still would have to face the Irishman in knowledge that his demonstration had become a laughingstock, but there were ways to counter such embarrassment. Perhaps, he thought, the presentation of twelve heads, each on a silver platter, would suffice.

If only his disciples had been more like Harrigan. A warrior who could best twelve younger men in combat, hand-to-hand, was worth recruiting, but he knew the Irishman had other loyalties, different causes to fight for. It was a pity, all the same. He could have taken over training for the novices and whipped them into fighting form. In time, he might have risen to challenge Tahir Arrani in the hierarchy of the sect.

And where, precisely, was Arrani now? He had been gone for hours, long enough to scour the trail along a two-day march, and there was still no word. The prospect of an ambush did not phase the sheikh. He knew it was unlikely, first of all, and if Arrani came to harm, it might not be the worst thing that had happened to the Old Man of the Mountain.

Of late, Arrani had been growing arrogant, self-satisfied, although he took great pains to keep his shifting attitude a "secret." It required no special insight for the sheikh to recognize the younger man's ambition, his desire to mount the throne of Alamut. If he had *not* desired control, *not* lusted after greater power, then the Old Man would have worried. As it was, he recognized his danger and would guard against it, keeping one eye on Arrani all the time.

Of late his thoughts had turned to the selection of a worthy heir, someone to carry on the work when he was gone, but he would not be hurried to the grave by brash young men with hungry eyes. At first he had believed Arrani might be perfect for the role of his successor, but the Old Man's attitude had changed. His second-in-command had grown ambitious out of all proportion to his worth, his capabilities, and so the sheikh had come to question his selection of Arrani as the heir apparent to his kingdom.

They were men of power, certainly, with all that role implied, but they were also stewards of a sacred trust passed down across a thousand years to Allah's chosen few. If there were profits to be made along the way, so much the better, but the cult of the Assassins was not—and had never been— the private army of a single man. They were the army of jihad, in thrall to Allah, and he would not let a brash successor blunt the holy sword, divert the thrust that would, in time, destroy the infidels.

In time.

But he was running out of time, and none of those who flocked around his banner now were worthy of the throne. Arrani might still find himself, find Allah in his heart, but there were ways to deal with a subordinate who overstepped his bounds. Ten headless bodies in the courtyard testified to that. If he was challenged by Arrani—or by anyone—the silent dead would soon have company.

There were other problems to contend with at the moment, not the least of which was Bryan Harrigan and his proposal from the IRA. Tonight they would discuss the details of his scheme, the costs involved. Sheikh al-Jebal had no precise idea of what the Irishman desired, but it would be a challenging assignment, that was certain, and the buyer's confidence would not be strengthened by this afternoon's performance at the training ground. The mission might demand a record price, but he was ill prepared to ask a fortune from the Ulsterman while memories of ignominious defeat still hung between them.

He would wait to see what Harrigan proposed. If necessary he might offer to perform the mission at a discount, thereby building up goodwill and spreading word of his professional integrity. The IRA could be a major customer in years to come, with its unending war against the British crown requiring new blood, new approaches. There was only so much money to be made from killing Jewish children in the Middle East.

Besides, the war against the Zionists was still jihad, the holy cause ordained by Allah through his messengers on Earth. The rest of it—in Europe, in America—was all a sideshow to the main event, assassinations and disruptive actions executed in an effort to support the cause. And if the Old Man of the Mountain made his fortune in the process...well, it was a fact of life that Allah would reward his faithful servants.

Yes, he thought the Irishman might be entitled to a discount, but he would let Harrigan describe the mission first. There was no question of declining, under any circumstances, adding insult to injury, but there were still logistics to consider, plans to finalize.

Where was Arrani when his talents were most needed? Rambling about the mountains in an effort to convince Sheikh al-Jebal that Bryan Harrigan was not the man he claimed to be. It seemed preposterous, but nothing was impossible, and granting the request had been a simple way to shed Arrani's clutches for a while. And, in addition, it was good to show him that business could proceed without him. He was not yet indispensable.

Sheikh al-Jebal was still in charge of Alamut, and if Arrani's quest proved fruitless, it would be a good excuse for cutting back on his responsibilities around the palace, shortening his leash a fraction. If, by contrast, he should somehow prove his wild assertions, it would still require approval from the Old Man of the Mountain to interrogate—or, in the worst scenario, to execute—their guest. *His* word was law, and he would countenance no usurpation of his powers while he lived.

And he was not dead, yet.

15

"You're sure they weren't suspicious?"

Sarah shook her head, the ebony tresses rippling across her shoulders. "It is quite routine," she said.

On the return trip from the training compound, Bolan had requested that "Shari" be allowed to help him pass the time until he and the sheikh met for dinner and discussion of their business. There had been no opposition from his host, but he had been relieved, in spite of everything, when Sarah Yariv had arrived.

"How are you coming on that exit?"

"I have not had time or opportunity to search the garden, but I do not think we could escape that way, in any case. The mountainside is far too steep, too rugged, for descent in darkness."

Bolan had been troubled by the same idea. He didn't relish clambering down cliffs without a rope, at midnight, while the world exploded overhead. The climb would have been tough enough in daylight, given trained associates and proper gear.

"That leaves the stables, if we make it that far. What about the other women?"

"I trust only two or three of them. The others have the mentality of slaves. They would betray us in the hope of winning favor with their master."

"Can you take the trusted ones aside? I don't want any friendlies left behind, if I can help it."

"I will try." Her frown was thoughtful. "Do you believe we have a chance?"

"To get away?" He shrugged and forced a smile he did not feel. "I'd say it's eighty-twenty in the Old Man's favor, but you never know. Once bombs start falling, anything might happen."

"If the planes arrive."

"They'll be here if you activate the homer."

Silence hung between them for a moment. Sarah was seated on the edge of Bolan's bed, the soldier in a wooden chair directly opposite.

"What's the matter?"

"I was thinking," she responded, "that the time I have spent here has been wasted. Everything that I have done…"

"That's nonsense," Bolan told her sternly. "They'll be hanging on your every word when you get back to Tel Aviv. If any of these basket cases get away tonight—or if they find another group active, somewhere else—the information you've collected will be vital. I imagine you could close the books on half a dozen major raids right now."

"Perhaps. But I had hoped to have a hand in seeing all of this destroyed."

"You will," the Executioner reminded her. "No homer, no surprise, remember? You're the quarterback on this play."

"Quarterback?"

"Forget it."

There was something on the woman's mind, and though the soldier had a fair idea of what it was, he let her get there in her own way and her own good time.

"This morning, in the garden—"

"Sarah—"

"No, please listen. I have been there many times, in seven months, with many men."

"This isn't necessary."

"I believe it is. I need to have you understand that there was nothing in my heart for any of them, ever."

"I believe you."

He had seen the symptoms time and time again, the guilty burden borne by female warriors who were forced, at times, to use their bodies as a weapon in the everlasting war against the savages. It was a natural reaction, and the only cure was time, perhaps the opportunity to talk it out with someone who could understand.

"I am committed to the defense of Israel," Sarah told him, something of the old fire shining in her eyes. "The things that I have done were necessary—for my country—and they have not touched my soul."

"I know a little bit about the way you're feeling," Bolan answered. "Sometimes when I close my eyes, I see the faces of the men I've killed, the ones who got their tickets punched because they trusted me and tried to help. We all have extra baggage that we carry, but the trick is not to let it weigh you down."

"I see the faces, too, and wish that I could kill them."

"So tonight you get your wish."

"And will that make them go away?"

"It never has for me."

"My family was murdered by the PLO in 1980. I was seventeen and still in college. I was at a party when they died."

"No way you could have stopped it, even if you'd been there. Would your country be a better place if you had died beside them?"

Sarah thought about it for a moment, finally found an answer she could live with. "No," she said. "I think it is a better place because I live and fight against our enemies."

"Damn straight."

"You are a wise man, for a soldier."

Bolan grinned. "I have my moments."

"Yes, you do." Her smile was hesitant. "This morning, when we—"

"Sarah, really—"

"It is not polite to interrupt." Her voice was stern, but there was mischief in it, too. "You still have time, before your meeting with the sheikh, and it may seem suspicious if your bed is not disturbed."

"I'll turn the covers down."

She shook her head. "I am afraid that will not do. Ismaili guards are very thorough. They would immediately see through such deception."

"If you have any other notions—"

"One or two, perhaps." She was already on her feet and drawing back the coverlet, the blankets, on his king-size bed. Before he had a chance to speak, the sequined vest and filmy harem blouse were lying on the floor beside the bed, and she was naked to the waist.

"This isn't necessary," Bolan told her, even as he felt himself responding.

"Yes, it is. I have not made love with a man by choice in seven months. I choose you. Now."

He joined her on the bed without further invitation, shrugging off his robe. She came into his arms with eagerness that was entirely different from their staged encounter of that morning. For the soldier's part, his own response was different as well, but no less ardent. For a timeless moment, Alamut and all its dangers faded like a bitter nightmare, losing substance, giving way to the superior reality of here and now.

So caught up was he in the moment that he did not hear the enemy approaching, had no warning of their presence in the hall before his door swung open to admit Tahir Arrani and a flying squad of riflemen.

"You will, I trust, excuse the interruption, Mr. Harrigan?" The Arab's tone was mocking, and the extra emphasis he placed on Bolan's cover name could only mean bad news. "His majesty, Sheikh al-Jebal, desires your presence in the banquet hall. Immediately."

VICTORY WAS SWEET, and it was all Arrani could do to keep from laughing as his captive scrambled out of bed.

"What's this all about?"

"Your questions may be answered by the master, if he chooses—after *you* have answered certain questions he will pose."

"You call this hospitality? What kind of questions?"

Ignoring the impostor for a moment, he addressed the frightened woman. "Dress yourself and go about your duties. You have no more business here."

She hastened to obey, aware that she was in the presence of a dead man, keeping eyes averted from Bolan. From the look of her, she could already feel his touch of death upon her flesh.

The man who posed as Bryan Harrigan had ceased to bluster, dressing silently beneath the watchful eye of four disciples armed with submachine guns. They had been forewarned of "Harrigan's" performance at the training compound, and they were prepared to take no chances with him. He was desired for questioning—a session Arrani was anticipating eagerly—but if he made an effort to escape, he would be shot without a second thought.

Arrani's conference with the Old Man had been brief and to the point. He had explained about the Harrigan tattoo, his observations in the garden of delights, and he had laid his Polaroid photographs before the master as the coup de grace. Throughout his presentation there had been no interruption from the sheikh. When he was finished, when the master had examined every photograph in minute detail, he raised weary eyes to Arrani's face.

"The stranger has deceived us, then."

"His driver, also. They are both impostors."

"I must know who has employed them to invade our sanctuary."

"As you say, my lord, so let it be."

"They must retain no secrets when you finish."

"I will know the hour when their worthless mothers gave them life."

And so he would. When he was finished with the so-called Irishman and his disreputable driver, he would know precisely who they worked for, what they had been paid, their mission and objectives. He would know their fondest hopes and deepest fears, the names of women they had loved and lost. They would be willing to betray their families at his command. And still it would not save them.

The woman finished dressing, gave the prisoner a wide berth as she exited the chamber in a swirl of gossamer and silk. The tall impostor watched her go, already dressed and waiting, eyes devoid of either disappointment or surprise as she abandoned him without a backward glance.

So much for love, Arrani thought, and smiled in satisfaction as another of his personal beliefs was proved out. The woman was a piece of property, no more significant—although, perhaps, more pleasing to the eye—than any other piece of furniture in the castle. She would do as she was told, with whom it might be ordered, and she would feel nothing for her recent lover, doomed to agonizing death.

The rat-faced driver was the only missing piece required for swift completion of the puzzle. He would still be in his chambers, and they would take him by surprise with little difficulty. He was unarmed, and he did not appear to be a formidable hand-to-hand combatant, like the bogus Harrigan. One guard should be sufficient to control the ferret while they brought him back to join his comrade.

"You," he told the nearest of his soldiers, "come with me. The rest of you will watch this man and kill him if he makes the slightest effort to escape." He spoke the orders first in Arabic and then repeated them in English, for the captive's benefit. It was important to him that the man should understand his life was hanging by a thread, that thread already stretched across the keen edge of a razor in Arrani's hand.

He left the chamber with the guard in tow, proceeding along the corridor to the ferret's suite. Arrani took no pains to move with stealth; it did not matter if the traitor heard their approach. Any major secrets would reside with "Harrigan" and not his underling. A killing, now, might not be inappropriate.

They reached their destination, and Arrani didn't bother to knock. He preferred to take his adversary by surprise, to push through the door with his escort close behind, prepared to spray the room with automatic fire at any sign of opposition. Rising apprehension gripped Arrani as he surveyed the empty room. The closed door yawned open, revealing the caftans hanging there and nothing more. He scanned the tiny bathroom in an instant, found it empty and took time to check beneath the bed before he put the suite behind him, barking orders to his escort.

"Rouse the captain of the guards, and quickly. Sound a general alarm and seal all exits from the castle. No one, save the master, may depart without my personal inspection and approval."

"To hear is to obey."

"Be quick about it!"

"Yes, my lord."

The runner scuttled off, his submachine gun clasped across his chest. Arrani watched him go and hesitated at the door of "Harrigan's" suite. It mattered little that the ferret had escaped him, momentarily. As long as he was trapped inside the walls—and there was no escape for prisoners of Alamut—his brief evasion was of no concern. It was a minor inconvenience, nothing more, and he would pay for it upon his capture.

If he fled the fortress, that would be another matter, but Arrani had no fear of such a failure on the part of their security. The traitor would be hunted down and captured. And before Arrani had finished with him, he would curse the day of his birth. Arrani had been clever in identifying the impostors, and he would not spoil it by letting one of them escape.

The man who posed as Bryan Harrigan had scarcely moved. He stood beside the bed and scrutinized his captors with a kind of flat disinterest in his eyes. He might have been a jaded student caught at cribbing answers rather than a spy confronting torture and, eventually, screaming death. Arrani vowed to shatter that composure, bring the true man out and test his mettle in the fire.

"Your comrade momentarily eludes us," he informed the tall man, watching for some trace of a reaction, finally rewarded by a shrug. "He will not be at liberty for long. While we are waiting for him to be found, you will accompany me."

The master had insisted on an audience with "Harrigan" before the questioning began in earnest. If his personality and magnetism could not drag the answers out of their impostor, it would be Arrani's turn to try. And he was looking forward to it with anticipation.

"This way."

The impostor fell in step behind him as Arrani headed toward the banquet hall, his escort bringing up the rear. He had no fear of "Harrigan," no apprehension that the man might spring upon him from behind before the guards could riddle him and drop him in his tracks. Whatever else the man might be, he did not strike Tahir Arrani as a fool.

He would present the captive to his master, watch and wait while the man refused to answer simple questions, and in time, he would be given charge of the interrogation. *Then* they would have answers, and to spare.

Within the dungeon of his mind, Arrani knew precisely how to handle the impostor, how to keep his body and his mind alive—alive and screaming—through the night. It would not matter if the necessary answers were obtained immediately, if the actual interrogation took a moment or an hour. He would not be satisfied until the ersatz Irishman was broken, mentally and physically. Until he begged for death.

And if the infidel was very, *very* fortunate, Arrani might decide to grant his wish. When he was finished. When he had extracted every ounce of pleasure from what promised to become a highly satisfying night.

THE ENTRANCE TO THE GARDEN stood unguarded, the sentries called away to other duties as a general alarm was raised. They might return to beat the underbrush, but scouring the garden would not be their first priority. They would be scrambling to find a second prisoner, and no one would suspect that he was hiding here.

She knew the American's accomplice had escaped. There hadn't been an opportunity for her to warn him, but she saw him scuttling in the direction of the stable as she left the sleeping chamber, dizzy from the shock of what had transpired. Somehow Arrani had discovered the American's identity, or he had learned enough to know that he had been deceived. Interrogation would supply the missing answers unless she could find a way to free the captive before it was too late.

But first, she had a job to do.

The American had given her his watch, and now the timepiece told her it was half-past six. The airborne strike was set for midnight, and she had to activate the homer now, aware that she might not be favored with another opportunity.

Any plan she devised to rescue the American was almost sure to fail. Unarmed, against an army, there was little she could do to help him, but she had to try.

She found the tree where he had clipped the small transmitter to a limb and jumped to catch the lower branches, locked her thighs around the trunk. She had not climbed a tree in years, but she was motivated now, and she was running out of time.

How long would the American survive Arrani's questioning techniques? More to the point, how long could he withhold the news of Phantoms poised to strike at Alamut? If she allowed him to betray that secret, everything was lost, and all her work, the degradation she had suffered, would have been in vain.

The bark was rough against her skin, but Sarah scrambled up the trunk and found the homer, concealed from casual scrutiny by leaves. By straining, she could reach the activation button with her fingertips, and pressing it, she was rewarded by a tiny click that told her she had done her job.

Eight hours. More than enough time, provided the Phantoms were on schedule, that there had not been a change of plans. She could not be responsible for other hearts and minds, not when her own were still in turmoil. She shrugged off the train of thought and descended swiftly to the ground.

She had to warn Michelle and Mari. It was a pity that she could not trust the other women, did not know the master's spies by name, but she could take no chances. There was still a chance her friends could help to save the American, and they were certain to cooperate once she had made it clear their own escape was linked inseparably to his survival. If he died, if he was broken by Arrani and revealed the secret of the air raid, they were all as good as dead.

But three against an army offered small improvement on her former odds, and Sarah knew that they would need a weapon, a strategic edge, if they expected to survive the night. Securing guns would be a decent start, and that would be a challenge in itself. She had been trained to fight—in military service, by Mossad—but to her knowledge, Mari and Michelle had never held a weapon, much less fired a shot at another human being. Sarah was convinced that anyone could kill, if suitably provoked, but there would be no time or opportunity to practice marksmanship, acquaint her gentle troops with firearms nomenclature.

Abruptly Sarah stopped herself. She had not spoken to the others yet, and she was picturing the three of them in combat, ranged against a troop of dedicated, skilled Assassins. Taken in its proper light, the situation was disheartening, but she refused to crumble in the face of overwhelming odds. While they survived, there must be hope, and worry only cost her precious time.

She must alert the others now, and formulate a plan for seizing weapons. After they were armed—assuming they survived that long and pulled it off—there would be time to scrutinize an angle of attack.

Arrani would convey his hostage to the cellars, where interrogation chambers had been fitted with implements of torture, both old and new. She had been "privileged" to view the chambers once, as part of her indoctrination in the harem, and although they had been vacant at the time, an atmosphere of latent menace, pain incarnate, made her glad to leave the musty rooms behind. If memory had not deceived her, the interrogation chambers were accessible by one route only, and the narrow staircase could be easily defended by a single man—or woman.

It was something, but she would not let herself be lulled into the expectation of an easy victory. Or any victory at all. They would probably be killed or captured when they tried to arm themselves. The one thing Sarah could *not* do was trust her life to chance, allow herself to passively accept whatever might befall her. Taking action here and now might mean her death, but sitting back and doing nothing whatsoever would be tantamount to suicide.

She had an opportunity, at last, to strike against her enemies, and she could not afford to let it pass her by. If she could stop one man, eliminate a single member of the killer cult, then she would not have thrown her life away without some purpose.

Moving with a new determination, Sarah hurried off to find her "sisters" and explain precisely what the three of them had to do.

16

They would be hunting him now, without a doubt. Hafez Kasm shifted in the musty darkness of the disused storage chamber, conscious of the fact that he would not be safe much longer unless he found a better hiding place. If he was cornered there, the hunters might—might not—choose to capture him alive. With Belasko in their custody already, he was more or less an afterthought, a loose end waiting to be tied...or cleanly snipped away.

His own escape, thus far, had been a fluke. Or was it fate? Perhaps the guiding hand of Allah? He had been relaxing in his room, if such was possible in present circumstances, when a sudden apprehension overcame him, urging him to cross the room and have a look outside. He was in time to see the raiders bursting in on the American, weapons testifying to the fact that it was not a social visit.

And he had fled. Without a backward glance. While there was time.

The memories of creeping along that corridor brought angry color to his cheeks. He was embarrassed by the fact that he was alive and still at liberty, of sorts. Instead of running, there had been the option of attacking the raiders from behind, empty hands against their submachine guns, desperately attempting to help his comrade. They would both be dead by now, of course; but as he huddled in the darkness, searching his mind for a plan, he wondered if his choice might simply have postponed the fate that was inevitably bearing down upon them.

Their situation seemed impossible, from every angle. Belasko was in custody and under guard, perhaps already facing stiff interrogation at the hands of men who thrived on pain and suffering. Hafez, meanwhile, was free...if being trapped, unarmed, inside the fortress of his enemies could be construed as freedom. If he stayed in place, they would inevitably root him out, and he ran an equal risk of stumbling across a hunting party if he tried to find another, safer, hiding place.

The Arab believed there was virtue in decisive action, even if that action, ultimately, might be wasted. He had promised the American he would try to save himself if anything went wrong, but he could no more leave his contact in the clutches of Sheikh al-Jebal than he could turn his back on duty, honor and self-respect.

There were, of course, substantial obstacles he would have to overcome before he had a prayer of attempting a rescue. The borrowed caftan he wore was totally inadequate as a disguise, his stolen army uniform no better. He could pass for an Ismaili gunman if he dressed accordingly—the palace force was large enough for some men to be strangers to their fellows—but he needed proper garb and armament to perpetrate the masquerade. In that disguise, he might be able to locate the chamber where Arrani and his men conducted their interrogations, might surprise them, and—

And what?

Annihilate an army single-handedly? Fight his way past sentries, through the fortress walls?

It seemed preposterous, but he was bound to try. He would need a weapon and the disguise that could be gained in one way only. Cautiously he cracked open the storage room door and peeked outside. The corridor was empty, but

Kasm knew a hunting party might appear at any moment, bearing down on him.

He thought about his wife and children, pushed their images away as he stepped out into the corridor. The tunnel suddenly reminded him of an esophagus, conveying him, a helpless scrap of food, into the dragon's belly. Still, a living morsel might find ways to make the diner feel uncomfortable, and foreign objects, swallowed rashly, might prove lethal to the largest, most invulnerable dragon.

Conscious of his footsteps echoing along the passageway, the Syrian proceeded northward, toward the mountain's heart. There was a reason for his chosen course: the hunters would be expecting him to try to escape, so they would be concentrating on the exits, leaving fewer troops to search the deep recesses of the castle. If his logic served, the chances of encountering a solitary guard were better once he turned his back on the massive southern door and stable exit, to the east, deliberately moving toward an area from which there could be no escape.

A moment later, while edging toward a hard right-angle in the corridor, he found his man. The guard was slender and young, attired in the standard turban, slacks and jacket of the sheikh's private army. He was carrying an AK-47 automatic rifle casually, as if he knew the danger had already passed him by.

Procrastination would be fatal now; there was no time to formulate a detailed plan. Head down, arms clasped across his belly like a man in pain, Kasm lurched into view, his footsteps dragging, shuffling along the stony floor. He staggered, groaned, threw out an arm to catch himself and missed the wall by yards, collapsing on his face.

The sentry barked an order at him, saw that a response was hopeless and approached with cautious strides.

"Who are you?"

The sentry's voice set his teeth on edge, and for the brief duration of a heartbeat, he was tempted to surrender, buy himself a little time, at least, by giving up his suicidal scheme.

Too late.

A rough hand settled on his shoulder and rolled him over on his back. The rifle muzzle grazed his cheek. He battered it aside with one hand, shot the other forward, rigid fingers digging for the sentry's larynx. Kasm was on the sentry in an instant, straddling his chest, knees pinning down the arms that sought to throw him off. There was no question of the sentry crying out, and with his rifle cast aside, his sole defense lay in his knees, and he pummeled his attacker's kidneys. Craning forward to escape the numbing blows, Kasm applied more pressure to his adversary's throat, and was rewarded by the bluish cast that crept across the young man's features, the obscenity of his protruding tongue.

It ended suddenly, as if a switch had been flicked off, the sentry disconnected from his life without a hope of resurrection. Glazed eyes stared beyond the Syrian, beyond the rugged ceiling, locked upon the infinite. Withdrawing, working on the painful cramp that had knotted his arm, Kasm mused, briefly, whether the dead man had, indeed, found paradise.

A door some yards beyond the kill zone opened at his touch. He laid the AK-47 on the dead man's chest, bent low to seize the body by the ankles and dragged it through into a room piled high with crates of ammunition and grenades. Unwittingly his quest had led him to a portion of the palace arsenal.

He stripped the soldier swiftly, shed his robe and uniform beneath the glare of naked bulbs, then slipped on the man's slacks and jacket. Kasm had managed to achieve the first phase of his plan. If he was not subjected to intensive scrutiny or questioning, he was convinced that he could pass for an Assassin.

He used the fallen sentry's knife to pry the lid off of a crate containing ammunition magazines. With trembling hands, he stuffed his pockets, tucking extra clips inside his belt. To these he added frag grenades from yet another box. He was aware that he might look suspicious with the extra hardware dangling from his waist, preferring firepower to perfect conformity at the moment. If he met a hunting party in the corridor, grenades might make the crucial difference between annihilation and survival.

He was ready to confront the enemy. Thus armed, Hafez Kasm offered up a prayer to Allah and went out to meet his almost-certain death.

SHEIKH AL-JEBAL WAS waiting when Arrani brought the infidel before him, flanked by guards with automatic weapons, tethered by a slender chain around his neck and wrists. The shackles on his legs prevented him from taking normal strides, but he maintained his bearing and revealed no sign of fear. Despite the proximity of death, there was defiance in his eyes.

"Where is the other?"

"We are searching for him now," Arrani said. "He was not in his room when we arrived."

"He must be found!"

"Of course, my lord."

The sheikh turned his attention to the prisoner. "What shall I call you?"

"Why not stick with Harrigan?"

"We know that Bryan Harrigan is dead."

"In that case, I don't think he'll mind."

"You have been sent against us by our enemies."

The captive smiled. "You haven't got a lot of friends."

Amal stepped forward, primed to slam his rifle butt against Bolan's skull, until the sheikh restrained him with a glance.

"If I was in your situation, facing certain death, I think that I would try to spare myself unnecessary suffering."

"I had a hunch you were a coward."

Rigid on his throne, the lord of Alamut absorbed the insult, felt the color rising in his face. It would be easy to command Amal or any of the other guards to kill the prisoner at once, erase the mocking smile with blade or bullets. But he realized that sudden death was what his captive had in mind. An execution—*any* sort of execution—would be infinitely preferable to the pain of the interrogation chamber. The infidel would not escape so easily.

"You are condemned to death for trifling with the will of Allah," he declared. "But first, I will have answers to the questions your presence here has raised. Defiance will prolong your suffering. The choice is yours."

The mocking smile was back. "Guess I might as well try it the hard way," he said.

"To the cellars!" Turning to his aide, he said, "Arrani, you will supervise the questioning to ascertain precisely who has sent this infidel among us and for what unholy purpose."

Bowing from the waist, Tahir Arrani smiled. "To hear is to obey."

Alone once more, the lord of the Assassins was beset by nagging doubts and questions. It was obvious that his security had been unequal to the task of keeping out intruders. Having failed this time, the system would be suspect in the future, making every new disciple a potential enemy. Could there be other infiltrators in the palace, even now? If so, how could he ever hope to root them out without revealing failure, losing face with those who worshiped him as Allah's voice on Earth?

It pleased him to believe that "Harrigan" had been a fluke, an aberration that would help him to improve security, strengthen his defenses against the day when other enemies would send their spies and their killers to destroy him. He could learn from the experience and profit from it in the long run, if he kept his wits about him.

He was not concerned about the missing driver. They would find him soon, and crush him like the scuttling insect that he was. Unarmed, without a prayer of slipping past the sentries on the gate, he was a cockroach in a maze, condemned to run the corridors until he was eventually cornered and destroyed.

But he was Syrian, and that was troubling. It left two possibilities: some portion of the Ba'ath regime had secretly turned against him, or the man was a traitor, on the payroll of some hostile Western government. In either case, the notion of a native Syrian betraying the Ismaili sect was a disturbing one. If nothing else, he should have been too frightened to participate in such a scheme. His courage—or insanity—might prove contagious in the long run, leading other fools to raise their voices or their hands in opposition to the will of Allah.

He would serve as an example, this one, and his body—what remained of it when they were finished—would be sent home to his village, graphic evidence of what lay waiting for the idiots and infidels who dared approach the walls of Alamut. His family and friends would understand the warning well enough, and word would spread like wildfire in the desert grass.

Already feeling stronger, Abdel al-Sabbah stood and moved across the dais toward his private exit from the throne room. Guards in the corridor snapped instantly to full attention, falling in behind their leader with precision born of numerous rehearsals. They would stand outside his sleeping chamber through the night, and if he left again for any reason, they would follow him wherever he might go.

His door was one of very few within the palace capable of being bolted from inside. He used the extra safety measure now, embarrassed by the apprehension that refused to leave him, hopeful that his confidence would be restored once the impostor was broken in mind and body, stripped of every conscious thought and hidden memory that might be useful to the cause. Debasement of his enemy would make him strong again, and once he knew the infidel's employers, he would have a means of wreaking vengeance on them in his own good time.

The prospect of revenge improved his humor, but he knew that it would be difficult to sleep. Hashish would help, but he would need his wits about him if his enemy began to confess. And while the drug was soothing, it possessed a tendency to cloud the mind, obscuring crucial details. It was well enough for soldiers on the eve of death to fire their courage by artificial means, but he could not afford that luxury.

It had occurred to him that he should witness the interrogation, but he had dismissed the thought at once. Arrani was entirely competent to conduct the questioning alone, and it demeaned the sheikh to deal with all the trivial details himself. When they were finished with the infidel, he would receive the information he sought, and he would base his retaliation on it.

The necessity of retribution, swift and lethal, was not open to debate. The means might be discussed, but a challenge to his power here, in Alamut, could not be left unpunished. If he had to strike at Downing Street or send his men against the White House, Abdel al-Sabbah would teach the Western governments that he was no one to be trifled with. Intimidation might impress the Russian bear, but Communists were godless fools, devoid of inner strength, the fortitude that only Allah could provide.

Jihad was coming; he could feel it in his soul. For years, the sheikh had been content to hire out his soldiers as mercenaries, raking in a fortune for himself while they paid homage to the will of Allah, wreaking havoc on the unbelievers. It was satisfying, and, above all, it had been safe.

The holy war had found him, had been brought home to his doorstep, and he could not turn away. His ancestors had steeled themselves through generations, waiting for the proper time to strike, and it would be *his* duty—his eternal honor—to inaugurate the holy war. If Muslim governments elected to support him, he would welcome their assistance. If they failed him, each in turn would find that Abdel al-Sabbah possessed a memory of great endurance.

But first they had to finish with the enemy at hand, and there was nothing he could do to rush the process. Proper questioning took time, a certain creativity and style. For all his ambition, all the doubts that he engendered in his chief from time to time, Tahir Arrani was a master at his craft, and he would have the hours or days required to properly complete his work.

The lord of Alamut had time to spare, and he could easily afford to wait.

"I THINK IT IS our only chance. If you have a better plan, I'm listening."

"How do we know the planes are coming? It could be a trick." Mari, as Sarah had expected, was the first to express doubt.

"To serve what purpose?" Her exasperation showed, and she was painfully aware of passing time. "Would anyone come all this way and risk so much without a reason? Would he throw his life away in such a fashion if he did not honestly believe the planes are on their way?''

"All right, then,'' Mari countered. "Let us take his word as truth. Why should we risk our lives to help this man, when we barely have the time to get away ourselves?''

"Because without him we would have no chance at all.''

"He is a man. He takes his pleasure like the rest, by force.''

"You speak from ignorance. He is an agent, forced to play a role.''

"I think that we should help him.''

Startled by Michelle's decision to participate in the discussion, Sarah smiled. "And I agree. You have a choice now, Mari. You can join us, or—''

"Be left behind, I know.'' Her frown was petulant. "Which means I have no choice at all.''

"You're with us, then?''

"I'd help the devil if I thought it would get me out of here.''

Despite the superficial similarities of their appearance— long dark hair and harem costumes—the three women posed a study in contrasts. Sarah was the oldest of the three, although their ages spanned a period of barely eighteen months. Michelle was French, a student who had taken time off from her studies for a bargain-basement tour of the Middle East. She had been picked up in Damascus and carried off to Alamut, her year-old disappearance still a mystery to French officials in the capital. Soft-spoken and apparently submissive, she had startled Sarah, in their early conversations, by repeatedly expressing her intention to escape the Eagle's Nest by any means available.

Mari, the final member of their trio, was a native Syrian, abducted from her village fourteen months before Sarah's arrival at Alamut. Mari was a lesbian, her casual contempt for men exacerbated into hatred by the various indignities she had endured under orders from the sheikh. After an initial overture to Sarah in the second week of her "apprenticeship," the slender Arab swallowed her rejection, and they had gone on to share a friendship based on mutual respect. While Mari shared Michelle's desire for freedom, she was fatalistic in her own acceptance of their hopeless situation. Still, she was a fighter, and Sarah was glad to have her on their side.

It would have been a shame to kill her as a guarantee of silence.

"Tell us, then," the Syrian demanded, "how are we to work this miracle against an army?"

Sarah told them, spelling out the details, and they heard her out without interruption, asking pointed questions when she finished. Neither of them seemed to doubt her premise, although Mari was convinced they would all be killed in the attempt.

"I do not care," Sarah told her. "I would rather be shot down than burned or buried by the rubble when the Phantoms come."

"A lovely choice. Such opportunities."

"And what about the others?"

"Can we trust them?" Sarah asked.

"Oh, yes—to get us killed."

"Let's do it, then," Michelle put in, "before I lose my nerve."

Sarah stretched out her hands and clasped those of her comrades. For a moment, they comprised a living circle, pledged to one another, to the death.

"All right," she said at last. "Let's go."

17

"All systems go."

Behind Grimaldi, the Israeli flight officer echoed confirmation. "All systems go."

They waited for clearance from the tower, Grimaldi chafing at what seemed to be another in the endless series of delays that had confronted him since he awoke in Tel Aviv that morning. They had time to spare, he knew, but it did not ease the nagging apprehension that had dogged his footsteps through the city, perching on his shoulder like a harpy during his last ride to the air base.

His last ride. And where the hell had *that* come from?

He made a conscious effort to relax. They were on time, the weather held no threats in store, and Bolan had never let him down.

And that, Grimaldi finally decided, was the problem. What if *he* let *Bolan* down? What if they found their target, right on schedule, and the rockets he unleashed against the target killed the man he admired above all others? How would he live with that . . . or would he care to try?

The Executioner had known the odds against him going in, and he had been in tighter corners. Hadn't he? Before he ever set the homer, long before he keyed it into life, the soldier would have mapped an exit from the killing grounds. No way in hell would Bolan hang around to see the fireworks from a ring-side seat. It would be suicide, and kamikaze raids had never been a part of Bolan's style.

The tower's clearance crackled in his ear, and Jack Grimaldi put the Phantom in motion, taxiing into position for takeoff. Another delay, while the traffic controller went through his procedures, and then they were clear. Throttle forward, the first, heady rush down the tarmac, velocity pressing the pilot and passenger back in their seats. Grimaldi kept one eye on the accelerometer and one on the runway, feeling the plane as it started to lift, hauling back on the stick to oblige the raw power of thundering engines.

Once airborne, they circled the field while the four other Phantoms took off, falling into formation with Jack on the point. They would first travel west, and then north, over water, until they were holding on station, just off the Syrian coast. They would wait there, regardless of whether the homer was working or not, until half-past eleven, at which time the flight would slip in under radar and close in on their target.

A strike before midnight was out of the question. If the homer was active upon their arrival, the Phantoms would wait all the same. Bolan's life was at stake. Jack had promised him midnight, and midnight it would be. He had weathered the flack from Mossad and the air force, suggestions that one man was always expendable given the mission's importance to thousands or millions of others. He held to the line, never budging in spite of their threats to proceed on their own, with a last-minute phase-out of troublesome Yankees. He had been persuasive, his phone calls to higher-ups reversing the Israeli decision. The strike would be laid down at midnight, no later, and anyone still on the ground could look out for himself or get fried.

The whole premise, of course, was dependent on Bolan. Achieving his optimum altitude, settling in for the ride,

Grimaldi had time to review all the myriad problems that might have defeated the soldier, prevented his placing the homer at all. If his contact had failed to appear, Bolan would have been forced to proceed on his own; he might never have pinned down the target—or come within miles of it—given the rugged, confusing terrain. There were bandits to deal with, assorted guerrillas with possible secrets to hide, not to mention the Assassins Bolan was seeking. In spite of official protection, the cult would undoubtedly lay out security screens of its own, to prevent casual intruders from stumbling into its stronghold.

It was no piece of cake, but then, Bolan was known to the select few as a can-do commando, the best and the boldest. Grimaldi had no doubt the homer would be there and singing its heart out before they arrived. It was Bolan who worried him, one man—or two, with his contact—against what might well be an army of die-hard fanatics. Some enemies scattered or folded when heat was applied; true believers would stick to the end, never counting the cost to themselves or their comrades. They reveled in death, in the prospect of giving their lives for "the cause," and that meant every one of them had to be killed. Bolan might not have adequate hardware to carry it off. Hell, he might not have time.

Clearing land, Grimaldi went to his instruments to plot their course, holding radio silence. His wingmen were pros, with enough years of combat between them to tote up a century, all of them itching for action, a crack at the crazies who listened to Allah and heard only shrill cries for blood. They were anxious, but they were committed to following his lead, and Grimaldi had no fear of anyone peeling off early to follow the transmitter's beam on his own. They would wait, and when time came to strike, they would go as a team.

Only Bolan, afoot in the darkness, would be forced to go it alone.

As Jack Grimaldi led his flight of Phantoms toward their holding point, the Executioner was neither on his feet nor in the dark. The ceiling fixtures of the cellars were larger and brighter than the scattered bulbs that lit the corridors above. It had been clearly reasoned that the torturers would need sufficient light in which to do their work.

As yet, the rack was not especially uncomfortable. Bolan's ankles were securely fastened at one end with leg irons, while his arms were stretched above his head, wrists bound to something that resembled a giant cogwheel, manually operated by a handle on one side. The rack itself was made of unfinished timber, which was rough against his skin without the buffer of his camo shirt and pants.

He knew about the rack. There were different styles and cultural refinements, but they all performed the same grim function: stretching muscles, joints and tendons until something gave, the body or the mind. A stubborn subject might be physically dismembered, but the soldier thought that it would seldom go that far before the victim started babbling everything he knew.

A charcoal brazier stood to one side of the rack, assorted branding irons and metal tongs protruding from the heap of glowing coals. If stretching did not do the trick, Arrani was prepared to try his hand at other means.

At the moment, he was alone. The sheikh's second-in-command had supervised his placement on the rack, the fastening of cuffs and clamps, the stoking of a fire inside the brazier. Then, surprisingly, Arrani and his ghouls had withdrawn without a word about half an hour earlier. In the interim, there had been time for him to think, anticipate pain and listen to superheated metal clicking in the brazier. Ample time to be afraid.

And that, of course, had been the point. Whatever else Tahir Arrani might turn out to be, he was apparently a student of psychology. He knew that the imagination was a potent weapon, magnifying pain beyond the scope of physical reality. Some victims, Bolan knew, would break before the questioning began, their fear denying them the opportunity to test their thresholds.

Shrugging off his fear, he used the time to test his bonds for any slack. The leg irons were unyielding, loose enough to chafe his flesh without allowing him to wriggle free. The screws that held them firmly in their place were long and tight, the hasps secured by metal clips resembling clothespins. At the other end, his wrists were bound with leather cuffs that buckled tight enough to hold him fast without cutting off the circulation. Bolan's hands would not be numb if one of his interrogators felt the urge to pull his fingernails.

Without a prospect for escape, the warrior turned his mind to tactics of resistance. What would his interrogators want to know? His name and nationality, for openers. The names and nationality of his employers. Finally his contacts, mission and objectives. In short, everything.

He was experienced enough with torture to be conscious of the fact that every human being had a breaking point. No man or woman could resist indefinitely; every person had a weakness which, discovered by the enemy, would make them infinitely vulnerable.

He would talk, beyond the shadow of a doubt. The only concerns were the timing and the extent of his disclosures. It was roughly ten o'clock, by Bolan's estimate, and while he might be able to withstand interrogation for two hours, it was not entirely necessary. In the last analysis, he could afford to tell his captors *anything*, as long as he did not reveal the existence of the homer. While the small transmitter was secure and sending out its beacon, he could tell Arrani everything about the dead-end mission into Syria. His chance encounter with the IRA's ambassador would kill some time, and none of it would matter if he held them with his tales until the stroke of midnight. After that, they would all be dead, their lips forever sealed by fire from heaven.

Midnight.

Surely he could last that long.

Each moment that Arrani and his henchmen spent outside put Bolan that much closer to his goal. It might come down to moments, seconds, in the end, as he began to lose control. Strategic leaks along the way could buy more time, with the interrogators forced to verify and question every word before they could accept his statements as the truth. A major drawback in the use of torture was that victims might confess to anything, and they would make things up, if necessary, to alleviate the pain. All humanitarian concerns aside, enlightened nations had finally abandoned torture, on the whole, because it was notoriously inefficient as a means of gathering reliable intelligence.

The trick, then, was to time the break—if such a thing was possible—and make it count. With footsteps in the corridor betraying the return of his interrogators, Bolan wondered if he would be equal to the challenge.

Two more hours.

If he could last until midnight, he would have it made.

THERE WERE TWO OF THEM, and Sarah cursed beneath her breath. She had been hoping for a solitary guard, someone who would make it simple. Two was more than twice as difficult. It could be fatal, and she had no wish to die just yet.

"What shall we do?" Michelle sounded breathless, and her hands were trembling visibly.

"Stay here." It was a snap decision, made on instinct. "Watch us and be ready to come running if we need you. Mari, come with me."

"My luck."

"Just do what we agreed."

Their targets were approaching from the east, their rifles carried casually, but Sarah knew they could respond to any threat within a heartbeat's time. The trick would lie in mentally disarming them before she made her move, and now that it was time, she wondered whether she could pull it off.

No time for doubts or second thoughts. She had been turning in Academy Award performances for seven months, and this time she would not be called upon to follow through. She merely had to let the jackals think she was available and eager for their touch. A hint of pleasure yet to come, and let their imagination do the rest.

With Mari at her side, she moved along the tunnel on an interception course. The gunners saw them coming, instantly dismissed them as they might a piece of furniture. At Alamut, a woman's place was in the bedroom, or the garden, preferably on her back. Aside from sex, a dance or the occasional performance of domestic tasks, the female of the species had no role in an Assassin's life. Ismaili soldiers did not marry, did not procreate. Their love, if such it could be called, was finally reserved for Allah and their "holy cause."

But they were men, of flesh and blood, and they could be distracted on occasion. Possibly, on *this* occasion. Sarah's hopes this night, their chance for survival, were riding on the weakness of the flesh.

They had rehearsed their parts while searching for their prey. A giggle, that from Mari, quickly hushed by Sarah as they came in earshot of the guards. A glance from Mari toward the younger of the riflemen promised heaven in the offing if her chosen man could only spare the time. Impatiently Sarah took her companion by the arm, attempted to prevent her from embarrassing them both, but Mari pulled away. The younger guard was hesitating, staring at her, his gruff companion aping Sarah's role, the voice of reason.

Mari bowed her head, eyes huge above the veil that custom and a curious propriety demanded as a part of feminine attire. Their vest might be designed for maximum display of cleavage, and their harem pants might be nearly transparent, but their faces must be covered at all times, except when they had been ordered up for duty in the garden of delights.

It was unheard of for a woman to speak first in such encounters, but her passion had attained such heights that Mari could restrain herself no longer. Sarah was surprised and gratified to see the gunman blushing, his companion startled, glancing furtively in her direction. They were on a mission for the master of the palace, true, but it appeared to be of no great urgency. There might be time . . .

Astounded by his rare good fortune, Mari's chosen target steered his "conquest" toward the nearest door. It opened on a storeroom filled with crates of canned goods, some of the emergency supplies Sheikh al-Jebal had gathered as a form of siege insurance, building up his stores against the day when Alamut might be cut off from sources of provisions in the valley. Once inside, the younger rifleman laid his rifle on a stack of crates, his hands all over Mari as he steered her toward a shadowed corner.

Sarah met the eyes of his companion, answering his silent question by moving toward him with her most seductive walk. His mind was elsewhere, and he did not notice as her right hand slipped behind her back, slim fingers fastening on the handle of the knife she had tucked inside her waistband.

They were touching close now, and the sentry brought up his free hand to cup her breast, rough fingers kneading through the fabric of her vest. She smiled, aware that he would never see it through her veil, would never know that death had smiled upon him in the final moments of his life.

A thud was immediately followed by a breathless gasp, as Mari drove her knee into the younger sentry's groin. Without a backward glance to see if it had been effective, Sarah brought her knife around and drove it home with all her strength beneath the gunner's sternum. He went rigid, wheezing as the six-inch blade sheared through his diaphragm and found the pumping muscle of his heart. A wrenching twist, and Sarah felt the hot blood spill across her wrist, her forearm, heard it spattering the stony floor around her feet. The man became deadweight, sagging in her grip, and Sarah let him go, the knife blade glistening as she withdrew it from its fleshy scabbard.

She pivoted and found the younger sentry on his knees, hands clutching wounded genitals, head down, eyes closed against the pain. Before him, Mari wore a dazed expression of her own, but she was thinking, searching for a weapon, reaching for his rifle even as Sarah stepped forward.

"Stop! No shooting yet!"

Without a second thought, she tangled fingers in the sentry's hair and wrenched his head back, laying bare his unprotected throat. Her blade sliced right to left, behind his larynx, and she put her weight behind it, sawing outward, grimacing and bearing down until the butcher's work was done. A little cry escaped from Mari as the crimson river lapped around her slippers, then she skipped aside as Sarah let the body fall.

"His rifle, quickly! And the ammunition magazines!"

Securing the dead man's AK-47 posed no problem, but the shapely Syrian proved squeamish when it came to stripping off his ammunition belt. Impatiently Sarah rolled the body over, retrieving the belt and passing it to Mari, moving swiftly toward the first man she had killed.

This one had worn a bandolier, and Sarah worked it off over his head. She slipped it across her own shoulder, repressing a shudder as canvas steeped in blood made clammy contact with her flesh. She pried dead fingers from his automatic rifle and tucked it under her arm. She was rising when she saw the pistol in his belt, with extra magazines in leather pouches. Michelle would need a weapon, and Sarah took the extra time required to strip the side arm from her kill.

"Come on! We have to hurry."

Michelle was waiting for them in the corridor outside, pacing nervously. She grimaced at the sight of so much blood on Sarah's hands and clothing, but she took the pistol belt when it was held out to her, adjusting it to fit her slender waist. The pistol looked big in Michelle's hand, and Sarah spent a moment briefing her on its mechanism, chambering a live round and working the safety, showing her how to insert a fresh magazine. In spite of mounting agitation, fear that they would be surprised by other sentries, Sarah took the extra time to instruct Mari in the workings of the Kalashnikov, as well.

"How do you know all this?" Michelle inquired, when she was finished.

"I had brothers in the army."

It was the truth, and Sarah had neither the time nor patience for a longer, more precise description of her training in the military arts.

"What happens if we meet more guards?"

"We kill them and keep moving. To the cellars."

"I'm afraid."

"That only proves you're not insane."

"Are you?"

"Insane?"

"Afraid."

"Of course. It makes no difference. We must still go on, or die."

They went on.

HAFEZ KASM FELT as though he'd been roaming through the tunnels for hours, though he realized it had not been that long. On two occasions voices had alerted him to the approach of hunting parties, and he hid in empty rooms until they passed. Thus far, the search appeared to be restricted to a sweep of corridors, without a thorough search of each room along the way.

He had been lucky, but the longer he relied on luck, the less he had to spare. As he approached the cellars, homing on the staircase that would lead him into the bowels of the mountain, he was bound to stumble over sentries he could not evade. If they were startled by his heavy armament, alerted by his poor disguise, he would be forced to kill them on the spot, and any small advantage he might still retain would vanish with the first report of gunfire.

It had been about an hour since the American had been taken prisoner. The torturers might know his secrets by this time, but while a chance of helping him remained, Kasm would not turn his back. And if he came too late to keep

Arrani from discovering their mission, he could still release his friend from pain, prevent the torture from continuing.

No stranger to the ways of death, Hafez Kasm still had doubts about his own ability to frame Belasko in his sights and pull the trigger of his captured weapon. In the last analysis he knew that he could do it as an act of mercy and a token of the friendship he had developed for the tall American. And, with the help of Allah, he would also wreak a bloody vengeance on the jackals who had made it necessary.

He stepped around a corner, saw the group of sentries bearing down upon him and momentarily froze. He recovered immediately, proceeding with a stride that was meant to be casual and making a hasty head count of the opposition. There were four, two armed with submachine guns, and two with automatic rifles. They were muttering among themselves, although he had not heard their voices this time. He was watching them as the point man looked up and saw him.

For an instant there was something close to recognition in the sentry's eyes, and then it soured, turned into doubt. A double take took in the stranger's armament, the cartridge belt encumbered with grenades, and the sentry was frowning, hesitating, turning toward his comrades with some comment on his lips.

Kasm could not afford to let him speak, aware that the four men certainly outgunned him. He snapped his rifle up and squeezed the trigger, knocking down the point man with a ragged burst of automatic fire. A second rifleman was wounded by the bullets ripping through his comrade, the impact spinning him around and painting blood tracks on the granite wall.

The Syrian dropped into a combat crouch before the others could react effectively. He cut their legs from under them and hosed them with rifle fire as they fell, their bodies twitching as he pumped lead into them.

The sole survivor, gravely wounded, had his bloody cheek pressed against the wall. He might have fallen otherwise, yet he was not prepared to yield, his spastic fingers groping for the pistol he carried on his belt. Unmindful of the racket now, Kasm held down the trigger of his weapon and emptied the magazine, his target dancing, sprawling in the awkward attitude of death.

They would be after him in moments, and he had no time to lose. Reloading as he rose, Kasm sidestepped the fallen bodies, holding to his course. The staircase to the cellars lay ahead of him, no more than twenty yards away.

With Allah's help he might survive to see it, and if not, so be it.

Hafez Kasm closed his mind to thoughts of death and went to meet his destiny.

18

"I can assure you, Mr. *Harrigan*," Arrani said mockingly, "in time you will be pleased to tell me everything you know."

"I will be pleased to tell you squat."

"The rack can be a most persuasive instrument." He half turned toward Amal, who stood beside the lever that controlled the wheel. "Begin."

The rack gave off a groaning sound, which might have testified to age or long disuse. The first sensation Bolan felt was a distinctive tightness in his shoulders, hips and knees, the major points responding to a sudden tension. It was something short of pain, but he could see the rack's potential, and he closed his eyes, prepared to bear the coming agony in silence.

At a signal from Arrani, the cogwheel slipped another notch. And there was pain this time, as Bolan's spine was tightened, lifted off the rough bed of the rack. He clenched his teeth, refusing to surrender. It was early yet, and if he started to spill his guts now, he might not buy the time Grimaldi needed for his strike.

"The name of your employer." Arrani's voice was soft, seductive, in his ear.

"Forget it."

The wheel creaked another notch, and Bolan was acutely conscious of the perspiration beading on his forehead, glistening on his chest and shoulders. Angry fire was kindled in his joints and muscles, spreading rapidly. He realized that in a few more moments, in a few more turns of the infernal wheel it would be difficult for him to breathe.

"Your mission?"

"Kiss my *aaagghhh*!"

The cry was wrenched from Bolan's lips as two more notches on the cogwheel made their grim rotation. Now his spine and limbs were bowstring taut, his only contact with the rack maintained at wrists and ankles, where he was securely bound. His vertebrae were straining, and he wondered how much tension was required to snap the fragile spinal cord. Would death be instantaneous, or would his torturers defeat their own sadistic purpose by accidentally deadening his pain, paralyzing him with a twist of the wheel?

It was a notion that amused him, and he smiled, unconsciously, despite the pain.

"What is it that you find so entertaining?" his interrogator barked.

"Your mother."

"Once again!"

The rack gave off another groan...or was it Bolan? Suddenly aware of cataclysmic roaring in his skull, he was not certain whether he had made the sound or not. It didn't matter in the long run. He was nearly ready to begin the game now.

"Your assignment?"

"Search and destroy," Bolan gasped. There was no need to simulate pain.

"Search for *what*? Destroy *whom*?"

"Are you really that stupid? You must know the answer to that one."

"Again."

It became more difficult, each time, for the wheel to turn. Bolan's body was resisting, halting its progress, retarding its motion. With part of his mind standing outside the pain, Bolan wondered how long he could hold it before wood and steel got the better of flesh and bone.

"Search for what? Destroy whom?"

"Search for *you*. Destroy *you*."

"You are arrogant. How can one man hope to vanquish an army?"

"You cut me loose, pal, and I'll give you a demo."

Arrani let that one go by, his face close to Bolan's, smiling with animal pleasure. His breath was a draft from a crypt. "Your employers?"

Too soon.

"What's the difference?"

"Again."

Bolan shuddered as his joints were tested, at the breaking point. How many pounds per square inch would it take to separate a shoulder? Wrench a hip out of its socket? Snap a spine?

"Who sent you?"

"The Israelis."

It was close enough, and if his hazy element of passing time was even partly accurate, Arrani and his ghouls would have no chance to act upon the false intelligence in any case.

"But you are not Israeli."

It was not a question, and he saw no point in bluffing. "Free lance," Bolan hissed between clenched teeth. "They pay, I play."

"A mercenary?"

"Hey, you sound surprised."

"And your companion?"

"Just a contact. Prearranged. I never saw the guy before."

"A Syrian?"

"I didn't ask."

Arrani was about to signal for another notch, but then he smiled, appeared to reconsider. "And where is he now, this friend you never met before?"

A gleam of hope. "You didn't get him?"

"He would be here if we had," Arrani said, scowling. "Where is he?"

"How the hell should I know? I was picked up first, remember?"

Arrani raised his hand, prepared to signal for the turn that would inevitably, separate the soldier's hips or shoulders, possibly his knees, but then hesitated.

"A professional," he sneered, "would prearrange his contact points, escape routes. You are a professional, I think."

"We never got that far." The pain was making Bolan dizzy, and he kept his wits about him with an effort. "He was new to me. I didn't know him from Adam. The way he talked, I figured he was on a kamikaze mission. Thought it might be rude to tamper with his karma."

"You were willing for your friend to die?"

"My contact. I'm a little short on friends these days. Besides, I thought he'd make a nice diversion."

"You have no honor."

"It's a luxury I can't afford."

"How did you find this place?"

"Your people brought me here."

"Again."

The pain was all-encompassing, apocalyptic. Bolan knew that it could not get any worse.

"Again."

Instantly it did.

"How did you learn of Bryan Harrigan's appointment with the sheikh? How did you find this place?"

"They had your operation spotted out of Tel Aviv. You'll have to ask my contact the particulars of how and when. The thing with Harrigan was pure, dumb luck. Our paths crossed, and I recognized him. Just put two and two together. Why else would he be here?"

"You insist on clinging to this flimsy lie?"

"It may be flimsy, but it's not—"

"Again!"

Bolan couldn't contain the scream that spilled from his lips. The pain had moved beyond his threshold. Before Arrani's henchmen could finish the job, he was interrupted by the unexpected entry of a guard.

The Executioner caught nothing of the swift exchange in Arabic, might not have understood the words if they were speaking English, but he recognized the sentry's panic, felt it strike a responsive chord in his interrogator. Something had occurred that demanded Arrani's presence elsewhere in the castle, and without delay.

Arrani barked an order to Amal, and Bolan braced himself, determined not to scream as he was torn to shreds. When nothing happened after several heartbeats, Bolan peered through slitted eyelids, studying Arrani's face.

"Your friend has chosen to resist," the sheikh's second-in-command said, frowning. "He will join you soon, if he survives. Perhaps you will be privileged to see him questioned for a time before I must return to you."

"Don't do me any favors."

"Rest assured that I will not. Before I finish with you, death itself will seem a favor, and it will be slow in coming."

Bolan forced a smile, despite the pain, his mental clock already running down the calculations. Sooner than you think, he thought.

"LISTEN!"

Sarah froze and waited for the sound to be repeated. When it came, there was no room for doubt; the distant echo, barely audible, was automatic-weapon fire.

Beside her, Mari tensed and took a tighter grip on her rifle. "What is happening? What does it mean?"

Sarah had no answers, just a driving sense of urgency that would not let her linger in the corridor. "We have to hurry," she responded. "There is no more time."

But as she moved along the tunnel, ready with her own Kalashnikov to take out any opposition, Sarah could not drive the haunting questions from her mind. If Belasko was in custody, then who were the Assassins firing on? And who was firing back? If his companion had escaped Arrani's dragnet, then they still might have an ally who was prepared to help them free the American.

Except that Belasko's accomplice would not know they were his allies. At a glance, they would be simply harem girls with guns, no less a danger than the sentries in the tunnels who were hunting him. A sudden meeting could be deadly, and while Sarah had no wish to kill the man she had seen but twice, and briefly, she did not intend to let him kill her, either.

"This way!"

They had reached a major intersection in the labyrinth, and Sarah led her comrades to the left, in the direction of the cellars. The underground layout of the castle had been filed away in detail in her mind, different sections memorized and studied over seven months. She knew their only hope of freedom lay behind them, but she would not allow herself to cut and run without at least attempting to deliver the American from the hands of his interrogators.

Forty yards, more or less, until the tunnel branched again, and they must once again bear left. From there, it was approximately fifty yards to the staircase that would take them into the bowels of Alamut. Despite her dedication to the defense of Israel, years had passed since Sarah had accepted literally the tenets of her faith. She could understand the Christian's concept of hell, and if hell *did* exist, she could think of no more fitting epicenter for it than the dungeons of the Eagle's Nest.

They were proceeding to the turn at a rapid pace when half a dozen guards appeared from nowhere, moving toward them on a hard collision course. There was nowhere to run, nowhere to hide. One of the Ismaili riflemen had seen them, confused at first, then galvanized by the peculiar spectacle of harem girls with automatic weapons in their hands. He barked a warning to the others, hit a combat crouch and swung up his AK-47, prepared to fire.

Sarah hit him with a burst that cut his legs from under him and bounced him off the stony wall, a rag-doll figure folding to the ground. His comrades scattered instantly, some of them diving prone, others huddling in doorways, flattening themselves against the wall, returning fire. The corridor became a shooting gallery with human targets ranged at either end and no-man's land between.

Already prone and wriggling toward the cover of a doorway, Sarah was surprised to see Michelle still crouching in the middle of the corridor and blazing with her pistol, features locked into a mask of grim determination. As a European, she had suffered much from the Ismaili pigs at Alamut, and now she seemed intent on evening the score. As Sarah watched, Michelle dropped one man, then another, twisted figures squirming on the floor as she continued squeezing off in rapid-fire.

Suddenly the action of Michelle's weapon froze, locked open on an empty chamber, lazy smoke curls rising from the breech. She squeezed the trigger once or twice without result, then jettisoned the empty magazine and fumbled at her waist for another.

Downrange, a rifleman popped out of hiding to release a short precision burst. The bullets stitched a line of bloody holes across her midriff, and she sat down hard, a stunned expression on her face. The eyes she turned toward Sarah had the glassy look of rapidly approaching death.

A second burst made tatters of her filmy blouse and sequined vest, erasing any hint of life and pummeling her body backward to the floor. Half blinded by her sudden and unwelcome tears, Sarah squeezed off a burst that dropped Michelle's murderer, left him writhing in his death throes while his two surviving comrades went to ground.

The odds were even now in terms of numbers, but the numbers scarcely told it all. The two Assassins had been trained to kill, indoctrinated to the point where they would welcome death in battle as a boon, a sweet reward. While Sarah's combat training might surpass theirs, her comrade, Mari, had no training whatsoever, and the rounds she had fired so far had threatened only ceiling-mounted fixtures.

They were still effectively outnumbered, and every passing heartbeat meant the possibility of reinforcements, more Assassins joining the ranks of their beleaguered brothers— even creeping up to take the women from behind. The sudden thought made Sarah glance across her shoulder, and she very nearly missed the charge of the Assassins when it came.

A thinking man would certainly have held his place, pinned down his enemy and hoped for reinforcements, but the two Assassins had been stung by near-defeat at female hands, and they were confident of their ability to take the women now. With planning, with a bit of stealth, they might have pulled it off, but chauvinism and an overdose of confidence dictated that the riflemen would make their play with absolute disdain of their opponents.

Sarah snapped a warning to Mari and sighted down the barrel of her weapon as her adversaries broke from cover. Firing as they ran, the two men sprayed the corridor chest-high, unmindful of the fact that their opponents had already gone to ground. Their rounds went wild, caroming off walls and spraying chips of stone before they whispered along the corridor.

Holding down the trigger of her AK-47, Sarah caught her target at the waist and dropped him, his body twisting, jerking with the impact of the slugs. Across the hallway, Mari's man was down and dying, but he still had strength enough to use his Uzi submachine gun, and the probing rounds were falling closer to their mark. A short burst took his head off, and the Uzi coughed a final spurt of death downrange before his finger slackened on the trigger.

Rising, Sarah moved among the dead, relieving them of ammo magazines, that she immediately tucked inside the waistband of her pants. There was no point in checking Michelle; the second burst had killed her outright, and her sightless eyes were open, as dull as fractured marbles in the artificial light.

"Let's go!" she snapped at Mari.

"But Michelle—"

"Is dead. We're not. We still have work to do."

"For the American?" There was a hint of bitterness in Mari's tone.

"For *us*. We need him if we're going to get out of here alive."

"All right, then."

Sarah led the way and wondered how much truth her words contained. Could Belasko help them get out of the Eagle's Nest alive? Was *he* alive, or had they come too late? Did it make any difference in the long run?

Doubts and questions spinning in her mind, the lady from Mossad struck off along the corridor. The hour was late, and she had nowhere left to go but down.

HAFEZ KASM HEARD the anxious voices just ahead and knew that he was coming to the cellar stairs. There would be guards, of course. He had been counting on it. But it would be helpful if he knew their number, their position in the corridor beyond his line of sight. A blind assault was a double risk, and he could not count on taking out all his enemies before one had a chance to bring him down.

The corridor curved gently, and Kasm would be within their range of vision if he took a few more steps—too far away to rush them with any chance of success, near enough for them to fire on him when he showed himself. It was a hazardous position, either way. He could hear troops hot on his heels, men intent on tracking down the gunner who had killed their comrades.

His situation made the choice, removed it from his hands. It would be suicide to stand and wait, to allow the enemy to catch him in a pincers, pin him in a cross fire with no hiding place. If he was bound to die, at least he could initiate the contact, take a number of Assassins with him when he fell, instead of waiting to be slaughtered like a bullock in the charnel house.

He tucked the AK-47 beneath one arm and removed two frag grenades from his cartridge belt. He yanked the pins on both, his fingers holding safety spoons in place, and edged his way along the curving tunnel, halting when he caught a glimpse of his assailants at the limit of the curve.

It was a tricky shot, left-handed, and he wouldn't have a second chance to get it right. If either hand grenade fell short, rebounded on him, he would have to scramble for his life, directly toward his angry pursuers.

He pitched the first grenade, a looping underhand, and saw it strike the wall, bounding toward his enemies. The second followed in a heartbeat, and he dropped to a crouch, clutching at his rifle as the hopeless warning shouts erupted just beyond his line of sight. The patter of scrambling feet, and then the shock wave of a double detonation rocked him on his heels, a roiling haze of smoke obscuring his advance.

There had been five of them, at least, and three were down, two of those writhing, clawing at their wounds. He concentrated on the men who were on their feet and knocked them over with the AK-47, short precision bursts designed to clear his way without expending too much precious ammunition. He would be needing it before the night was over, and he didn't have a round to spare.

The stairwell leading to the cellars lay open before him, seemingly unguarded. He had made it this far, but he was not ready to descend. Not yet.

Angry voices swelled behind him and drew inexorably closer, trackers answering the sounds of battle, homing on the kill. They would expect to find him dead or dying, their comrades avenged, but he would have a small surprise in store for them when they arrived.

He unhooked the last frag grenade from his belt and freed the pin, his fingers tight around the lethal egg as he crouched to wait. The hunters were approaching rapidly, were almost on him now. Kasm imagined he could smell them in the corridor, which reeked of smoke and death. Soon...

The first Assassin blundered into view, and the Syrian let fly with the grenade, deliberately lobbing it behind the man. He swung up his rifle before the high-explosive charge touched down and was already firing, bringing down the first live targets, when another smoky thunderclap ripped through the tunnel. Two or three of them were moving, struggling to rise, and he dispatched them swiftly, emptying the rifle's magazine and ramming home a fresh one as the echoes of annihilation died away.

There would be others, but they would take some time to reach him. In the meantime, he was ready to hit the cellars.

Hafez Kasm offered up a prayer, and without a backward glance he started down the stairs.

19

At first, the sounds of battle came to Bolan like a dream, a hint of muffled thunder in the distance. When he tried to turn his head the effort sent a bolt of agony along his neck and down his spine, and he became conscious of his precarious position.

They had left him on the rack, limbs rigid, hips and shoulders straining, almost at the breaking point. It was impossible for Bolan to relax his posture, rest his back or buttocks on the rough-hewn wooden bed.

The soldier clenched his teeth and concentrated on the sound of automatic-weapon fire. Clear-headed now, he recognized that it was louder, closer, than he had initially believed. The sound of an explosion had roused him, and now a second went off nearby.

Grenades?

He had lost track of time, admittedly, but if Grimaldi and his strike force had arrived, their thunder would have shaken down the palace walls instead of merely echoing along a corridor and down the stairs.

He thought immediately of Hafez Kasm—still at large, according to Tahir Arrani—and the urgent summons that had drawn Arrani from his toil. There was a possibility that the Syrian had escaped the hunters, armed himself somehow... but why would he be fighting near the dungeon? Bolan's orders had been terse, explicit: if their cover was destroyed, Kasm should do his best to save himself, escape and carry word of the Assassins to his contacts in the Company. The Syrian had grudgingly agreed.

But had he kept his word?

Bolan recognized the telltale rattle of an AK-47. Footsteps sounded on the stairs, but his position on the rack would not permit a clear view of the staircase. He was braced for anything as boot heels clomped across the stony floor, relief disarming Bolan as he recognized the visage of Hafez Kasm.

"You're supposed to be long gone," he growled, but without conviction.

"I was unavoidably delayed."

Kasm attacked the buckles on the cuffs, and Bolan let himself go limp as tension on his spine and shoulders was released. He ached from head to toe, but a preliminary shakedown told him there had been no lasting damage. If he could manage to stand and keep himself in motion, he should be all right.

Kasm had knocked the pins out of the shackles, and the soldier flexed his aching legs, allowing circulation to return before he sat upright, swung his feet over the edge of the rack. He stood, tottered for an instant, caught himself and took a few exploratory steps to gain his balance.

"Here."

The Syrian had found Bolan's clothing, and he waited as the soldier dressed, supporting him when the warrior staggered while slipping on his trousers. When his combat boots were laced, the Executioner stood tall and tried to loosen up with a few tame calisthenics. Rapid visuals confirmed his first suspicion that no weapons had been left at his disposal.

"We should go now."

Bolan frowned. Kasm was right, of course; they had no choice. But he didn't enjoy the thought of roaming through the tunnels empty-handed, bumping into hunting parties with no means of self-defense. There was the Tekna, but he had no realistic hope of getting close enough to stab his enemies.

"I feel a little naked."

"Here, take this," the Arab offered, holding out his own Kalashnikov. "I'll find another on the way."

"No, thanks. I'll bag my own. Let's roll."

He turned back toward the stairs...and froze. Amal was watching from the bottom step, his submachine gun trained in their direction, almost casually. He muttered something to Kasm and wagged the stuttergun for emphasis.

"We are commanded to surrender," the Syrian told him simply, lowering his rifle until it was pointed at the floor.

"No way. We've got to take him down. On three."

"I am not certain—"

"One."

Amal was scowling at them, glancing rapidly from one man to the other.

"If I miss him—"

"Two."

The enforcer barked another command. There was murder in his eyes, as he raised the Uzi to his shoulder.

"Three!"

As Bolan pivoted and hurled himself away, intent on drawing the squat Assassin's fire, he knew that he was betting heavily against the odds.

The roar of automatic weapons buffeted Bolan's ears and followed him down.

FOLLOWING THE BEACON'S homing signal, Phantoms holding tight formation on his flanks, Grimaldi prayed that everything was on schedule at the target. Obviously Bolan had been able to secure the homer, but that told Grimaldi nothing of the big guy's present situation, his ability to bail out of the dragon's lair before the sky came crashing down around his ears.

At their present air speed, it would take less than fifteen minutes to reach the target. The strike would be dead on schedule, the jets coming in beneath the coastal radar, avoiding major population centers as they skimmed across the rocky landscape. Dead on schedule, and Grimaldi knew that he couldn't delay the strike for Bolan's sake, not even by a moment. It was do or die, and Bolan knew the rules by heart. Hell, he had written many of the rules himself.

The rules said that every soldier was expendable; no individual was more important than the mission of the moment, and combatants in the field were expected to sacrifice themselves, if necessary, to ensure the operational success of their assignment. Simple, right.

Until you got to know the soldier, one-to-one. Until you recognized Mack Bolan as a friend, the man who turned your life around when it was going nowhere fast and kept you on the track until you found yourself again. When friendship was involved, where righteous love came into play, the game plan wasn't simple anymore.

But Jack Grimaldi knew his role, and he would play it out, whatever the result. He knew he'd grieve if the warrior bought it, but he would not allow the loss to break him down. He knew, as well as Bolan, that the war they fought was constant, everlasting, and a midnight raid in Syria would no more constitute a final victory than it would guarantee world peace.

But it would be a start, another holding action won against the savages, and in the last analysis, a transient victory was all that they could hope for. While the human race included savages and sadists, venal men and venomous fanatics, there would always be another field of conflict, one more battle to be joined. And if the Syrian excursion closed the file on Bolan, finally, then Jack Grimaldi would be standing by to help take up the slack.

He checked the servopneumatic and radar altimeters, scanned the fuel gauges, killing time. The moonlit desert sweeping past his undercarriage called up memories of moonscapes, astronauts with golf clubs. What was the message they had left behind? *We came in peace, for all mankind.* Grimaldi might have said the same, without excessively distorting truth. The problem was that sometimes, lasting peace could only come about through war.

Negotiation was a great idea, he thought—for politicians, diplomats, committee chairmen. When it came to dealing with fanatic terrorists, however, logic took a holiday, and words had no more impact than they would upon a rabid animal. Swift, decisive action was required, and personal survival was the top priority.

The Phantoms were prepared for swift, decisive action. Each was fitted with a 20 mm cannon in the nose, its cyclic rate of automatic fire fine-tuned to approximately 6,000 rounds per minute. Deadly, it was small potatoes in comparison to the destructive payload the Phantoms carried underneath their wings. This time around, each aircraft carried two Sidewinder missiles, two Sparrows, and four of the big Phoenix blockbusters. They were equipped to demolish their target, with hellfire to spare.

The Israelis were good at search-and-destroy missions, the long years of terrorist warfare conditioning pilots to follow their orders and never look back. If an enemy hit the Israelis, Israelis hit back, and if paybacks appeared to go overboard once in a while, they were speaking a language their enemies understood only too well. If the terrorists plucked out an eye, the Israelis would take the whole head, bump the ante, defying the hostiles to put up or fold.

It was war to the knife, and the knife to the hilt, with a nation besieged on all sides. It had lasted four decades, with no respite in sight, and occasional cease-fires had not made a damned bit of difference. Grimaldi could feel for them. But this time the war had turned personal; a friend's life was at stake right along with the rest of it.

Scowling, the pilot put thoughts of Bolan behind him. Duty remained, as it always did, guiding him toward the next confrontation with death.

At the moment, his duty was calling him in to ground zero, with seven minutes to spare.

COMING OUT OF HIS SHOULDER ROLL, Bolan was braced to attack Amal, ignoring the odds. But the gunner was down, bloody tracks on his chest testifying that Kasm had got to him first. Bolan glanced at his ally, watched slow-leaking crimson discolor one sleeve of his tunic.

"How bad are you hit?"

"Just a scratch."

"I'll buy that."

Bolan scooped up the Uzi and wrestled the cartridge belt free of the Arab's lifeless body. He took a moment to buckle it on, double-checking the stuttergun's load, then followed Kasm to the staircase.

"The stables?"

"Beats walking."

Kasm took the steps two at a time, Bolan hard on his heels. They were halfway to ground level when two figures appeared at the head of the stairs, guns in hand, blotting out the dim light from above. Bolan sidestepped and flattened himself against the wall, his finger about to depress the Uzi's trigger.

"Don't shoot! Hold your fire!"

The voice belonged to a woman, familiar despite the distortion of strain. He relaxed slightly, reaching out to rest a hand on the Syrian's tense shoulder.

"It's all right, Hafez. They're friendlies."

Kasm looked confused, but he eased off the trigger, reluctantly following Bolan to meet their new comrades in arms. Bolan half smiled at Sarah and rested a quizzical glance on the other woman.

"This is Mari," she told him. "A friend."

"Fair enough. Any others?"

"No more."

"We've got no time to sparc, and we're trying the stables," he told her. "Let's move out."

By his rough calculations, the stables lay nearly a half mile away. Bolan was fully aware that Grimaldi might bring down the roof on their heads at any moment, their margin of safety exhausted. There might be a chance, if they got to the stables in time...

Voices carried to them as they rounded a corner, giving no time for a retreat. Time spent hiding was time they would never regain, and each second was crucial now that they were down to the wire.

Bolan tried for a head count and gave up at seven, eyes locked on the weapons that swiveled to greet him. No time for a warning, as instinct took over, the warrior responding on cue to a threat from the enemy. He was aware of Kasm fading back in a crouch, his Kalashnikov spitting out short, measured bursts. The hostiles returning fire now, muzzle-flashes winking like fireflies as Bolan and the women cut loose with their weapons.

If they made it no further, at least they would go down fighting. The missiles would strike any time now, and Bolan was ready. If this was his time and his place, he would take it, and let the chips fall where they may.

TAHIR ARRANI SCANNED the corpses, searching for the American's companion, finding only loyal Ismailis, the dark blood pooled beneath them bonding them in a kind of grim mosaic. A collage of death.

Somehow, the son of jackals had surprised them, caught them unawares. It was the only explanation, and he grasped it eagerly. One man could not defeat four gunners under normal circumstances. There was little comfort in the thought, but it was better than admitting that his troops were negligent, incapable of running down a single man when the odds were on their side.

Where would he go? It stood to reason that the man would be searching for an exit from the castle, but his track, so far, had led them in the wrong direction, toward the center of the mountain. It was possible that he was merely lost, disoriented by the tunnels, but Arrani did not think so. It would be too pat, an explanation made to order to allay his fears, and innate pessimism kept him from accepting such a tailor-made solution.

The intruder knew where he was going, and that certain knowledge chilled Arrani, made his blood run cold. The little ferret would attempt to free his comrade from the dungeon, might be with him even now, the slaughter in the tunnels serving as a grand diversion to draw off Arrani's troops.

It was a decent plan, all things considered, but it was not foolproof, and Arrani had been wise enough to cover all his bets. Amal would greet the worthless peasant when he arrived to save his friend, and both of them would scream their lives away before Arrani finished with them. They had much to answer for, not least of all the lives of the loyal Assassins stretched out on the floor around his feet.

The infidels would die by inches, pleading for oblivion's release, and he would grant them no mercy. The secrets they cherished would be his; their wildest hopes and dreams would be laid out before him, open to inspection, and he would dissect them, piece by piece, until the jackals realized that there was no hope left, no sanctuary in a universe of pain. He would destroy them utterly. And it would be a pleasure.

Sudden gunfire erupted at his back, from the direction of the dungeons, and he hoped Amal would leave the infidels alive. It would be disappointing if he found them dead when he arrived, and yet, sometimes these things could not be helped. Death was inevitable when the unbelievers set themselves against the will of Allah.

An instrument of Allah's mighty will, Tahir Arrani hoped he might be able to participate in the elimination of the infidels. If not, he would content himself with laying plans for punitive attacks on the Israelis, who had organized this whole fiasco from the outset.

More reports of gunfire, and Arrani thought the point of origin seemed slightly different. How was it possible? How could the little ferret trick Amal and flee the trap they had laid to snare him?

Instantly, as if in answer to his silent question, automatic-weapon fire was heard from two distinct and separate points. Arrani stiffened. Whatever might be happening, the Syrian they sought could not engage Arrani's hunters at two places simultaneously. Somehow, though it seemed impossible, he had enlisted aid.

But how? And *who*? There were no other strangers in the Eagle's Nest, no infidels he could recruit to do his bidding. It could not happen, but Arrani's ears did not deceive him:

small-arms fire from the direction of the cellar stairs; explosive sounds of combat farther off, but clearly emanating from a tunnel to his right. He had at least two enemies inside the fortress, and he would have to find them both, destroy them before they could inflict more damage on the chosen warriors of jihad.

It was his duty, and he must not fail.

With sudden panic welling in his breast, Arrani barked commands that split his force of riflemen, sent some of them toward the sounds of angry gunfire. The remaining troops would accompany him to the dungeon.

With the bloodsong pounding in his ears, Tahir Arrani hastened off.

20

Abdel al-Sabbah was worried. It was an uncomfortable, unaccustomed feeling, and the lord of Alamut was angered by the weakness he perceived within himself. Sheikh al-Jebal, the Old Man of the Mountain, should be in command of every situation, and the fact that he was not had shaken him.

Two strangers, enemies, had wormed their way into his confidence. When he had tried to rectify the situation, one of the men had slipped past his Assassins, vanished into the bowels of the castle. Somehow that single enemy had armed himself, and from reports, he had been raising havoc with the troops.

Humiliation, heaped upon dishonor, seemed to weigh down the Old Man and it was only with a conscious effort that he managed to sit upright on his throne. Aside from breaching the defenses of the Eagle's Nest, his enemies had brought discredit on the proud Ismaili order. First, the infidel who posed as Bryan Harrigan had shown his prowess over twelve trainees, demoralizing all concerned and forcing the sheikh to execute a crop of new Assassins in an effort to save face. No sooner had the tall man's masquerade been revealed, than his companion disappeared and set about annihilating soldiers on his own. Eight men were dead, and almost by the moment there were fresh reports of gunfire here and there throughout the tunnels, seemingly defying any single man's ability to move so far, so quickly.

The possibility of mutiny had crossed the sheikh's mind, but he dismissed it out of hand. His men were trained, indoctrinated in the faith, and each had tasted paradise, renewing personal devotion to their leader. To jihad. If anyone had planned to overthrow him, others would have given up the traitor, vying for the honor of delivering his head to the master.

So Sheikh al-Jebal believed. He gave no thought to female enemies, because a woman's place was in the harem, or the garden of delights, and none would have the courage or resourcefulness, the sheer audacity, to rise against him. Better to believe that his defenses had been penetrated by an outside force, perhaps the SAS, Mossad or CIA. It was a notion he could live with, something that would not shatter his sense of social equilibrium.

He should be hearing from Arrani soon. His second-in-command had been dispatched to gather information from the impostor, but had been interrupted at his task by gunfire in the tunnels, the discovery of slain disciples. With an army at his beck and call, Arrani would eliminate the threat before it went too far... but Abdel al-Sabbah was troubled nonetheless.

He did not wish to leave the Eagle's Nest, but it was painfully apparent that his enemies had found him. Elimination of solitary infiltrators—even raiding parties—posed no great problem, but he had to think beyond the present. Hostile nations might bring pressure on the Ba'ath regime to root him out, deny the Assassins a base of operations.

It grieved him to imagine the ancestral fortress standing empty, the abode of rats and spiders, and he recognized the loss of face that would attend his flight from Alamut. Where would they find another setting so ideal for training and indoctrination purposes? How could another garden of delights be nurtured in the hostile world outside?

If he was forced by circumstances to flee his home, there would be no peace in this life, or in the next, for any of his enemies.

All things considered, exile—within established limits—could be good for business. If the Syrians could not protect him, he might try Khaddafi. It would be difficult, at first, to reconcile their egos, but with time and space—the latter plentiful in Libya—there might be room to grow. Khaddafi's hatred of America and Israel gave them common ground, and Abdel al-Sabbah was fairly confident that he could woo the colonel into offering asylum to the Assassins.

But first there was the business of survival, the elimination of the men who now threatened to destroy him. Evacuation might not be required, if he could wrest victory from defeat. The sheikh smiled. He might be bloodied, but he was not beaten, and he would teach his enemies a thing or two about the risks of tampering with Allah's will. It was a lesson that, unfortunately, none of them would live to pass along.

The Old Man of the Mountain stood slowly, waiting for his bodyguards to flank him. He had reinforced his private guard when it became apparent that Arrani had allowed one of the infidels to slip away, and he was thankful now, with the sounds of battle ringing through the tunnels, offering a stern reminder of his own mortality.

But he was a survivor, and he was not ready to surrender. Before that happened his opponents would be forced to overpower him, demonstrate conclusively that he was not the master of the Eagle's Nest. With Allah's help, that day would never come.

He led his loyal disciples from the throne room toward the sounds of raging combat. It was time for him to join the battle and assert himself as ruler of the Assassins. Sheikh al-Jebal was moving out to face his enemies and to grind them beneath his feet.

HAFEZ KASM FIRED a ragged burst in the direction of his enemies and ducked back into the cover of a slightly recessed doorway. Angry hornets whined around him, gouging chips from the walls and spattering his face with shards of stone. The American had taken cover in another doorway, but Kasm couldn't see the women. For all he knew, they might be dead.

It had seemed easy, at the outset, even though the guards had seemed to come from nowhere. The Ismailis had been talking among themselves, and the initial burst of automatic fire had left no more than half of them in fighting condition. The mopping up should have been easy, but they hadn't counted on reinforcements being close at hand.

The second wave had come prepared for battle, drawn by sounds of gunfire in the tunnels, and there were about a dozen of them.

If only he had more grenades, the Arab thought, he might have pinned down their adversaries long enough to risk a countercharge. Instead, *they* were pinned down, and it wouldn't be long before more troops arrived, perhaps on their flank to crush them in a pincer movement.

It was time to go on, at any cost. He slipped the empty magazine out of his AK-47, fed a fresh one in and worked the action, chambering a live round. It took a moment, but he caught the American's eye and tried to signal his intentions, nodding toward the enemy and brandishing his weapon like a lance. He dared not voice his plan in case one of the enemy might comprehend a smattering of English, and he hoped Belasko understood him well enough to lend a hand.

Across the body-littered corridor, his comrade smiled and nodded, ramming a fresh magazine into the pistol grip of his Uzi. Bolan glanced downrange, flashing a hand signal that told Kasm at least one of the women still survived. And if two guns were good, he knew three guns would be better—as long as the inexperienced women did not panic and shoot him in the back by accident.

He smiled at that. With so much death around him, his survival hanging by a thread stretched across a razor's edge, it would be perfect irony if he was shot down by a member of his own small troop.

He flashed five fingers at the American and started counting down. His heart was in his throat, his stomach churning. He was ashamed to find his hands were trembling.

Four.

The hostile fire had abated, but the Assassins would be waiting, rifles trained along the tunnel, ready for a target. To charge the guns seemed suicidal, but they had no options.

Three.

He braced himself, controlled the trembling in his hands by wrapping them tightly around his weapon. If his time had come to die, at least his enemies would never have the opportunity to say that he had died a coward.

Two.

His heart was hammering against his ribs, but Belasko caught his eye, and the American was smiling. Was he frightened? Did the certainty of sudden death weigh heavy on his shoulder as it did upon Hafez Kasm?

One.

He took a breath and held it, braced to run, afraid that he might freeze at the final instant and disgrace himself.

Go!

Adrenaline roaring in his ears, Kasm charged the enemy, his weapon spitting short, selective bursts. One of the Assassins had been rash enough to break from cover, and the Syrian stitched a line of holes across his chest. The straw man was slammed backward, a stunned expression on his face.

Kasm cut down another, and another, sensed the bullets slicing through the air around him, plucking at his clothes. One round inscribed a fiery line across his hip; another burrowed beneath his arm, deflected by his ribs, and very nearly knocked him off his stride.

Nothing mattered now, except a continued advance and the rifle spitting in his hands. The American was beside him holding his own, and he could hear another weapon, two, as both the women joined the sprint toward the gates of hell.

A bullet clipped his shoulder, staggered him, and he went down on one knee. Refusing to release the rifle, stubbornly returning fire, he riddled the Ismaili who had wounded him and struggled to his feet again, aware of warm blood plastering the tunic to his skin.

The women had passed him, and he picked up his pace, refusing to be left behind. The Assassins had broken ranks, were running away like frightened children. But they could not outrun bullets, and one by one they toppled, sprawling to the ground in awkward attitudes of death.

And suddenly they were alone.

He scanned the battlefield for other adversaries, giddy from the loss of blood and the smell of cordite. He realized he had not released his breath since he emerged from cover and gasping like a diver too long out of breath, he fumbled for another magazine.

"You're hit."

"A scratch."

"You're losing blood."

"We have not far to go."

Bolan searched his eyes for several heartbeats and finally nodded.

"Right."

A straggler could kill them all, and he did not intend to place himself in that position. If he felt that he could not keep up, Kasm would break away and find a place to make his stand, content to buy them time by slowing down the enemy who would be sure to follow.

They had come this far, but they were not yet free by any means. The stable lay before them, possibly guarded, and there was still the open courtyard, as well as the gates they could never hope to open on their own.

So pointless, but his spirit would not let him wallow in dejection and surrender. Better to die in combat, fighting for his honor, than to gain an extra hour by submitting to his enemies.

A hundred yards, more or less, would bring them to the stables. He could make it that far. After that, it might not matter.

A hundred yards, and Hafez Kasm knew that he was privileged. Few men were favored with the gift of measuring their lives with such precision.

BEFORE HE REACHED the bottom of the stairs, Tahir Arrani knew he was too late. The bodies in the corridor had been a warning; the gunsmoke, hanging in the stairwell like a whiff of grim disaster in the offing, was confirmation.

The American was gone.

Amal had failed to stop them; his death was no real consolation. The infidels were again at liberty, and they were obviously armed. They would be killed, of course—they could not hope to stand against an army—but the very fact that they survived to this point was a humiliation for Arrani. He was losing face with every moment that his enemies remained at large; each soldier lost in the pursuit was one more stumbling block for his campaign to one day rule the Eagle's Nest.

Where would they go? Two strangers in the labyrinth might easily be lost, but he could not afford to put his faith in chance. Thus far, the infidels had managed to defy the odds of probability. They were resourceful, ruthless, deadly. And he knew that they would have a plan by now, however desperate and hopeless it might seem. They would not wander aimlessly around the tunnels, waiting to be ambushed and annihilated.

Would they dare to try the entrance they had used upon arrival? It was guarded, they would know that much, but in a pinch, they might have no alternative. Arrani thought the force on duty at the palace entrance was sufficient, made a mental note to keep in touch with them by runner and began to consider alternatives.

On orders from Sheikh al-Jebal, the infidels had not been watched as closely as they should have, and he had no way of knowing whether they had sniffed out other exits from the castle. Surely they would not have found his secret passage to and from the garden of delights, but there were other avenues—the stables, for example—that his enemies might be aware of. Three exits came to mind, and while a token force had been assigned to each, Arrani knew they needed reinforcements.

He turned to the riflemen around him, selected runners, issued orders and watched them disappear. They would alert the sentries on the farthest exits, gather reinforcements and return to join him when their work was done. They knew where he would be.

The nearest exit opened on the stables, and Arrani meant to lead the hunters there himself. He had no reason to believe the infidels would choose that exit over any of the others, but accessibility, the need to act, made up his mind. If sentries on the stable gate had seen no strangers, he would reinforce the post and carry on the hunt. In time, he knew, his path would cross the American's, and he would be victorious.

It was a pity that he would be forced to kill the jackals outright, rather than resume his interrogation, but he would not risk more damage to his battered reputation. There would be no second chance for his enemies to escape.

At least, he thought, the interrupted torture session had borne meager fruit. He was prepared to take the tall man's word about an accidental meeting with the Irish terrorist, who had been en route to Alamut. Israeli sponsors were believable, as well, and it made sense that they would use a mercenary this time, after losing other agents in their past attempts to track the Assassins. Arrani had disposed of one himself, and knew that Syrian police had snared another in the recent past. The American's Arab comrade was a problem, hinting at the possibility of other traitors searching for the Eagle's Nest, but it was a problem he could deal with, given half a chance.

When he had found the jackals, finished them, there would be ways of insulating Alamut against impending danger. Contacts in the Ba'ath regime would help identify the Syrian, his friends and relatives. A hunting party could be sent to clean the slate before unfriendly eyes discovered what was written there.

The prospect of annihilating families improved Arrani's mood, but first he had to find the infidels. Their heads, on silver platters, would be helpful in restoring his position in the eyes of Abdel al-Sabbah . . . but would it be enough?

Of late, the Old Man had been looking at him strangely, with a sort of wariness, as if he harbored dark suspicions, sought some reason to mistrust Arrani. Given the disaster that now confronted him, there was a possibility that he would be deposed, relieved of duty by the sheikh, replaced with someone who had wooed and won the Old Man's favor.

If it came to that, what were his prospects for survival? Earlier that day, Sheikh al-Jebal had ordered death for twelve disciples on the basis of a bungled training exercise. How much more serious was his predicament, with intruders at large and armed inside the castle?

Moving through the tunnels with his squad of riflemen, Arrani knew that he was in a desperate situation. Even a successful hunt might leave him facing execution, and he did not plan to offer up his own head to pacify the master. If it came to that, he was prepared to make a rather different sort of sacrifice to Allah.

With the outsiders killing anyone they met, it would be tragic—but predictable—if one of them should meet the sheikh. Quite by chance, of course. It would be touch-and-go, with bodyguards around him, but the mercenary and his companion had already slaughtered ten or twelve disciples that Arrani knew of. It was conceivable that they could drop the palace guards, eliminate the sheikh . . . and if they died in the exchange of gunfire, riddled bodies laid out at the scene, who would be rash enough to question Allah's will?

In the event of such a tragedy, it would be only natural to seek immediate replacement for the chief of the Assassins. And who better to accept the post than one who had been faithful to the sheikh for years on end, a loyal disciple, well versed in all the projects their sect had undertaken on behalf of clients in the world outside? Who had a better right to occupy the throne?

It would be risky, but the prize was worth the gamble. At the moment he had everything to gain and nothing but his life to lose.

Before he could inaugurate his new regime, however, he would have to find the outsiders. From there, he could proceed with the elimination of Sheikh al-Jebal, his bodyguards and the Assassins who were witness to his treachery. Perhaps two dozen lives in all.

It would be, Arrani thought, a vital new beginning for his personal jihad.

21

"We are approximately thirty yards from the stables."

Bolan hesitated, glancing back along their trail, where angry voices echoed in the tunnels. At his side, Hafez Kasm seemed to be maintaining his composure, but the crimson stain beneath his arm was wet and glistening, more than triple its initial size. If he had not yet begun to feel the blood loss, his time was running out. Debilitating weakness was not far away.

All the more reason, then, for them to make their move as quickly and decisively as possible. The Executioner had no idea how they should play it once they reached the stables, but he knew they could not afford to run in place. As long as they were moving, they were still alive, and there was hope.

Sarah was intently studying the corridor that stretched ahead. Her friend, Mari, wore a nervous look, but she was hanging tough, and Bolan counted her as a survivor, street-wise, ready to confront an unforgiving world on any terms. Kasm was fading, and Bolan did not like the little smile that played across the Arab's features. He had seen that look before, on dying men.

"We're going," Bolan told him. "Are you with us?"

"With you? Yes." He pushed off from the wall and raised his AK-47. "To the stables."

Bolan shared the point position with Kasm, concerned about reaction time if they encountered sentries unexpectedly. Already, he could see the Syrian responding sluggishly to questions, like a man who's had one drink too many. He was still in control, but fractions of a second could be life or death in point-blank confrontations, and the Executioner did not intend to sacrifice four lives in the pursuit of saving face.

They reached the final elbow of the tunnel unopposed. Beyond that point, they would be moving through a free-fire zone, and Bolan couldn't risk even a glance around the corner to assess their opposition. Listening, he was rewarded with a dismal silence that could mean anything...or nothing. A battalion could stand silent if the troops were disciplined and motivated, or the total lack of sound might simply indicate an empty corridor. If he could only poke his head around the corner once...

"I'll go." The lady from Mossad had sized up his dilemma at a glance. "They'll think I'm lost in the confusion. If there aren't too many—"

"No. It's my turn." Mari had removed her cartridge belt before she finished speaking, and she was around the corner before they had a chance to haul her back. A futile curse beneath his breath, and Bolan held his Uzi ready. He couldn't control the situation now, but he could try to make the best of it.

Beyond his line of sight, he heard the woman speaking rapid, frightened Arabic. A male voice answered sternly, then another. Clearly the appointed sentries on the stable entrance had no sense of chivalry where duty was concerned.

"On three," he told the others, conscious of the fact that there could just as easily be twenty guns as two, around that corner. Counting down, he put his faith in the advantage of surprise, and knew that once the sentries were disposed of there would be no time to stop and count their options. They would have to keep rolling, blind and possibly outnumbered, killing anyone who tried to stop them.

Bolan didn't even want to think about what happened *after*, if they survived the next few moments, managed to secure mounts inside the stable. He couldn't allow himself to dwell on the mammoth gates, the walls with riflemen on top, the courtyard teeming with Assassins.

"Three!"

Bolan made his move, Kasm behind him, Sarah bringing up the rear. Two sentries, who were now outnumbered, saw Death approaching but refused to break and run.

They carried folding-stock Kalashnikovs, and both were firing as their enemies emerged from cover. Mari lunged against the one on Bolan's left and grappled for his weapon, taking half a dozen rounds at skin-touch range, which flattened her on impact, left the guards wide open.

Bolan hosed them with his submachine gun, heard the automatic rifles of his comrades chiming in. Another heartbeat, and their enemies were dancing jerkily, like puppets with a drunkard or a madman on the strings. Bright splotches were painted on the door and wall behind them as they fell. Bolan didn't have to call a cease-fire; there was no one left to kill.

There was no time to check on Mari, who was obviously dead. Bolan rushed the door, reloading on the run, aware that every second counted. Death might be waiting for them just beyond the threshold, but there was no other way. The heavy door was built to open inward, and he pushed against it with his weight, prepared to feel the impact of a bullet in his face at any moment. Crouching, Bolan scuttled through the opening and hit a flying shoulder roll to spoil his adversaries' aim. He came up on his knees, the Uzi braced for action ... and discovered that his "opposition" was a solitary stable hand.

The man had seemed dumbfounded for an instant, but he was a trained Assassin, like his fellow cultists, and he bounced back swiftly, groping for the rifle that was propped beside him in a corner. Bolan helped him get there with a lethal figure eight that punched him forward like a rag doll, slamming him facefirst against the wall.

They were alone, but only for the moment. "Hurry up! Get mounted!" Bolan snapped, suiting words to action, as he moved toward the stalls where horses stood.

None of them were saddled, and the gear was stowed at one end of the stable. The warrior moved with long, determined strides to fetch the minimal equipment he would need. A set of reins, for starters; a saddle would be nice, but time was short and Bolan was prepared to rough it, if he had to. Reins were crucial, though, if he was going to control the horse, and he draped a set across a shoulder, moving on to choose a saddle.

He could hear the numbers falling in his mind, but Bolan forced himself to work methodically, with steady hands. There might be faster ways to do the job, but they would likely dump him on his butt before he traveled fifty feet, and riding into hell was bad enough. He had no wish to try the journey on all fours.

As he was tightening the cinch beneath his horse's belly, watching Sarah snug her saddle into place, he was startled by a shouted warning from Hafez. A single fluid motion put the Uzi in his hand, and he was pivoting to face the enemy as three of them burst through the outer doorway to the stable. All were armed with automatic weapons, and they read the situation in a glance, their rifles snapping up and into target acquisition.

Bolan broke away from the animal, tracking right across their line of fire, determined not to let his adversaries shoot the horses by mistake. Their only hope of getting out alive was standing in those stalls, and one stray round would force them to begin the saddling procedure from square one.

Kasm was standing tall and firing at the three Assassins, even as echoes of his warning died away, eclipsed by the staccato bark of automatic weapons. One of the Ismaili gunners staggered, fell, and Bolan saw a second going down before he could align the Uzi's sights with living flesh.

It was the third who found his mark, the bullets ripping through Hafez Kasm as he held the Uzi's trigger down, too late. A storm of parabellum manglers punched the solitary gunman back and out of frame, but he had made his score in passing. Twisted like a scrap of cast-off clothing on the stable floor, the Syrian was finished. Bolan had no time to say goodbye.

"Get mounted!"

Sarah was already clambering aboard her animal as Bolan barked the order, moving toward his own. He had the reins in hand, one foot up in the stirrup, when a crash of thunder shook the Eagle's Nest to its foundations, startling the horses as no gunfire had been able.

Midnight, and the Phantoms were on time.

The Executioner could only pray that *he* was not too late.

SHEIKH AL-JEBAL WAS a survivor. From his ragged childhood, through his service with the fedayeen, to his position as the master of the Eagle's Nest, he had possessed the necessary traits that saw him, more or less intact, through every hostile confrontation. Wit and wisdom. Ruthlessness. Intelligence. Imagination. Part of being a survivor was accepting the reality of an occasional defeat. You learned to walk away before your losses became insupportable. Above all else, you saved yourself.

And so the time had come for him to leave.

He had reports of gunfire from the cellars, from the stables, and his hunting parties had discovered Ismaili corpses scattered through the tunnels. He did not believe that two men could accomplish all of that and still survive against an army numbering more than a hundred men. Somehow his fortress had been breached, and there was nothing he could do to save it now. The first priority was preservation of his leadership as figurehead and mentor to the Assassins.

The whole disaster was Arrani's fault. The son of a syphilitic jackal had been placed in charge of all security for Alamut, and any breach of that security was his direct responsibility. It was a pity there would be no time to punish him as he deserved, but if, by chance, Arrani managed to survive this night, the sheikh meant to see him hunted down and slaughtered for his failure to protect the voice of Allah.

In the old days, when their treasury was empty and their name anathema to every Muslim government on Earth, escape from such a situation might have been impossible. His enemies were in the stable, cutting off his access to the horses, and he could not risk the courtyard, where the vehicles were parked. He might have been cut off, but he was not, and as he called his palace guards together, the sheikh released a silent prayer of thanks for the wonders of technology.

It was a short walk to the heliport, and he could be away from Alamut in moments, soaring like a bird of prey. He had another nest prepared, but no one knew of it, other than a handful of his trusted servants. He had kept Tahir Arrani in the dark about his secret hideaway, in case withdrawal from the Eagle's Nest should someday be compulsory. His hidden lair was not a palace, in the sense that Alamut had been, but it would serve him in his hour of need, and there was always room to grow.

A true survivor learned from each defeat and memorized his own mistakes, the better to avoid repeating them in future. Sheikh al-Jebal had learned from his experience this night to trust in no one and suspect all men, however loyal they might appear when speaking to his face. It was a timely lesson, and he took it to his heart.

Maintaining contact with his clients wouldn't be a problem, though he counted on a brief disruption of communication while his new retreat was fitted with equipment. All the names and places, the assignments waiting to be carried out, were filed inside his mind. It might take time for him to build another strike force capable of serving foreign clients, but he thought that there were bound to be survivors from the night's fiasco, and it would be relatively simple to make contact, rally them around his standard once again, when he was ready to proceed.

The garden of delights would be most difficult to re-create, but given time and patience, cash and ingenuity, he would surpass the most elaborate achievements of his predecessors. He would build a fortress, sow a garden that would stand for generations as a symbol of almighty Allah's wrath against the infidels.

But first he must escape the trap his enemies had laid for him at Alamut.

His ears picked up a sound like summer thunder, and he felt a faint vibration, a trembling in the stone beneath his feet. Before he had a chance to place it, the sheikh was staggered by a violent tremor, nearly deafened by the roar of high explosives.

He recognized the sounds of thunder now, immediately realized that there would be no saving Alamut. Somehow, his enemies had called an air strike, and it was in progress.

The flying wedge of guardsmen hustled him along the corridor at double-time, brushed past the sentries on the giant doors and bulled their way across the courtyard toward the helipad. His message had been sent ahead, and he could see the rotors turning, gathering momentum, winking at him with reflected firelight.

Alamut was burning, and the midnight sky above his head was ruled by swooping harpies, demons of the air who rained destruction on the fortress that his father had built. An explosion behind him sealed the entryway with fire and tumbling stone, the shock wave driving him and several of his guardsmen to their knees.

The Old Man struggled to his feet, helped up by clutching hands, and staggered toward the helicopter. There were mere seconds left, perhaps, before a lucky—or deliberate—shot destroyed his only hope of getting out alive.

The helicopter was a Cobra, purchased on the international black market and stripped of its original markings. It was fitted with a machine gun, courtesy of the supplier, but an airborne dogfight with the snarling Phantoms would be more than ludicrous. His only hope lay in a swift and unobserved escape.

"No lights!" he ordered the pilot, as he strapped himself into his seat. His riflemen were grappling with seat belts, closing off the entry hatch. He heard the rotors straining into lift-off, knew when they were airborne by the hollow feeling in his stomach.

There was still a chance, with Allah's help and guidance.

Still a chance.

And why, then, did he feel as if a part of him was dead already?

JACK GRIMALDI SAW the stationary chopper on his first pass, and he let it go. He used his Sparrow missiles on the castle proper, one eye on the Phantom's situation display indicators as he sent the stingers on their way. They struck what he presumed to be the second story, blossoming in fire and thunder, slinging blocks of jagged stone into the yard below.

The courtyard was illuminated by strategic floodlights, but the Phantoms were not halfway through their run when someone on the ground got wise and pulled the plug. By then, the light from leaping flames was adequate to mark their target, and Grimaldi knew it would be hell down there. He thought of Bolan, trapped inside the mountain like a mole, and pushed the grisly thought out of his mind.

Somehow, the helicopter had lifted off in the interval before his second pass. Grimaldi gave the pilot points for courage under fire. He almost hated to destroy a guy who showed that kind of guts. Almost.

But it was obvious that someone in authority was counting on the chopper as his ticket out, a free ride to the nearest safety zone. Grimaldi had no way of knowing who might be inside, but he couldn't afford to let him slip away. Annihilation was the game plan, and the pilot didn't want a fumble on his record. Not with so much riding on the outcome of the game.

"The chopper's mine," he told whomever might be listening, and then he took the Phantom down. He stroked the target designation switch and froze the Cobra in his sights, his finger tensing on the trigger that would spur his 10 mm cannon into blazing action.

In the fraction of a heartbeat that remained before he made his move, Grimaldi caught a mental image of a tethered goat, staked out as bait for a marauding tiger. There was nothing the goat could do to save itself from rending claw and fang. It could only stand and watch death coming for him with a hungry snarl. He wondered, as he squeezed the trigger, whether anybody in the helicopter might have felt that way.

At nearly a 100 rounds per second, human senses couldn't register the cannon's rate of fire. Grimaldi felt a distant shudder, and imagined that he heard the faintest hint of canvas ripping, but his mind was on the target as it came apart, disintegrating in midair. Its shattered listing body spilled guns, seats and bodies toward the courtyard, where they mingled with the rubble and the dead. Instinctively he let the trigger go and watched what was left of the Cobra—describe an awkward corkscrew spiral toward the earth.

He took the Phantom up to get back into formation for another run. He still had business with the living, and it would not keep. The Sidewinders this time, he thought, for some variety. And finally the Phoenix fire.

And may the gods of war have mercy on us all.

22

As another shock wave rippled through the tunnel, Tahir Arrani fought to keep his footing, offering a silent prayer for the swift annihilation of his enemies. It was a futile prayer, he knew, because the infidels had aircraft, and Alamut could not compete with horses and a single helicopter.

They were finished, but Arrani was continuing toward his objective with the single-mindedness of a fanatic. At the outset, he had meant to reinforce the stable exit, close it to his prey, but now he had a different goal in mind. Survival was the key, escape from the vindictive thunder of the war-planes overhead. It did not seem appropriate for him to die there, in the tunnels. Arrani knew that he was meant for greater things, and he did not propose to thwart his higher destiny by giving up, allowing his unworthy adversaries to destroy him.

At a glance, the crumpled bodies of the guardsmen scarcely registered. It was the blood, thick rivers on the floor and speckled abstract patterns on the wall, that finally brought him back to grim reality. The stable door yawned open beyond their twisted forms, beckoning. The scream-ing voices of the jets were much closer here.

Arrani felt a pang of sudden fear, and knew at once that he could not afford to surrender to his feelings. Instead of backing off and ordering a rifleman to check the stable out, he cocked his automatic pistol, stepped across the bodies of the fallen lookouts, crossed the threshold with his men in tow. If this night brought his death, the least that he could do was to face it as a man.

There was yet more carnage inside the stable, bodies sprawled in awkward positions. He recognized the impostor's Syrian companion, tunic dark with seeping blood, and he was pleased that one of them, at least, had been eliminated. It would please him to destroy the other personally, but his mind was on escape now, and the hunt would only slow him down.

A high-explosive charge was detonated somewhere overhead and to his right, immediately followed by a second and a third. The ancient stone was crumbling; he could hear the slabs and boulders tumbling to the courtyard, impact vibrating like aftershocks from the explosions.

In the end, it was the jets with their rockets, that made up his mind to flee on foot. The horses, trained to tolerate the din of gunfire, were uneasy with the new cacophony of unfamiliar sounds. Some of the stalls, he saw, were empty, their occupants bolting to seek their freedom in the courtyard.

He would have a better chance on foot. Once he was through the gate he could make his way down through the valley unobserved. The peasants, if they dared to show their faces, would be dazzled by the light show on the mountain, and they would not notice him. If someone tried to stop him, he would die, and somewhere on the way, Arrani would acquire a means of transportation for himself.

But on the way to *where*?

Arrani had no destination in mind, no time to think it out. The riflemen could tag along or stay behind and die; it did not make the slightest difference to him. He briefly thought about the sheikh, decided that the Old Man could get out of this one by himself. A brand-new day was dawning, born in fire, and with the help of Allah, he would take the place of Abdel al-Sabbah as leader of the Assassins. But first, before he could rebuild, he must escape.

Without a word, he passed the empty stalls and skittish horses, stepped across the bodies in his path. The courtyard was in chaos, men with rifles and machine guns firing at the planes without a prayer of doing any damage, others scrambling for cover, cut off by explosions any way they turned. A hundred yards distant, he could see the gate, unguarded, waiting for him, and he knew that any further hesitation might be fatal.

He had scarcely cleared the stable when he saw the American, on horseback, with another mounted rider at his side. Unless Arrani's eyes were playing tricks, the second rider was a woman, dressed in harem garb, and while he could not see her face, he thought he recognized the whipping mane of raven hair.

Another chance! He could destroy the infidel and leave this place a hero. Moving with a new determination, he struck off toward the riders, watching as the man raised an Uzi submachine gun, toppling a pair of sentries from the wall above. The woman had a rifle, but he did not care. The odds meant nothing. Allah would protect him as he made his sacrifice of love.

He fired from sixty yards out. The echo of his pistol shot was lost in the confusion of the air strike, but his target seemed to feel the bullet's passage as it missed his head by inches. Turning in his saddle, the impostor picked out Arrani in the milling crowd, swung around his mount and charged.

It seemed like something from a fable, with Arrani self-cast in the role of hero, standing firm against the infidel crusader, offering his life for Allah and the message of His holy word. He held the automatic braced in both hands, sighting down the slide and squeezing off in rapid-fire, his target drawing nearer, growing larger by the second. He could see the muzzle-flash from his opponent's weapon, felt the parabellum manglers eating up the ground around him, knew he was invincible, immortal.

And it came as a complete surprise, therefore, when he was stitched across the abdomen by bullets, impact forcing the air out of his lungs. Collapsing to his knees, Arrani found he could not breathe, but he refused to lift his finger off the automatic's trigger. Kneeling in his own life's blood, he finished off the magazine and was rewarded as the charger faltered, stumbled and began to fall.

Too late.

The animal's momentum had already carried it too far. It was on him, the heaving body flecked with blood and perspiration, looming over him and falling, falling, blotting out the light of soaring flames.

Tahir Arrani was surprised to find he still had time to scream.

GRIMALDI USED HIS FIRST TWO Phoenix missiles on the upper levels of the castle, taking satisfaction in the rock slides he created, knowing it would be pure hell inside. They might not bring the house down, literally, but with five Phantoms working on it, they would come damned close. They would definitely make the hideout uninhabitable for the survivors.

He would have given anything, just then, to know where Bolan was, be certain that the guy was either dead or running free and clear. Uncertainty was always worst, but he couldn't allow the doubts to cloud his mind or stay his hand. He had a job to do, and he was far from finished.

People were dying in the courtyard. The shrapnel from exploding rockets—shattered chunks of stone that varied from the size of gravel to a few great boulders—was raining down on the courtyard, claiming casualties with every new explosion. Two or three of the Israelis had already tried their hands at strafing runs, the 20 mm cannons spewing death, projectiles cutting trails of blood and dust across the crowded yard.

If Bolan *had* survived, *had* managed to escape the castle, it would be grim irony for him to die among his tattered enemies, another of the human silhouettes in Jack Grimaldi's shooting gallery. There had to be a way—

And then he had it.

"Listen up!" he barked into his microphone. "I'm taking down the front gates. If I can't finish it with what I've got, someone will have to help me."

"Why the gates?" one of his wingmen asked, confused. "You'll let them get away!"

"The gates?"

"This isn't a debate, goddamn it! I was put in charge of these festivities, and I said hit the gates!"

The air went silent, all dissent cut off immediately as Grimaldi nosed his Phantom into the approach. His wingmen might not understand the order, might resent his pulling rank, and that was fine. He frankly didn't care if they were happy with his leadership, as long as everyone remembered who the boss was on this run. As long as everybody did his job.

He knew that bringing down the gates would give the Assassins a chance to break away, but he was also conscious of the fact that they could never hope for absolute annihilation. Ground support would have been mandatory for a perfect clean-up, and the fact that they were striking deep inside a hostile country meant they had to settle for whatever they could get.

And some of the Ismailis would survive. There was a chance that they might set up shop again, in time, and start the nightmares over, but the pilot was not psychic, and he long ago had given up telling fortunes. There was just a chance that Bolan might be down there, in the milling, shouting crowd, and while that chance remained, Grimaldi would do everything he could to save the big guy's skin.

He had his sights fixed on the gates, his finger on the trigger, ready to release his last Phoenix missiles.

"I hope you're down there, guy," the pilot whispered, feeling sudden tightness in his throat. "God keep."

And then he fired.

THE FALL HAD SHAKEN Bolan, and jarred the Uzi from his hand. It was nowhere to be found as he regained his feet. His mount was clearly dying. Its forelegs pawed weakly at the ground, and Arrani's arm protruded from beneath the animal's bulk. No point in checking for a pulse; the guy was either dead or dying.

A number of Ismailis had observed the duel, had seen Arrani die. Some of them were closing on the soldier now, many curious, a few apparently determined to exact revenge. The screaming Phantoms slowed them, kept them glancing at the heavens—or across their shoulders, toward the castle. But they were advancing, all the same, and they would be upon him in a moment.

Bolan turned to face the rush of footsteps on his flank and had to sidestep as a scimitar sliced through the space where he'd just been standing. Going low, inside the swing, he drove the rigid fingers of his right hand underneath his adversary's rib cage, emptying the man's lungs and leaving him wide open for the knee that spread his nose across his face.

The scimitar felt awkward in his hand, but an exploratory swipe or two convinced him he could handle it. A second cultist rushed him, brandishing his empty rifle like a club. Bolan dropped him with a slice across the abdomen that left him kneeling in the dirt, trying to hold in his intestines.

Bolan was halfway to the gates when one of the attacking Phantoms seemed to veer off course. Its missiles streaked toward the wall, the giant gates, on a collision course with Bolan. There was time for him to hit the dirt, then the world exploded in his face, the shock wave rippling around him, tugging at his hair, his clothes. A flaming timber fell beside him, showering his back with sparks and embers. Bolan wallowed in the dirt to smother them, then scrambled to his feet.

The horse came out of nowhere, Sarah holding the reins with one hand, her AK-47 with the other. As she galloped through the milling crowd, he watched her fire off bursts to left and right, her targets toppling like bowling pins, their passing scarcely noticed in the scene of chaos.

"Hurry!" she commanded, as she reined her charge to a halt in front of him. The lady didn't have to tell him twice. He got one leg across the horse's rump, had slipped an arm around her waist, when yet another Phantom made its pass, unloading rockets on the ruined gates.

This time, one of the missiles struck the juncture of the gate and ground, its detonation clearing half the obstacle in one great burst of fire and flying lumber. Fractions of a heartbeat later, number two impacted on the wall beside the gate, and showered masonry upon the faithful who were close enough to catch the major fallout. As the smoke began to dissipate, Mack Bolan saw that half the gate was gone, the tattered remnants charred and smoking.

"We've got to try it," Bolan told her, shouting to be heard above the noise of droning jets and automatic-weapon fire.

The woman nodded, took a ragged breath and spurred their mount in the direction of the ravaged gate. She had no way of knowing if the horse would brave the flames or rear and dump them in the dust before it ran for safety, but it was a chance they had to take. Their options were exhausted, and a blowout at the finish line would be no worse, all things considered, than the fate that awaited them if they stood their ground.

Ten yards to go, and Bolan fought the urge to close his eyes. Three of the cultists were approaching, running on a hard collision course to cut them off. Bolan threw his scimitar, was rewarded for the effort when it struck the point man's leg a glancing blow and brought him down, the others tumbling on top of him.

They were at the gate, flames leaping in their faces, and he felt the sudden, searing heat as Sarah urged the horse to greater speed. It would be now or never, and the soldier held his breath, one arm locked around the woman's waist, as they took wing.

Their charger cleared the leaping fire with fractions of an inch to spare. Then, as if by magic, they had crossed the threshold, galloping through darkness with the sights, sounds and stench of mortal combat at their backs, receding as the brave horse carried them away.

Behind them, moments after they had cleared the gate, another Phantom made its run and slammed two rockets into the massive gateposts. Sarah reined in the horse after she had put a hundred yards between themselves and the inferno. They watched as a portion of the high protective wall collapsed, its rubble sealing off the courtyard's only exit.

"Let's go," he urged, placing one hand on Sarah's shoulder, gently turning her until she faced the valley, dark and silent to the south. The trance was broken.

"Yes," she said, and then she hesitated, glancing back again. "So many lives."

"They made a choice," he told her. "They can live with it."

"Or die with it?"

"It's all the same."

But as the soldier spoke those words, he knew that they were wrong. There was a world of difference between the living and the dead, the builders and the savages who sought to prey upon mankind. One tended fire and tamed it as a friend; the other used it as a weapon, and in time, would be consumed by cleansing flame.

The soldier closed his eyes as Sarah gave their mount a gentle nudge and started on the journey south. He didn't fear the darkness that surrounded them. It held no terrors that could match the restless phantoms in his heart.

They were alive, and for the moment, that was victory enough. There were occasions when a warrior could expect no more, and this was one such time. He left the butcher's work to Jack Grimaldi and the others, thinking of Hafez, Mari, all the men whom he had killed or helped to kill this day.

More ghosts. As if he did not have enough already.

Bolan made his mind a perfect blank and concentrated on the swaying rhythm of the horse. He would not sleep for fear of falling, but he could detach himself from his surroundings, cautiously replenish his reserves of energy.

With any luck at all, he would not dream.

EPILOGUE

Daylight overtook them in the mountains, high above the desert floor. Mack Bolan had been walking for the past two hours, leading Sarah's horse by starlight on a narrow trail that hugged the mountain crest. The fires of Alamut were far behind them, and the coastline was a hazy smudge on the horizon to the west.

"Where will we rest?"

"Just up ahead," he told her. "I see trees and boulders. We should be all right, with cover."

He didn't believe that anyone would pursue them, but it stood to reason that the army would investigate the target of the air strike, and he didn't wish to be discovered accidentally. A lone American would have been bad enough, but an American with an Israeli...well, Damascus might have thrown the key away on that one, and the Executioner did not intend to spend his future in the kind of squalid cubbyhole that passed for Middle Eastern prison cells.

"How will you find your way back home?" she asked, intruding on his thoughts.

He smiled and shook his head. "I was supposed to have a guide."

"This land is dangerous for strangers."

"So I've noticed."

"I could help you," Sarah offered. "You could stay with me, until we reach the border."

"Maybe."

"I will need some different clothes."

"I like the ones you've got."

"Perhaps, but they are not for traveling."

"We won't be traveling this afternoon."

"We must conserve our energy."

"Of course."

They traveled on in silence for a time, as rosy dawn touched the sky. In the middle distance, he could pick out details of the trees and boulders now. It seemed a perfect place to pass the day, secure from prying eyes.

"If you would come with me to Tel Aviv, my sponsors would be pleased to meet you, I am sure."

"We'll talk about it later."

"Yes. We still have time."

Hafez had been supposed to hand him off to contacts in the Company, but all of that could be forgotten now. The long trek south to Israel would be time consuming, fraught with peril, but he thought that there might be rewards along the way.

"Okay."

"Okay?"

"We'll do it your way . . . to the border, anyhow."

It was Sarah's turn to smile. "But first, we must conserve our energy. I hope that we are almost to the trees."

"Almost," he promised her, and made a point of picking up his pace. They had a long, hot day ahead of them, and he was looking forward to a respite from the road. "How long until we reach the border?"

"Traveling by night, perhaps three days. Or four."

"I'd vote for four," the soldier said, and led her horse into the shelter of the trees.

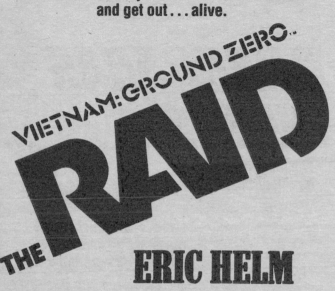

THE BARRABAS SERIES

The toughest men for the dirtiest wars

JACK HILD

"Jack Hild is just simply the best and gutsiest action writer around today."
—**Warren Murphy, Creator of The Destroyer**

Nile Barrabas was the last American soldier out of Vietnam and the first man into a new kind of action. His warriors, called the Soldiers of Barrabas, have one very simple ambition: to do what the Marines can't or won't do. Join the Barrabas blitz! Each book hits new heights—this is brawling at its best!

Available wherever paperbacks are sold.

SOBS-1A

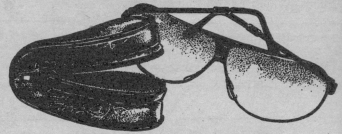